THE MOTHERLAND SAGA

The Epic Novel of Turkey

VOLUME THREE

COMING OF AGE

1939-1983

THE MOTHERLAND SAGA

The Epic Novel of Turkey

VOLUME THREE

COMING OF AGE

1939-1983

HUGO N. GERSTL

PANGÆA
PUBLISHING GROUP

COMING OF AGE: 1939 – 1983
Volume Three - The Motherland Saga
The Epic Novel of Turkey

www.HugoGerstl.com

ISBN 978-1-950134-24-3
Pangæa Publishing Group
www.PangaeaPublishing.com

Cover image: *Istanbul twilight © Daniel Boiteau, Dreamstime.com*
Inside images: *Border © Antsvgdal, Dreamstime.com*

Cover design and typesetting by
DesignPeaks@gmail.com

For information contact:

Pangæa Publishing Group
25579 Carmel Knolls Drive
Carmel, CA 93923
Telephone: 831-624-3508/831-649-0668
Fax: 831-649-8007
Email: info@pangaeapublishing.com

To those writers, artists, and editors in every age and in every land who keep the flame of truth alive at a time when those whose need to dominate others try to quench it; To those who will stand, even as one, against a million or more to preserve another's right to freedom and justice; and to those whose courage and morality help to repair the world: May your footsteps never falter and the work of your hands never fail.

AND FOR MY LORRAINE,
WHO MAKES IT ALL WORTHWHILE

HUGO N. GERSTL

THE MOTHERLAND SAGA

The Epic Novel of Turkey

Do not miss them on your shelf!

For Hugo N. Gerstl's complete novels list and descriptions, go to www.HugoGerstl.com

PROLOGUE

The second volume, *EMERGENCE*, like the second movement of a symphony, was the relative calm before the storm. As we enter Turkey's *COMING OF AGE*, World War II is tearing Europe to shreds, a holocaust like none other in history will result in the annihilation of two-thirds of the world's Jewish population, and plans are being made for sea-changes in the balance of international power if, when, the World War II finally comes to an end.

But the world as we know it, will never be the same, as we move into a New World Order.

PART FIVE:

THE STORM 1939–1946

1

The remains of Turhan's wife and nascent son were returned to Istanbul, where, after a dignified, simple funeral service, they were buried on a small rise overlooking the Bosphorous. For a brief instant, Turhan had pondered whether to take her back to Suvarli, the village of her birth, but Halide had managed to convince him this was the last place on earth to which she'd want to return, even in death. After Sezer's funeral, Turhan remained in Istanbul. He was torn by conflicting emotions he could not understand. He could make no sense of his wife's demise. At first, he blamed himself. He'd never been an observant Muslim. Perhaps this was Allah's justifiable retribution. He recalled their last words and felt tremendous guilt.

"If you stayed here, I wouldn't need to go. Why don't we both just stay in Ankara?"

"That's not my way, Sezer."

Halide, ever practical, disabused him of such feelings. "Do you think, my friend, that out of forty-five thousand men, women and children killed in Erzinjan there weren't an equal number of holy men and scoundrels? Or that Allah, who created the world, is responsible for its maintenance and perfection?"

"But if I'd stayed home, she would never have gone. We'd be together now. And our baby..."

"Turhan, many years ago, you told me about your friend, Ibrahim. Did he ask to lose his woman? Did I ask to lose Metin? Am I an evil woman because I was raped? Does an earthquake make any more sense than a war?"

Strangely, tears remained unshed, and he could make no sense of that either. Sezer had been a loyal, loving companion all the days of her life. Their marriage had been steady, solid, unexciting. He harked back to that conversation he'd had with Jalal, that day in Diyarbakır.

"What does it mean to love?"

"There's no way to explain love. You can't talk about it with the same detachment you'd reserve for cutting a lamb carcass into component parts. It's clear that all your previous experiences have not prepared you for love, else why would you have needed my counsel?

"You'd better realize some of the dangers when someone of your character embarks on such a journey. You are an intensely ambitious man, Turhan. I question whether you will ever allow yourself fully to give your heart to another human being."

Jalal had died a year ago. His words haunted Turhan. He heard other words, angry words.

"You are my wife, Sezer. Do you forget where you'd have been without me?"

"I'd be exactly where I am now, doing exactly what I'm doing today. Building Turkey."

Turhan fought the rising feeling within him. He was a truthful man. For him to deny his emotions would be to turn his back on the ideals he'd fought for, and it became harder and harder to ignore what he felt in the midst of his guilt. Relief. Freedom.

As the months crept by and Europe descended into the maelstrom of war. Turhan busied himself at *Isharet.* Halide worked harder than ever, recruiting, building, raising funds and teaching those who would teach others. While Nurettin Shihan, now her vice president, traveled the length and breadth of Turkey, acting as spokesman and lobbyist for Yujel Orhan Teachers' College, Halide, as president of the growing institution, stayed in Istanbul, acting as marshal, general and sergeant in her own war against illiteracy. A war for the minds of her adopted motherland. The original one-story wooden buildings were now flanked by two concrete-and-steel structures. Each month saw a greater influx of young men and women, more than matching the outflow of those returning to the villages to bring learning to Turkey.

July 15, 1941 was as hot and sultry as any day Turhan could remember. By sunset, the breeze coming off the Bosphorous had filtered its way as far inland as Beyoğlu. Still, Turhan was perspiring by the time he'd walked the mile from Taksim Square to the Park Hotel. He, Nadji and Halide had been meeting each Tuesday evening at eight, in the hotel lounge, for the past year. Nadji, a full colonel, was now head of military security for Turkey's entire northwest sector. He was posted in Istanbul. He and Aysheh were still separated, but neither had instituted divorce proceedings. His two closest friends were diplomatic enough not to bring up anything about Aysheh in conversation.

The Park Hotel was anything but imposing from the street, a low edifice, of indeterminate age. Its elegance was evident only when one entered the portals held open by white-gloved doormen. Turhan was always amused that he had to take the elevator two stories *down* to have one of the most dramatic views in the city. The Park had been built into the side of a hill overlooking the Bosphorous. Years ago, an enterprising young architect decided, with a stroke of genius, to position the lounge at the lowest point of the hotel. The result was a large, deep room, that floated above the buildings on the street below. As Turhan entered the place, he marveled for the hundredth time at the sweeping view. Immediately below him was *Kabatash*, the sea-bus pier. Less than a mile across the Bosphorous he could see the lights of Üsküdar on the Asiatic side of the city. To his left, Dolmabahche Palace dominated the horizon. His two friends were at their usual table, engaged in intense conversation.

"*Iyi akshamlar*," Turhan said. "You seem more interested in your own discussion than in the nightly spy circus."

Earlier that year, Turkey, neutral since the beginning of the European conflict, was forced to allow so-called 'commercial' ships of the warring nations to travel through the Turkish straits. Since then, the Park Hotel's lounge, with its unobstructed view of the passage between Europe and Asia, had become the most exciting place in Istanbul. Spies of every European nation gathered here each night and watched the passage of traffic through the Bosphorous. If a particularly large ship hove into view, there was a flurry of activity at the Park's bank of telephones.

A violin, piano and string bass trio completed "The Blue Danube" for the thousandth time that year. The audience applauded politely. The three white-haired musicians bowed stiffly and left the room. Turhan ordered a double shot of *rakı,* which he drank neat, unusual for him. "Troubles?" Nadji asked, raising his eyebrows.

"You've got it. Our brave government has turned the screws on the press."

"You mean the *Vatan* affair?"

"It's a real scandal if you ask me. Article 77 of the constitution guarantees no censorship of the press. Unfortunately, cabinet ministers can suspend a newspaper indefinitely, without any form of court judgment, once the articles have been published."

"Surely they've got to have grounds for such drastic action," Halide said.

"Anything deemed 'harmful to the national policy.' Two weeks ago, *Vatan* published pictures from Charlie Chaplin's film, 'The Dictator,' with sharp comment under the photographs. Von Papen protested vigorously. The government, anxious to protect its neutrality, and its lucrative sales of chrome and manganese to both sides, suspended *Vatan's* publication for ninety days."

"How's Yalman going to meet his payroll?" Nadji asked, mentioning the daily's publisher.

"Istanbul's publishers have put part of their earnings into a fund to help him out. We're distributing daily installments of a book he's writing along with our papers and charging a *kurush* more for the major dailies."

"Can they get away with that?"

"The government can't suspend *all* the papers, can they? The people would bring the assembly down."

"Why are you so upset about this?" Nadji asked.

"The game's no fun with the war going on. The government used to threaten us, but we had warnings when anything was going to happen. Any of us can take a two week suspension. If *Vatan* gets ninety days, it's only a matter of time before someone condemns *Isharet.* Von Papen knows how I feel about Hitler. There's been bad blood between us for years. I had protection while Atatürk was alive. Now that Germany seems to be doing well in the war, the Reich ambassador has influence in Ankara."

"What do you intend to do?" Halide asked.

"I thought I'd take a brief holiday. Sezer's been dead a year-and-a-half. I've managed to put by enough to live for a while."

"What about your work at *Isharet*?"

"After Selimiye died, Fahri Dikkat became publisher. He's made it very clear that *Isharet's* a *news*paper, not a platform for editorial opinion. I'm sure he won't miss me. I am, to use the European phrase – a 'loose cannon.' Dikkat's told the staff that anyone responsible for even one day of suspension can pack up and leave."

"With your following, you could go to *Vatan*, or just about anywhere else," Nadji said.

"Not so easily done. Fame is one thing, but the owners don't want to gamble their money on a 'star' who can make the sky fall. What were you two talking about so seriously when I came in?"

"Later," Halide said. "It's too crowded in here. Could you come up to my house in Belgrade Forest tomorrow? I've got something that might interest you more than a long vacation."

"You sure you can't tell me now?"

"One never knows who's listening."

Although Turkey was neutral, Inönü's government, faced with threats of invasion, first by Russia, then by Germany, drafted one million men and doubled the nation's military budget. Turkey had been an important land bridge for three thousand years. Now, more than ever, its location was critical. Von Papen asked permission for German troops to cross Turkey enroute to the Middle East oil fields. Inönü refused. Although the straits were "officially" prohibited to all military shipping, the combatants' submarines regularly slipped through the Bosphorous and the Dardanelles. There was little the Turkish navy could do to stop them.

Next morning, as Turhan and Nadji drove onto the semi-circular, gravel driveway of Belgrade Palas, Turhan remembered the first time he'd seen the house. It had been a one-story affair then. He'd helped Halide plant pine and oak seedlings. Now, after numerous additions, the house was an elegant, two-story, gray stone villa. The trees had matured and provided shade from the hot summer sun and privacy from the street noise a hundred yards away. Unlike Yeniköy, which had recently become a neighborhood of wealthy foreigners, *Belgrat Ormani* was still wholly Turkish, a neighborhood of quiet, dignified grace. It was far enough away from the Istanbul's bustle that it maintained its pristine greenness, yet one could catch the passenger ferry or take a *dolmush*, the shared community taxi, at Sariyer and arrive at Galata Bridge within an hour.

Halide introduced them to a short, balding man of fifty, with a thin moustache, dressed in a lightweight, brown summer suit. "Turhan, Nadji, I'd like you both to meet Samuel Kovalevsky of HIAS, the worldwide Hebrew relief agency," Halide said.

"My pleasure, Kovalevsky Effendim," Turhan replied. "I trust you're part of the reason we're here."

"That's true, Mister Türkoğlu." He lit a cigarette. Turhan saw, from his nicotine-stained fingers, that he'd lit many cigarettes in his life. "May I have your assurance that what I tell you gentlemen is received in confidence?"

"You realize I'm a newsman?"

"I'm also aware that journalists have a strict code of honor when it comes to preserving confidences."

"Very well, you have my word."

"Mine, too," Nadji said.

"You're a military man," Kovalevsky remarked.

"And an honorable one," Halide said. "I'd stake my own reputation on Colonel Akdemir."

"That's certainly good enough for me. We must take some things on trust."

Halide took a small key from her pocket and unlocked the middle drawer of her desk. She pulled out a folder and handed it to Turhan. Inside the folder were two typewritten pieces of paper and a page-and-a-half of handwritten notes. Turhan read the papers. He turned pale. "This is monstrous. I can't believe that anyone – not even Hitler – would agree to this."

"That's what I said," Halide replied. "But Mister Kovalevsky apparently has information from a number of sources, some quite reliable and highly-placed."

"And the Europeans have the nerve to call *us* 'barbarians!' Are you certain of your facts, Mister Kovalevsky? If this ever got to the newspapers..."

"It won't. Even if you hadn't given me your promise of confidentiality, von Papen has warned the Turkish government that any mention of this so-called 'final solution,' would be condemned as libel, and that Germany would consider this a reason to declare war on Turkey."

"And these 'extermination camps?'"

"They're mostly outside Germany itself. The latest, and largest is being built at Oswiecim in Poland. The Germans call it Auschwitz. There are others, Dachau, Bergen-Belsen, Maribor, Sachsenhausen, Majdanek, Treblinka. Read for yourself."

Turhan did. He gazed levelly at the Hebrew agency man before he spoke. "How can they possibly believe they'll be able to exterminate an entire race? This could simply be western propaganda. What proof do you have this is any more than suspicion on your part, Mister Kovalevsky?"

"Mister Türkoğlu, we cannot account for a large number of our people. The list of missing persons grows each day. German authorities have told intermediaries there's a delay in paperwork due to the war effort, and they're certain when the records of the 'resettlement' are complete, a comprehensive list will be available. I don't believe for one minute that Hitler intends to publish such a list. Colonel Akdemir, your general staff has learned, through French underground sources, that there's a new, highly efficient means of disposing of 'non-Aryans.' A gas, Zyklon-B, is attached to the pipes of the camp's showers. When inmates arrive at the camp, they are directed to these showers, so they'll be 'vermin-free' after their long and difficult trip. The moment the 'showers' are turned on..."

"How ghastly!" Halide said.

"That's only part of what we've learned," Kovalevsky continued. "There are stories of strange 'medical' experiments that allegedly take place in the camps. Dog fetuses being implanted in a human uterus, lampshades made from human skin."

"Please stop, Mister Kovalevsky," Halide said, turning pale. "I think I'm going to be ill."

"The underground could be making up these stories to discredit the Germans, just as the Armenians try to blame us for all the troubles they've ever had."

"I'm certain they're true," the newcomer said quietly. "Mister Türkoğlu, you lived in Berlin. Colonel, you lived in Vienna. Do you really have any doubts?"

"That's abominable. Our government can't stop me from telling the world about these things."

"Tell that to *Vatan's* publisher. They'll stop you all right. You may be able to tell five hundred, perhaps a thousand, people about it before the newsstands are raided and the papers confiscated. Do you think

Dikkat wants to put his neck on the block and risk *Isharet's* permanent suspension from publication?"

"Surely we can do something?"

"We can, in our own small way," Halide replied. "That's why you're here. Mister Kovalevsky advised me that a few – not many – Jews somehow escape Germany and the occupied lands and make it as far as Turkey. Jews from Palestine – they call it Israel – have set up a network to smuggle these survivors into Cyprus and from there to Palestine. They work under cover of night, with a few ramshackle boats. One of those vessels is the *Mustafa Fazil Pasha*, the old tub that first brought me to Turkey in 1915. It's called the *Selah Shalom* now. Turkey is the closest unoccupied neutral country that hasn't set up a blockade. Over a thousand Jews have used our motherland as their bridge to a new life."

"What about Switzerland?" Turhan asked.

"The Swiss put up every barrier possible," Kovalevsky replied. "They're as anti-Semitic as Germany, Poland or Rumania, but they manage their prejudices in a civilized way, with every deference to legality. After all, they're willing to accept anyone's gold or bank deposits."

"How do the Jews get to Turkey?"

"The Czechs and Yugoslavs have been remarkably helpful. Bulgaria's nominally a German ally, but it's had a strong Jewish population for several hundred years. Greece is a leaky sieve. Russia's so big and has so many problems of its own to worry about that the Soviets have neither the manpower nor the desire to protect their borders from the incursion of a few Jews."

"Does Inönü's government know Turkey's being used as a staging area?"

"Let's just say," Kovalevsky answered, "that he doesn't know about it *and he doesn't want to know about it.*"

"You said something about us being involved?"

"I did. There are several way-stations, safe houses being set up for escaping Jews throughout Turkey..."

After Kovalevsky left, the three friends sat around Halide's kitchen table. The afternoon light filtered through the newly-installed venetian blinds. "When did you say you'd give him an answer?" Nadji asked.

"I didn't," Halide responded. "He wants a reply as soon as possible."

"What he asks is fraught with danger for us," Nadji said.

"But it has to be done."

"What if we're discovered?" Turhan broke in.

"Are any of us strangers to risk?"

"Halide, if we're caught, we could be tried for treason," Turhan said.

"And if those like us don't do it, the world will try our nation for gross inhumanity when this war's over," she snapped.

"Nadji, talk some sense into the woman." The colonel shrugged his shoulders helplessly. "You mean you agree with her?"

"She's right, Turhan. You know it in your own heart."

"How does it work?"

"There are more than a hundred military officers involved in the operation," Halide said. "Nadji's in charge of security for the northwest sector. He knows which frontier guards can be bribed or threatened, and where the 'protection' of our border checkpoints will be less than vigilant at any given time. Getting Jews into Turkey is not particularly difficult. Hiding them in 'safe houses' is another story. German tentacles reach deep into our nation. As the Nazis exert economic and diplomatic pressure on Ankara to crack down on these 'anti-neutral activities,' it becomes more and more difficult to have way stations throughout Turkey."

"Why Belgrade Palas?" Turhan asked.

"The life span of a safe house is very brief. If it remains in operation more than a year, the HIAS people call it a 'miracle house.' Belgrade Palas is neither on the main road from Edirne, nor on the Black Sea, but it's close enough to Istanbul to suit their purposes."

"No one would remotely suspect Halide," Nadji said. "To the outside world, she's a dedicated, apolitical teacher who'd never be caught up in such a thing. The 'Palas' is large and sprawling. There are uncountable places where one could hide to avoid detection."

"Kovalevsky said if I gave my approval, the HIAS people would immediately begin building false floors, ceilings, closets, and walls."

"I vote 'Aye,'"Nadji said. "We spend most of our lives thinking back to past mistakes we can't cure, or thinking ahead to dreams that may never happen. This is our chance to live in the present and do something. What do you think, Turhan?"

"What role would I play in this charade?"

"I'm at the teacher's college all day," Halide answered. "Nadji's constantly on the move between here and the frontier. We need an administrator. A *cheteh bashı*, a ringleader, who knows how to get things done, and who has important connections everywhere in Istanbul, from the high-and-mighties to the underworld. Someone who can oil the machinery to get Jewish refugees out of the city once they've gotten here."

"And I'm supposed to be this person?"

"You're the one who said the writing game's no fun anymore," Nadji replied. "Personally, I can't think of anyone better suited to the job than you."

"You seem to forget that my name, if not my face, is rather well known in this town. It wouldn't be hard for someone to discover me."

"You're supposed to be on an extended holiday, right?"

"So?"

"Yalman wrote about his world travels when *Vatan* was suspended. What's to stop Türkoğlu from making a similar trip?"

"Stop talking in riddles, Nadji."

"There's a very simple solution. I'll secure documentary evidence to demonstrate that Turhan Türkoğlu departed Turkey by air to Malta, and from there to Portugal. From Lisbon, he flew to London and met with his good friend, Edwin Baumueller, who invited him to come to the United States as the guest of the New York *World*. For the next year or two, you'll be touring *Amerika Birleshik Devletleri*, writing articles about everything from their national mania, baseball, to the Indians, for all I care."

"How do you know Baumueller?" Turhan asked.

"He was passing through Vienna during my time there. He said he'd met you in Berlin and was quite impressed. We actually spent quite a nice evening together at Sacher's."

"Sounds as if you've planned an entire military campaign, *Albay*. What if Baumueller doesn't go along with it?"

"*Eshek*! Donkey! He's Jewish and he's your friend. Do you really think he'll refuse when he knows the plan?"

"You want me to get in touch with him?"

"Of course. Ask if he'll have someone write a few articles under your by-line, and post them from various places in the United States to *Isharet's* office in Istanbul."

"How do I identify myself to authorities when they ask the identity of the Belgrade Palas caretaker?"

"Do you still have that diplomatic passport Atatürk gave you when he kicked you out of Turkey?"

Turhan grinned broadly. "So it's time for Orfez Halip to come back to life? You're certainly right when you say it's more exciting than traveling. What have I got to lose but my life? All right, *arkadashlar*," he said. "Count me in."

When Turhan asked for a leave of absence to travel the world, *Isharet's* publisher breathed a sigh of relief. Granted, Turhan Türkoğlu was the most popular columnist in Turkey, but he was fiercely independent. He made no secret of his extreme distaste for the Nazi regime and what he perceived as Turkey's not-so-neutral "neutrality." During the weeks that followed Turhan's supposed departure, "Orfez Halip" moved into Belgrade Palas. He and Halide soon had their hands full, helping dispirited, terrified men and women move toward a new life of freedom. When she wasn't busy teaching, Halide was cook, confidante, psychiatrist and mother to the lost souls who slipped through the Master Race's ghastly fishnet. From the latter part of 1941 to early 1942, more than three hundred refugees used Belgrade Palas as a way station between the Reich and the Promised Land.

One night in February, 1942, Turhan returned to Belgrade Palas after a full day's absence. He'd guided eight Jews to a decrepit Turkish fishing boat moored well south of Istanbul, and felt fulfilled. Halide greeted him at the roadway. "Turhan, before you come inside, perhaps you and I should take a walk. It's such a lovely evening."

"What are you talking about, woman? It's cold, wet and miserable."

"Call it what you will. I need to talk with you."

The journalist caught the urgency in her tone. Allah, had they been discovered?

They walked away from the house. "A new refugee came in late this afternoon."

He breathed a sigh of relief. They hadn't been caught. But Halide still sounded tense, strange. "A very sad case. Thin, obviously malnourished. Tormented, very withdrawn. As usual, I went through how we worked at the house, what we did, the preparations for the exodus to Palestine. Not a word until I mentioned you were our administrator – I used your real name, of course. A funny look came into her eyes. She said she knew you years ago."

Turhan felt a wild pounding in his heart. He didn't even have to hear the next words to know exactly what they were going to be. "*Her name is Rachela Friedman.*"

2

"Bernhard?"

"Dead, I assume. Last time I saw him was years ago," she said dully. "He was sent to Theresienstadt. I was sent east."

Turhan contemplated the haggard, still beautiful face, as Rachela continued. "We traveled for two days in a barred cattle car. No windows, no food, no water, no bathroom, a hundred-fifty in a car. We urinated, we defecated, we stank. It didn't matter. The second night the Russians or the Poles, I don't know which, attacked the train. I didn't bother to take notes," she said bitterly. "Someone opened the car door. I was pushed out. There was gunfire. I was too exhausted to pay attention to what happened. I heard the door of the cattle car slam shut. The train was on its way again, but I wasn't on it. The Germans left me for dead. My attackers looked more carefully. I was still relatively young, pretty enough for their purposes. I was a woman, I had the right equipment. That's all they cared about.

"Four days later they'd had their fill of me. They were filthy. I don't know who they were. I know they weren't Jewish. They'd not been circumcised." Her eyes had a faraway look. Turhan could tell she did not see him at all. "The sounds of shooting came from a nearby forest. One of their messengers said troops were combing the area and they'd have to move. I was left behind. I hid in the forest for the next few months, eating berries, leaves, whatever it took to stay alive.

"One night, I heard men speaking Yiddish nearby. When I investigated, I found they'd camped near where I was hiding. I didn't reveal myself to them for several nights. Finally, when I couldn't stand the loneliness any longer, I came out of the brush in broad daylight. My hair was a greasy, rotted tangle. What clothes I had were in tatters. I probably stank worse than they. I hadn't had a bath since Vienna.

"For the next year, I 'serviced' most of the men from time to time. It's not as if I were a whore. We were a small unit at war. Everyone, man or woman, did what they had to do. I ran weapons to the outskirts of Warsaw. Occasionally they sent me to visit one of their Polish or Russian informants. If they wanted me to spread my legs for a bit of information, I spread them. What difference did it make? My life had no value to me. The Germans had already destroyed it. If I could repay them by lying on my back, so much the better."

Turhan shuddered. He was horrified at the thought of the delicate little woman, who'd captivated him with her shoulder-length auburn hair and stylish black sheath dress, pinioned beneath sweating brutes, who'd used her as little more than a bucket into which to pour their seed. "How did you get here?" he asked.

"A man named Baruch came into camp. We became lovers. He knew of a woman in eastern Poland who helped refugees get to the Ukraine. By that time I'd concluded anything was better than the life I was living, even if I got raped yet another time by a Cossack or a Russian peasant. The woman got me as far as Kovarisch. A Russian farmer introduced me to a tailor who helped me move ten miles farther south. Men and women, Jews and *goyim*, helped me. Each night, I slept on a different pile of straw, in a different barn. Finally I got to Odessa. I was crammed aboard a coal barge headed to Varna, among a herd of scrawny cattle. I didn't eat for three days. Please forgive me, I'm tired. The memories are hard."

Turhan nodded sympathetically. "I'll get you some tea."

"Thank you. I'd like that."

After Rachela's arrival, Turhan found it hard to concentrate on his work. She occupied his mind every waking hour. She said little. She ate, not much, but some. She remained withdrawn, haunted by ghosts that inhabited a world she alone occupied. Turhan tried to remind himself that his job was to administer a way station, that he was but one step in Rachela's journey, a nameless, faceless farmer, merchant, 'man, woman, Jew or *goy*.' Ten days' maximum, then send them on their way, that was the rule. He couldn't let her go. Not until he'd helped her to heal.

Was it pity he felt for this desperately wounded soul? Or was it more? Much, much more?

3

"I love you, Rachela."

She was silent.

"I said, 'I love you.' I've loved you since that night in Berlin."

Her eyes filled with a look he was unable to fathom. She said nothing for a long time, and when she spoke, her voice was soft, well-modulated, almost as it had been the night he'd met her. "Did you love me or did you love the glamorous little girl-woman at a stupid embassy party? A coddled, pretty toy on the arm of a wealthy businessman? A cultured western European you could never hope to win? I'm a Jew, Turhan, and you're a Turk. Jews, Turks, Gypsies, Negroes, those of our kind don't love, Turhan, or didn't you know? We produce a million Little Black Sambos, or Christ-killers, or hook-nosed Shylocks and usurers whose sole purpose in life is to cheat good, upright *Christians* out of every *mark* or dollar or *pfennig* we can. We give birth to pickaninnies who dance and smile and have incredible rhythm. Soon we create a country filled with murderers who slice crosses in the bodies of *Christian* Armenians and *Christian* Greeks and *Christian* Austrians, and thank God and Jesus and Mary that the heathen horde was stopped at the gates of Vienna."

Turhan held his tongue. He waited until her rantings had turned to uncontrollable weeping. Then he rose, not knowing what to say, and left the room.

Halide and Turhan were seated in a small den on the second floor of Belgrade Palas. "I never felt so degraded in my life." Halide had listened in silence while Turhan told her of Rachela's rage.

"Words spoken in anger or in jest contain much more than a grain of truth."

Turhan stood, unconsciously reached in his jacket pocket and drew out his key ring. He walked over toward the window, playing with the keys, and gazed outside. A light mist softened the twilight, blanketing the new, light green leaves on the nearest trees. Halide said nothing. He heard a slight squeak as she slowly moved back and forth in the bentwood rocking chair. He took a deep breath, turned back and faced his friend of so many years. "She's right, you know," he stammered. "What I felt was – was guilt…"

Halide rocked back and forth, back and forth, slowly, steadily, maddeningly. "Say something!" Turhan snapped. "I know exactly what you're thinking. How could I have felt the way I did? Sezer was a beautiful human being who was absolutely loyal to me from the day we met to the end of her life. Rachela was something beyond that. How can I explain it? She was unattainable, someone I could never have if I wished for a lifetime." The rhythmical squeaking of the rocker was Halide's only response. "Say something, for God's sake!" he shouted. Immediately abashed, he mumbled, "I'm sorry, Halide. I didn't mean that. Allah help me, I shouldn't have said that to you of all people."

"What *did* you mean, my friend?"

"I don't know," he said. "I'm trying to mouth all the right words, to say all the right things. Expiate the guilt I felt then, the guilt I feel now. But I can't, Halide. I'd be lying to myself if I said I didn't love her, even then. Maybe it wasn't love. Maybe it was something men and women never talk about to one another. Whatever I felt – what I feel even now – is beyond my ability, beyond my desire, to comprehend or even to control. Yes, I felt guilt at betraying Sezer, not by an overt act, but by what I felt in my heart." He laughed dryly, a hollow sound, devoid of humor. "What was it that struck me about Rachela, Halide? Why did I find her so beautiful? Why did I find myself unable, unwilling to fight what I felt, when I knew how wrong it was?"

"I thought you said you did nothing, that you never even told her how you felt."

"It doesn't matter. For the past eight years, I've thought about her. Not so it interfered with my life, not every day. But sometimes, when I was making love with Sezer, I imagined Rachela in my arms. Allah help me, would that I'd have fathered sons out of both women." He paused. "I see I've shocked you."

Halide said nothing.

"And you despise me for my weakness?"

"Should I?"

He sat down in the large, comfortable armchair next to the rocker and looked into her eyes. There was neither anger nor judgment there.

"Turhan," she said. "What is weakness in a man or a woman? What is love? When we're first born, each of us is alone. Each of us takes many unexpected side paths in our journey through life. Did you really love Sezer less because you were overwhelmed by Rachela? God formed us, then left us alone to blunder from one mistake to the next.

Sometimes collectively, as we see in this horrible war. Mostly, though, the mistakes we make are the ones we don't discuss, the very private ones we hide behind the mask with which we greet the world. Sezer's dead, Turhan. Your guilt at what you *thought,* but never acted on, must die with her. You must bury Sezer and your love for her with the honor she deserves."

"That doesn't answer my question," he replied. "Why Rachela? Is she really as beautiful as I believe or is she beautiful because I created my concept of her beauty within my own soul?"

"What is beauty, Turhan? I don't know what Rachela looked like several years ago, in a different world, a different life. I'll take your word for it that she was quite attractive. From what I see of her now, Sezer was infinitely more beautiful, but the heart sees differently than the eye, and who am I to judge?"

The rocker had stopped moving. The room had become dark. Halide rose stiffly to her feet, walked over to a large floor lamp, and turned it on. The light cast soft, golden shadows in the far corners of the room. She returned to the chair and started rocking once again. "Some people say the deepest love is friendship that catches fire. But without the element of touching, holding, feeling, without attraction, there's no spark to set off that fire. God knows, I still cherish the memory of the night Metin and I were together so many, many years ago. You know, I can still smell the sweat and stink of him when I came into that headquarters building." Her eyes took on a faraway look. She was young again. And beautiful. "He smelled so fresh after he bathed. I can still feel him, Turhan. Was *that* only physical? Perhaps. Somehow that night, it was hard to distinguish the physical from the spiritual. No girl ever had a wedding night as beautiful as mine." She blushed, realizing what she'd said, then giggled delicately. "And we weren't even married except in God's eyes and our own."

"I don't understand what that has to do with Rachela and me, or with Sezer, for that matter?"

"Nothing. Nothing and everything. Remember when I said we all start out alone?"

"Yes."

"If each of us has the responsibility to journey through life, for the most part alone, doesn't that carry with it the right to determine what path we take on that journey?"

"No, Halide, it doesn't," he said quietly. "Did you have the power to save Metin? Or to avoid being raped that night near Galata Bridge?"

Halide looked thoughtful. "Perhaps you're right, Turhan. That's why it's so difficult for me to say what I'm going to say. No matter what you feel, Turhan, you must let Rachela go. We're not equipped to deal with her problems. We're stationmasters at a brief stop on their underground train, nothing more. The HIAS agents told us repeatedly never to become personally involved, never to let our feelings take over. We're dealing with mortally wounded human beings. Whether you believe it or not, her world is as foreign to you as if she lived on the moon. You can never share her nightmares."

"But we must try, Halide. If we love enough, we can overcome anything."

"Turhan, you're dreaming about something that happened nine years ago. She's not the same woman you met in 1933. She's – damaged."

"That's just it. She needs more than ever to be helped. She needs to know that someone can be gentle, can care for her, can love her."

"The Jews have doctors to deal with people like Rachela. It will take years to soften the memories. They'll never erase the terror. You can't possibly share what she's survived. You haven't had your soul destroyed."

"I've got to help her, Halide."

"When you try to play God, you only lose in the end. Let her go, for *her* sake as well as yours."

"I can't help myself."

"*Mashallah,*" Halide replied sadly.

4

During the next two weeks, Turhan's contacts with Rachela were minimal. She stayed in her room most of the time. When they spoke at all, it was in formal monosyllables, accompanied by a nod. Turhan felt choked up each time he saw her. He discovered an emotion he never thought he had. In the privacy of his own quarters, he wept quietly as he thought about what she'd experienced. As the tears flowed, he reflected on his own life, until, at times, it became difficult to comprehend for whom he was crying. His thoughts always started with Rachela. But often Shadran's face appeared. And Grandfather's, who invariably looked as he had the last time Turhan had seen him.

For the longest time he blocked out the one person he could not bear to think about. Visions and visions and visions. Jalal and Ibrahim and Gönül and Zeki. Sezer and women whose names he'd forgotten. Rachela and Rachela and Rachela. He thought about *almost* everyone and everything. A little lamb that had been slaughtered when he'd been four, and an innocent teacher who'd been slaughtered only a few years later. But he refused to confront the one apparition that haunted him.

And then one night, when he was weakened and tired, vulnerable and soul-weary, he no longer had the strength to fight it. He fell into bed, still determined to try to avoid what had been in his soul so long. But as he tossed and turned, sleepless, it came.

Was it her fault she'd reacted as she had toward him? Had he been even a little more understanding, would it have made a difference? He had worked two years for a wealthy butcher. He'd never wanted for food. His life, even at fourteen, had been infinitely better than hers. What had he done to help her in her misery? Had he even once visited her? Or sent her the slightest bit of food or a bolt of cloth to make her tragic life the slightest bit easier?

What kind of mother had she been to him?

WHAT KIND OF SON HAD HE BEEN TO HER?

Which of them had had the power to make life better for the other? And which of them had turned a blind eye, a stiff neck, a straight back to the other?

Turhan felt the hot tears of shame. What had his life amounted to until now? He'd ridden with a caravan, escaped death, seen more of the world than one out of every thousand of his countrymen. He'd been showered with praise, possessed wealth sufficient to carry him through the rest of his days in comfort. And it all meant nothing.

He'd reacted to life, been an observer, been moved hither and yon by events beyond his control. Is that what life was all about? Was man's journey simply a sea on which he bobbed like a cork, floating from place to place, event to event, until he died? Or could a man indeed be captain of his own soul? Was life nothing more than a test of universal suffering, how much a human being could endure? Or was it within Allah's plan that Turhan could somehow find salvation from the cruelty with which he'd abandoned his mother, the cruelty of placing his own ambitions above those of another human being?

An owl hooted in lonely solitude in the forest beyond his room. A branch shorn of last year's cloak of leaves and bearing the buds which promised new life scratched rhythmically against his bedroom window. He glanced at his Gruen watch, which glowed with an eerie green phosphorescence. Two forty-five. And Turhan started to pray as he had never prayed before. For guidance, for strength, for salvation. Eventually he fell into a fitful doze.

He was in a small room. There were two others with him, dressed in simple white shrouds. The woman was very old. The man had fierce mustaches, but a glint of humor in his eyes. "Time to greet the spring," Turhan heard himself saying. "Come, Alkimi, come Ibrahim Effendi. It's so green you'd never believe it. The land is so lush and fertile. We've only to open the door."

"No, Turhan," the old woman spoke sadly. "It is not for us to go with you. You must do what you must by yourself."

"I can't, Alkimi. I don't know how. I've never learned. Dear Allah, I never learned." He tried the door and found it locked. He fell weeping at their feet.

"Help me, please help me," he sobbed. "My life is nothing. Ibrahim, father of my heart, can't you help me?

The man lifted Turhan 'til they faced one another, and spoke softly. "I love you, boy. Long ago, I asked to you carry on for me. To make my spirit as proud as if you were the son of my loins. For you were the son of my heart. Have you cried out against injustice? Have you fought for what you believed to be right?"

"I have, Ibrahim. And it's still come to naught."

"Why, Turhan?"

"I don't know why, Effendi."

"What was my final and greatest testament to you, Turhan?"

"I... don't... know," he stammered miserably.

"Have you betrayed me, too? Have you forgotten my most precious legacy to you? The last words of my life? Think, my son. Think with your

heart, your soul, your being. What was the treasure with which I blessed you above all others?"

As quickly as it began, the dream dissolved. And Turhan was awake.

"I recall your words, Ibrahim, father of my heart, as clearly now as when you said them with your dying breath," Turhan said softly. "'*Carry on for me. Make my spirit as proud as if you were the son of my loins, for you are the son of my heart. Don't be afraid to show emotion. Cry out against injustice. Fight for what you believe is right. Most of all, don't be afraid to love. That is my testament to you. Be strong, my son.*'"

In the dawn, for the first time in many, many years, Turhan, faced what lay deep within his soul. Once again, he was sure he could make a difference. His mother had had no choice, no chance. She had survived the best she could. Sezer had been a loyal companion, a good woman. He had crushed her gently, through his own selfishness. Rachela had had no more opportunity to avoid her fate. If Turhan could, through love, save Rachela, would not Allah forgive him for what he'd done to his mother and his wife?

By turning inward, he had found the answer. And in the end, he knew what he would have to do.

"I love you Rachela."

"Don't," she said. Her eyes were hard, dry. "Words mean nothing. You want to make 'love' to me, is that what you mean? Spread your legs, Rachela, lie quietly Rachela, I'll bring you happiness, Rachela, is that what you mean?"

"No, Rachela."

"How can you speak of love?" she said. "Weren't you even listening when I talked to you however long ago it was?"

"A few days," he said, quietly.

"Do you want me to say it again? What do you know of love, Turhan Türkoğlu? What do you know of suffering? You're successful, your life's not threatened. You're in the majority here. How easy it is for you to confuse pity with love."

The Turhan of a few days ago would have reacted harshly. Not now. When he spoke, it was a different Turhan, one who'd thought and prayed that what he said would come out right. "Rachela, I've listened and I've heard you. Would you please listen to me for only a few minutes? I don't ask you to believe me, to feel for me, to pity me. If you don't feel you can listen now, only tell me, and I'll leave you be."

"Go ahead," she said stonily. "I've nothing better to do with my time, and since you're here and have been kind to me, I see no harm in listening."

"I love you, Rachela. You're absolutely right when you say I can never understand your suffering. I won't insult you by pretending to fathom the depth of what you've experienced. And I will tell you that in a way my love for you is selfish. I can't bring back the yesterdays you were never allowed to have, nor can I promise you what tomorrow will bring, because that would be playing at being God. But if somehow I can bring you happiness, if only for this moment, I might be able to face my own guilt."

"What do you mean?"

"Once upon a time – only it wasn't once upon a time, it was forty-five years ago – in a nameless village in Southeastern Anatolia, a sixteen-year-old girl, who was unprepared for life, and who thereafter never had the chance to live, gave birth to a bastard son… She was ostracized, banished from her village, and her son was raised without her until he was sent to Diyarbakır on the orders of the provincial governor. By that time, she was making a poor living in the only way she knew how – the only way an abandoned, unschooled woman could make a living." Turhan told her the story of his mother's life. When he had finished speaking, Rachela found something she believed had been lost forever. The ability to weep.

Rachela continued to suffer in a nightmare universe of her own. But Turhan believed in his heart that if he loved her enough, he could help them both find salvation. Whenever they had an opportunity to be alone, there were mostly long silences between them. Finally, Rachela said, "Everyone else is leaving for the south. Why do I get better food, finer accommodations than anyone, fresh fish, meat, fruits that are out of season?"

"Do you want to leave for Palestine?"

She shrugged her shoulders. "For what purpose? To see hundreds like me, the living dead? To exist among withered souls and experience my own guilt every day because I somehow survived?" The distant blast of a ship's horn on the Bosphorous interrupted the loud chirping of birds. The paleness of the weak winter sun had given way to a bright spring day, and there were fresh, light-colored leaves on the trees in the garden outside.

"You could start a new life there. Be with people who've lived through the nightmare, who feel as you do."

She laughed harshly. "So you'd put me in the sanitorium they're calling Israel, is that it? A nice, safe place for sick people who somehow aren't equipped to deal with civilized society any more?"

"I didn't mean that at all," he said, gently. "I just thought that you'd feel..."

"I've forgotten how to feel, remember?"

"Do you believe I'm keeping you here as a prisoner, against your will?"

"Not really."

"We haven't spoken at all since the time..."

"There's nothing I want to say."

"Would you mind very much if I held you for a moment?"

"Do what you will. I've no control over what happens to me."

He held her against him for a very long time. Her body was stiff, lifeless. He stroked her hair with his fingers. There was no reaction. When he released her, she said nothing. Three days went by. One evening he brought her a glass of tea. He listened quietly as she retold the chilling story she'd told him the first night. At the end, he took both her hands in his and held them.

"Rachela, come to Pamukkale with me."

"Is it farther south?"

"It's south of Istanbul. And it's a very, very special place. I think you'd like it."

"How much time do I have to decide?"

"As much time as you need."

Later that spring, the flowers were in full bloom. Turhan sneezed from the pollen in the air as he and Halide walked along the pathway in back of 'Belgrade Palas.' "How long will you be gone?"

"A month, maybe a little longer."

"I wish you wouldn't."

"Halide, I love her more than anyone I've ever loved in my life. This happens once in a lifetime, maybe never. You know what it's like. You had Metin."

Halide held Turhan's hands in her own. "My heart's friend, you are not dealing with a whole human being. Have you – been with her?"

"No. I don't need that to convince me I'm insane with love for her."

"Are you in love with Rachela Friedman, 1933, or are you in love with love? Or do you feel you must avenge some great wrong?"

"I'm in love with her the way she is now, in 1942."

"Do you know what goes on inside her?"

"I'm aware of all I want to know," he said stubbornly. "You'll see. When the trip is over, she'll be a changed person."

"People don't change."

"There. You've said it yourself. People don't change. She can return to what she was ten years ago."

"That's not what I meant, Turhan. Go if you must. Go with Allah, God, Whoever. I pray your wishes are fulfilled. But whatever happens, know that I am your friend."

In May, Turhan and Rachela left Istanbul. They said little on the ferry that took them across the Sea of Marmara, making brief stops at the pine-covered Princes' Islands. They debarked at Yalova, and drove through rolling hills covered with the reds, oranges, purples and golds of spring flowers. Rachela began her tale again. Turhan listened in silence. When she concluded, he said, softly, "You're in Turkey now, Rachela. The war is in Europe, a thousand miles away."

She closed her eyes. Turhan breathed in the overpowering, sweet floral bouquet from fields on either side of the road. Soon Rachela was snoring. Her face contorted into ugly shapes, and she whimpered. When her face relaxed for a very brief period, she looked like a little girl. After dinner that night, they spoke for a long time. They slept in the same room, but not together.

Rachela emerged from the bathroom next morning. For the first time since he'd seen her nine years before, she'd applied a light coat of makeup. She wore a simple tunic in bright spring colors, a gift from Halide. When she saw how his eyes were filled with the vision of her, Rachela smiled. In that moment, he knew he could never let her go. They drove along the Aegean. South of Izmir, they turned east. The road wound through lush green hills covered with olive and fig trees, into the Meander River valley. Villages perched on terraces, climbing hundreds feet above the flood plain. "Earthquakes and floods hit the valley every five years or so," Turhan explained. "Towns are built on high, flat ground to avoid these disasters as much as possible."

"Can nature bring about any greater disaster than man?"

Late in the afternoon, they reached Aydin. Turhan hired a suite of two rooms overlooking the Meander River. That evening, they strolled the beautiful meadows that descended to the river's edge. For the first time, she reached out and held his hand. She did not speak of the years just past. She told him of her childhood in Berlin, of dances, horseback rides, and holidays in the Hartz mountains.

They returned to their suite later than night. Turhan watched, not a little regretfully, as she closed the door to her room behind her. Soon he heard water running in her bathroom. He tried to picture what it would have been like – what it could one day be like – to be married to her. Enough of such thoughts. He settled into bed and started reading.

He heard a faint sound and felt a presence in the room. He looked up. Rachela stood at the foot of the bed wearing a white, filmy nightdress. He rose quickly, went to where she was standing, and held her. There were no words. He buried his face in her hair, breathing in the unbelievably fresh smell of her. He kissed her brow, her cheek. Rachela was so tiny, so delicate. His voice was hoarse. "You know, if we do this, our lives will be changed forever."

She nodded solemnly. He looked into her eyes. Her beautiful, beautiful green eyes flecked with pale gold. She smiled. Turhan took her hand, as gently as an infant reaching out to its mother for the first time, and silently led her to his bed. Moments later, they lay in each other's arms, lovers at last, grasping for one another, straining to reach beyond the limits of earthly love. Yet they were as gentle as two fawns frolicking in a field. When, after a long time, it was over, he lay awake, feeling her gentle breath as she lay curled about his body. Moments later, soft tears flowed down his own cheeks as he drifted into the sleep of the blessed.

Several hours after they left Aydin, they saw what looked like a large white stain on the side of a nearby mountain. As they passed through Denizli, the road began a steep climb. "My God!" Rachela gasped, as she beheld a sight that had transfixed travelers since ancient days. Nature, as if apologizing for the earthquakes and floods it sent to the region, had compensated mankind by the gift of Pamukkale. From the summit of the mesa, hot, calcium-rich water gushed out from everywhere at once, flowing down, fanning out like veils, carving the rock into terraces and basins. As the water overflowed these hot pools, it spilled down to the next level, and from there to terraces below, all the way down to the valley below. There were countless lagoons, pools, caves, and islands. Over thousands of years, the water had formed stalactites that descended a fifth of a mile down the side of the cliffs, creating softly rounded caves, white as snow, a landscape like none other on Earth.

Easy trails led from one level to the next. Water that erupted at near boiling temperature from limestone fissures gradually cooled as it mixed with outside air. Pamukkale was a fairyland, a millennial playground. The mineral-rich water provided soothing balm for bones, muscles, joints and skin. The myriad hideaways created a secret world for lovers.

As bountiful as nature was, it could also strike with sudden cruelty. There were fallen pillars, arches, and statues in several of the pools. Temples built higher up the mountain had come tumbling down when challenged by nature. Over the centuries, the ruins became one with the water. No one removed the man-made stone columns. To swim among two-thousand-year-old ruins added to the awesome majesty of the place.

Rachela shouted joyously. Her voice echoed down the mountainside. She called out again and again. Turhan's name. Her own. Childish gibberish. There was not another human being in sight. "Oh, Turhan, I can't wait to dive in. Let's not go to our villa yet!" With that, she stripped off her tunic, posed like a small Aphrodite, ran to one of the terraces, and jumped into the water, immersing herself in its luxurious warmth. "Turhan Türkoğlu, if you don't come in this minute, I'm going to drag you in here!"

He needed no second invitation. He shed his own garments and joined her. They jabbered nonsense, like happy monkeys, jumping up and down among the pool's cascades, submersing one another, touching, feeling, electrifying each other with intimacy hotter than the water. They could not grasp each other tight enough, hold the other close enough. Inside a nearby grotto, they found a shallow pool, with soft limestone ledges, no doubt carved eons ago for precisely what they had in mind. The soft, smooth stone matched the contours of their bodies. They made love in the warm water and on the ledge surrounding it. Then, they made love again, and yet again until they collapsed with fatigue. Afterward, they lay on a warm ledge, hidden from view, drifting into and out of blessed sleep.

Like children, they played, they laughed, they loved. Days and nights blended in an incalculable rush, filled with walks through Hierapolis, the ruined city that had been a world-famous spa in the days of ancient Greece, and still more passionate, life-giving lovemaking. If only time could have stood still! The two of them would happily have existed in their own world, devoid of the need for anyone else, forever. The month sped by. It was a fairy tale, and like tales told to children everywhere, it had to end. On their last night in Pamukkale, Rachela cried bitterly. "Why the tears at such a happy time?" he asked.

"Because something this wonderful cannot be real. It's a dream that never happened."

"We'll make it our reality."

He quietly handed her a small box. Inside the box, wrapped in cotton, was the most exquisite piece of jewelry she'd ever seen. It was a necklace of hammered gold chain. The centerpiece was of gold filigree, in the shape of two letters, "R" and "T", intertwined with a six pointed Star of David. In the very center was a single, perfect blue-white diamond. Inscribed on the reverse side were the words "I will love you longer than this will last. Forever, T."

They walked above the falls in the warm, spring evening. A stream flowed gently by the side of the meadow where they walked. Turhan had brought a blanket and they made love once again. Afterward, they wrapped themselves in the cover to watch the moon as it cast silver blades of light on the rivulet. The night was alive with the chirping of crickets, the gentle flow of water, the faint night breeze, the millions of pointed lights in the sky.

"*Shema Yisroel*, dear God, don't let it ever end," she prayed.

"It won't," he promised. "I will cover you in a blanket of love, for eternity."

Much later, when the night had turned cool, they returned to their rooms.

As they neared Yalova, where they would embark by ferry to Istanbul, they experienced the loveliest sights and fragrances of the early Turkish summer. Women in white shawls and *shalvar*, the copious, tent-like pantaloons, looked like so many white poppies as they worked in the fields. It was the same in every village they passed. The women worked. The men either rode small, overloaded donkeys, or played *tavla* – backgammon – in the coffee houses. These were Turhan's people. So had they lived for generations and so would they live for generations to come. The meadows, colored with dark green growth, presaged the coming of bountiful crops, corn, tobacco, tea, grapes. The rolling foothills leading to the mountains of the Turkish interior were dry and rocky, giving an added sense of life to the fruitful fields below.

On both sides of the road, white-shawled women and men wearing dark trousers, plaid shirts and black fisherman's hats, sold an assortment of the season's fruits, bright red and green apples, stacked haphazardly one atop the other, ruby-colored cherries, as large as small apples, and *sheftalı*, the incomparable Turkish peaches so brimming with sweet nectar it was impossible to bite into one without the juice running down their chins.

"You haven't said a dozen words since we started out this morning," Turhan said. "Is something the matter?"

"No," she replied, absently.

At a particularly lovely rise that overlooked the Sea of Marmara, several miles ahead and below them, Turhan pulled the car to the side of the road. "Rachela, have you given any thought to our future together?" She said nothing. "I've thought a lot about it during the past month. Perhaps it's time I let others do some of the work."

"What do you mean?" she asked.

"I never thought I'd say these words until you came. Please, hear me out before you say anything. I always believed I could change the world, make it a better place for everyone. Turhan Türkoğlu, champion of the emerging Turkey, savior of the little man. But I've changed. If I were to retire tomorrow, devote my life to one person, devote my life to bringing you happiness, that would be enough to make my life worthwhile. A long time ago, a man who meant the world to me told me never be afraid to love. Some years later, another man said he doubted I'd ever be able to fully give my heart to another human being. You've taught me I can do that.

"I'm a wealthy man by Turkish standards, Rachela. Not nearly as rich as you were in Berlin, but I've saved enough that I need never work again. Somehow I'm saying this the wrong way, and I don't mean to, but it's the only way I know how." He noticed he was speaking faster and his heart was pounding. "I've been thinking of purchasing a small home in the hills south of Izmir. It's far enough away that the world need never intrude on us."

He'd avoided looking at her while he'd been speaking. Now he saw her lovely face, half-hidden in shadow. "Turhan, dear, dear Turhan," she said softly. "You have your hopes, your dreams, your whole life still ahead of you. If only I could share your spirit and your dreams."

"You can, Rachela," he said earnestly, terrified lest she draw away. "They can be *our* dreams. In time we might even have children..."

"Would you really want to bring children into a world such as this?"

"They're our hope for the future, Rachela, the only way we can affirm our faith there will be a future."

"There's no future, Turhan," she said dully. "There's only what's past."

"I don't believe that, darling," he said, holding her hand to his chest. "I don't ask that you commit to anything. Only try to share my dream for a little while, let me bring you what love I can."

"Oh, Turhan, Turhan," she said, and he could see soft tears rolling down her face. "You're so good, so honest, so childlike. And so precious to me. So very, very precious."

"Then you'll give me a chance to show you the world's not such a bad place after all?"

"I don't know that I can. Let me think about it," she said.

"Take as much time as you need. A lifetime if that's what it takes."

As quickly as she'd fallen into the quagmire of her private despair, Rachela's mood lifted. She'd been eating well during the past month, and there was a healthy color to her cheeks. There was no question in Turhan's mind that although there were jagged peaks and valleys in Rachela's mood swings, at least there were moments when she exhibited genuine happiness. Ibrahim had been right. Love was, indeed, the greatest gift, and given without reservation it could heal anything, anyone.

Theirs was one of the few cars shoving onto the ferry at Yalova landing, but they had to drive through a multitude of goats and fat-tailed sheep, oxcarts and scruffy ponies to get to their reserved spot. "Welcome to the real Turkey!" Turhan said in mock exasperation. "Every smell and sound and more commotion than you could imagine. Praise Allah, I've got you close to me to ward off the foul odors. You still smell of peaches, you know."

Rachela's mood swung down again. "At least theirs is the stench of life," she said. "They say the air around the crematoria where they burn Jews smells very sweet and fragrant."

"Rachela..." He stopped himself. Who was he to pre-empt her memories? And if he loved her, truly loved her, how could he do anything but listen in silent sympathy. He squeezed her hand gently.

An hour-and-a-half later, the ferry reached the midway point of their journey across the Sea of Marmara. Rachela cried out in wonder, "Look to the left, Turhan!" Half a mile to port, the pine forests of Büyük Ada, largest of the Princes' Islands rippled in friendly greeting.

"We've got an hour lay-over here, darling," he said. "Would you care to stretch your legs and walk through the town?"

"I think I'd like that."

They alighted, and after a late lunch of lamb kebabs and spring water, Turhan and Rachela strolled a century back in time. The buildings in town were of the kind that had been popular in the days of the Sultans, two-story, gaily painted wooden structures with bay windows hanging over the floors below. There were no cars to be seen anywhere on the island, although numbers of horse-drawn carriages propelled men and women of every station over the cobblestoned streets. As he had so many times before, Turhan felt the grace of another age.

"This is positively charming," Rachela said. "And what fitting names – the Princes' Islands."

"Not if you'd have asked the princes who lived on them."

"What do you mean?"

"The sultans had a long, vicious history. Each sultan had many wives, and sired sons by each of them. You can well imagine the palace intrigues as each mother fought to insure that her son succeeded to the Tulip Throne. As long as a competing half-brother lived, there was always the threat of overthrow. The easiest way to avoid that was murder."

"How ghastly," Rachela remarked. "I imagine the servants were kept busy cleaning the bloodstains from every room."

"Not at all," Turhan replied. "Muslim law strictly forbade the shedding of so much as one drop of royal blood. The chamberlains, or the eunuchs, or whoever was in charge of such things would invariably approach the unsuspecting victim from the rear and strangle him with a silken cord." He observed Rachela's own choked look and quickly added, "It wasn't long before the sultans found a more civil way to treat with their relatives. Instead of resorting to murder, they exiled their various brothers and half-brothers to these islands, hence the name Princes' Islands. The pretenders to the throne had all the comforts they could want, beautiful scenery, fine food, women or young boys to satisfy their needs – everything, that is, except access to Istanbul or the rest of Turkey. So they lived out their days in a golden prison."

"It looks to me as if those days are preserved here."

"They are. To this day, no automobiles are allowed on the streets and all the buildings are constructed from the pine and fir that grows naturally on the islands. Istanbulus flock here in droves every summer to escape the oppressive heat of the city, and since it's less than two hours away by cheap ferry, it's all many of them can afford."

"Who'd need more?" she asked.

"Turhan, I can't tell you how happy I am to be proved wrong," Halide said a week after he and Rachela had returned to Istanbul. "She's gained weight, she looks radiant, and she seems to be coming out of it. Maybe love truly is the elixir of hope you said it was."

"I'm sure it is, Halide. I've got to remember she's not well yet. It will take years, maybe the rest of our lives, to ease the memories of what happened to her." Turhan had taken time out from a busy day to beard the lioness in her own den. It was his first visit to Yujel Orhan Teachers' College in several months. The place seemed to sprout new buildings every time he came. Workmen, apparently oblivious to the bright summer sunlight, were busy putting the finishing touches on the new, three-story brick administration building.

"So you plan to take up residence on the Aegean, my friend?"

"Yes. I thought we'd spend the summer here, give you a chance to find someone to take over running the house, help train him, and then ease my way out of your life for a while."

She smiled, and Turhan noticed she looked a bit tired. "You really think you could escape my clutches, Mister Türkoğlu?"

"Not hardly. Nor would I want to. When this war's over – and it will end some day – I'd expect you to visit often and enjoy our view from the hills above Izmir to the Greek islands beyond."

"You're serious about retirement?"

"Never more so in my life."

"And Rachela?"

"It'll take time. But we've got our whole lives ahead of us and a world of unhappiness to conquer."

"You know," Halide said thoughtfully, "I truly didn't think something like this would happen. When I warned you, I'd read many books, spoken with many so-called experts on the subject and every one of them said the same thing. These poor, sad people must exist in the shadow world left to them. We can only watch and offer sympathetic comfort. Maybe love is the answer after all."

Although he missed the warmth of her sleeping next to him, propriety decreed that Turhan and Rachela continue to sleep in separate rooms each night. Not that they avoided making love, but they were circumspect, lest they disturb the routine of the safe house. Turhan continued to shuttle the survivors to the quiet harbors at Serağlio Point, from which they'd depart for the south. Rachela stayed at the Belgrade Palas, cleaning, walking about the grounds, occasionally visiting Halide at the college. Healing.

Early in July, she experienced uncomfortable stomach cramps and found she had trouble sleeping. For some hours after she awakened each day, she felt a slight nausea and dizziness. She said nothing to Turhan about this for several days. Ultimately, when she mentioned it, Turhan insisted she consult a Jewish doctor he knew in Shishli. He accompanied her on the first visit and sat nervously in the waiting room while the doctor, a short, middle-aged man with an engaging smile and a look of being overly well-fed, poked, probed and tested. He was both thorough and very gentle.

"I'm certain it's nothing serious, Madame Türkoğlu," he said to her, "but I can understand your nervousness." He measured out a small jar of white pills which he handed to her. "These will help you to sleep," he said. "I'm giving you the entire bottle because medicine's gotten frightfully expensive on the open market. We're always given samples, so it's no great gift. One a night should be plenty, two if you really have problems. These should last you a month, and I hope you'll have no need of them afterward. I'll want to see you again in two days when the tests come back."

In the outer room, he told the anxious Turhan, "I'm sure there's nothing at all to worry about. Probably just nerves, but it's best to make sure. I've told your wife to come back in two days." Neither said anything to disabuse the doctor of his belief that he was dealing with "Madame Türkoğlu."

"I suspected as much," the doctor said two days later. "But I simply wanted to be sure. Congratulations, Madame Türkoğlu!" He smiled broadly.

"What do you mean, doctor?"

"The tests have come back. If everything goes as I believe it will, you will become a mother in a little less than eight months. As the Turks are fond of saying, 'Inshallah, may it be a healthy boy!'"

Rachela's mind reeled as she walked up Istiklal Caddesi to Taksim Square shortly after noon to catch the *dolmush* back to Belgrade Forest. *My God*, she thought, *I'm with child. Turhan's child. Maybe he was right. Maybe we must have faith in the future.* She was so busy daydreaming, she hardly noticed where she was going, until suddenly she bumped into someone on the street, and came instantly awake. "Excuse me, I'm so sorry," she said to the back of a tall man immediately ahead of her.

"That's quite all right," he said, turning and raising his hat to her politely.

Rachela gasped and turned pale. She knew that face! A reminder of her past.

"Frau Friedman, is it not? I'm certainly surprised to see you in Constantinople," he said, using the old European name for the city.

"H... Herr von Papen...?" she said, trembling. It was all she could do to keep from fainting right there.

"Mister Ambassador," he said coolly. "But then again, you wouldn't exactly call me *your* Ambassador, would you?" he said. "I believe you are a 'stateless person?'"

She stared at him in stunned silence. "Ah, yes," he continued airily, "one of the little fish that swam through the net when her husband was 'resettled.' No matter. We need a few of you to remain 'at large.' How could the Reich survive if there were no Jews remaining alive to be scapegoats?" He smiled icily, then continued. "But don't get the idea that you're entirely free, Gnädige Frau. We've got friends everywhere in Turkey – even, for that matter, in Palestine – and we manage to keep account of whoever we want. Our friends advised us, for example, that you and that *scheissdreck* reporter for *Isharet* went on a jolly little vacation together. Wonderful combination, a Turk and a Jewess, eh, Frau Friedman? *Auf wiedersehen*."

He tipped his hat and disappeared into the lobby of the German consulate.

That night, Rachela locked the door to her room before Turhan came home. She lay on her bed, and thought back to a time so long ago. Waves lapping over her toes the first time she went to the *Neuer See* in Berlin's Tiergarten. She'd been five years old. Papa had bought her a small, stuffed animal and delicious, sticky candy. God, life had taken her along strange roads since then. She was forty years old now. Her body was almost as trim as it had been before she'd been defiled. Small, uplifting breasts. Pink nipples, not brown like so many of the cows she'd seen in the partisan camps. She still had auburn hair that fell in soft waves around her freckled face. It had not yet gone gray.

When she'd been with Bernhard, she'd loved to admire herself in the mirror. She knew other men had undressed her with their eyes, in Berlin, in Vienna, even in the godforsaken hellholes of Poland. She and Bernhard had lived in the nicest section of Berlin, with servants to succor their every whim. Freedom to come and go as she pleased, whenever, wherever.

Damn it! Why did it have to go so wrong? Damn the God who'd made her Jewish, who'd made her desirable, who'd made her a woman! Damn Him to hell!

Turhan was a good man, but what did he know? Had he endured the indignities? If he lived a hundred years, he'd never know the agonies she'd suffered. So many were dead. Because they were Jews! Because they *said "Shema Yisroel Adonay Elohenu"* instead of "Hail Mary, Mother of God, Blessed art Thou among women and blessed is the fruit of thy womb, Jesus." It was not right that so many millions should perish, while she alone survived. Surely a just God would see that all His children must be treated equally.

What did stupid men know anyway? They felt they could protect you, save you from the pain of existence. Turhan actually wanted her to have his child. Now, in time, she would do that very thing, bring a child into this endless hell. What kind of bizarre punishment would that be to inflict on an innocent baby?

Let me be your lover, let me be your friend, let me bring you comfort. But there is no comfort. Move to Palestine and face a life among the dead? Live with Turhan so they could suffer knowing that one day, when they least expected it, the octopus would consume them, destroy their child? No, it could not happen. It must not happen. I must sleep now, she thought. Maybe then it will be better. She was calm. She lay back and fell asleep, a smile of childlike innocence on her face.

She still wore the same smile when Turhan found her next morning. The small pills, her only real friends, had done their work well.

5

She was gone. Never again would he feel the warmth of her body nestled against his. No more laughter, no more anguished tears. Gone was the pain so intense it could kill, the passion so profound it could give life anew. Death had made the decision that could not be made in life. His mother was gone. Sezer was gone. Now Rachela was gone. His soul had been cut out of him. It could never be replaced. Turhan found a rustic house on the outskirts of Izmir. There, like a fatally wounded animal deprived of its mate, he went into seclusion to die.

Time passed. How much, he didn't know or care. *Rakı* did not erase the memory. Cursing Allah did not help. Alone with his memories, he mourned, shunning contact with the outside world. His body shriveled. He cried endlessly, wrote a few lines, cried more, contemplated joining Rachela in death. Yet each time he brought himself to the precipice, he drew back.

What use had his life been? He'd written a few articles, spoken a few words, helped a few people to read. So what? If it hadn't have been him, another human being would have filled the role, perhaps better than he. Ibrahim had been wrong. Jalal had been wrong. He'd loved beyond his ability, beyond anything he'd ever felt in his life and what had it accomplished? Rachela was gone, never to return. He'd destroyed everyone he'd touched. His mother. Sezer. And Rachela.

Months passed. Turhan cut wood, harvested what vegetables grew on the plot of land surrounding the house, prepared for the colder season. His body was leaner, more sinewy than it had been. Hands whose hardest previous work had been typing copy became calloused, roughened. Despite his every effort at self-destruction, he was in better physical condition than ever. Rachela haunted his every moment. Yet, as days gave way to months, memories grew softer, more distant. In spite of his grief, Turhan's heart kept on beating. He slept each night and awoke each day. The world refused to come to an end.

Nadji was reassigned to Ankara in September, 1942. Halide was left to run the Belgrade Forest sanctuary on her own. A month after Turhan's departure, there was a knock on her door. When she opened it, she found herself looking into the brown eyes of a sharp-faced man a head taller than she, who wore a checked, open-necked shirt and dark slacks. She estimated he was forty-five, her age. He was chunky, solid-looking.

"Yes?" she said. "How may I help you?"

"You are," he removed a card from his jacket pocket and read, "Halide Orhan?"

"That's correct. Who might you be, Effendim?"

"My name is... Ahmet Haratürk. I understand you need someone to manage the house you're running to help my people."

"Who are you?" Halide asked, suspiciously.

He took out a single-page, typed letter and handed it to her. Halide could make out Hebrew letters and an address on the letterhead. Except for the words "Jaffa, Israel," "Ahmet Haratürk," "Abba Habonim," and the typed in signature "Moshe Olmelech," she couldn't understand a thing. She looked up blankly.

"My letter of identification from the resettlement agency in Israel, Hatzma'odt. I assure you, Miss Orhan, you are free to check my references. I would prefer you do so."

"How do you know I need a new administrator?"

"Word filters through various channels."

"You hesitated when you said your name was Ahmet Haratürk."

"I haven't used that name in many years," the man said. "I emigrated to Israel in 'thirty-six. Like most settlers, I took on a new name, in my case Abba Habonim. Life is hard in the Promised Land, but if one is astute there's a very good living to be made. I shipped citrus fruit to Western Europe. Within five years, I made a fortune. I felt it morally imperative that I return here to help my fellow Jews any way I could."

"Why didn't you go directly to the HIAS people?"

"They'd undoubtedly want a monetary donation from me, but I'm sure they would otherwise spurn my help. I'm well known in Israel, in fact, all over the Middle East. The Germans, I'm sure, consider me a criminal, to be caught and hanged. I understand our – your – Turkish government doesn't want its neutrality compromised in any way. My organization, which is not connected with HIAS, has heard of your good work."

"I can't pay you much, you know."

"I don't need money. My resources are such that I could easily pay you what it costs you to run this home. I simply ask that you allow me to prove myself to you."

"Abba, Ahmet, whatever your name is, I'd like to check it out with HIAS. I'm not saying you're not welcome. Now, more than ever, I need all the help I can get. But I'm certain you're aware of an event that took place thousands of years ago on the eastern side of the Dardanelles."

"You mean *Chanakkale* – Troy – when the Greeks brought in the wooden horse as a gift to the Trojans."

"Precisely. You may be everything you say, but I suggest you and I speak with the HIAS agent when he returns from the United States next month."

"Surely there's some work I could perform in the interim to show my good faith?"

"I suppose there's no harm to be done in that short a time. Very well, Abba."

"Ahmet is better, now that I'm back in Turkey."

"Have it your way, Ahmet. You can start work right now."

From the beginning, Haratürk was a godsend. He worked tirelessly, day and night. Before long, the paperwork was better organized than it had ever been. However, after he started, Halide received word from her counterpart on the Asiatic side of the Bosphorous, that a smaller number of refugees than usual was getting through to Cyprus.

When Nadji visited Istanbul, he and Halide met at the Park Hotel lounge. Nadji told her his contacts had warned him that internal security police were watching her home rather more than was necessary. They talked about Turhan, who, they hoped, would finally emerge from his self-induced exile in a few months. Halide told him about the journalist's replacement. The colonel became suspicious. When she described Haratürk, his eyes hardened. He asked if she could arrange for him to see Haratürk without his knowledge.

The next day, Halide sent Haratürk to the post office just north of Taksim Square to pick up a parcel she told him was being sent from her agents in Izmir. The large, ornate old building bustled with the usual morning crush of postal patrons. Haratürk took no notice of a small group of Turkish officers, Nadji among them, waiting for their own mail in the line to his left. Even before Haratürk's return, Halide received a telephone call from Nadji. "Meet me at five this evening, usual place," he said, and hung up the phone.

When she arrived, Nadji said, "Let's walk up Istiklal Caddesi." She could feel from the insistent tug on her arm he did not want to talk in the lounge. She followed obediently. When they were in the midst of the early evening crowd walking up Istanbul's main shopping avenue, he said, "I know your administrator. I've known him for twenty years. His name's not Ahmet Haratürk."

"I know. His Israeli name is Abba Habonim."

"He's not Israeli. His name is Abbas Hükümdar. He was the policeman that came to your rescue on the night you were raped. Very pro-Nazi. Deputy Minister of the Interior. One of the most militant voices insisting publicly that Turkey remain neutral. Privately, he has several business dealings with the Reich. He's been a frequent visitor to von Papen's Ankara residence. I'm surprised your HIAS people haven't discovered him."

"They've been too busy with their own problems to visit much, lately. Come to think of it, Haratürk – Hükümdar – reported sick when they came through." The realization suddenly struck Halide that Nadji had uncovered the leak in the underground system that was putting the refugees in jeopardy. She stiffened. "What must I do?"

"Send Hükümdar on an important errand, preferably one that will take more than a day. I'm certain his police are making careful note of anyone who comes to Belgrade Palas. I'll have to stay away to avoid detection. Get in touch with the HIAS people immediately. While Hükümdar's out, get rid of anything that can implicate you in the effort to facilitate the refugees' transit through Turkey. The cover's exposed. We'll have to dismantle the house."

"But Nadji, after all the good we've done?"

"It's no longer 'we.' It's 'them' or 'you.' Kovalevsky will understand that. You have to act immediately. It's only a matter of time – maybe even days – before Hükümdar gets a search warrant. The Jewish agency is used to such disappointments. This is not a failure. You've helped hundreds come through. Your house lasted longer than most."

"How can I let those good people down?"

"Do you really have a choice?"

The following day, Haratürk – Hükümdar – telephoned Halide early. "I know you need me now of all times, but my mother's taken seriously ill in Ankara."

"But Ahmet, as I told you, I'd planned for you to meet HIAS' chief of mission this evening. He'll only be in town for a little while. I've told him so much about you. He'll be terribly disappointed." She winked at the five Jewish agency representatives who were busily packing the records.

"I'm so sorry, Halide. I know I missed them last time as well, but I'm sure they'll understand. I'm calling from the railroad station in Üsküdar. My train leaves in ten minutes. The woman is seventy-five. I've seen her only once since I returned from Israel. I'll be back in three days, four at most. Please make my apologies."

"All right, Ahmet," she replied, feigning exasperation and weariness. "I suppose there's nothing else I can do."

Within five hours of the call, it was as if the way station had never existed. Every record had been shipped out. False walls, beds and cots, even excess toiletries had been removed. The operation was terminated as rapidly as it had begun. Halide settled in for the night and was just falling asleep when she heard pounding on her door.

She put on her robe and answered, only to find herself staring into the face of her administrator, Ahmet Haratürk, who announced in formal tones, "Halide Orhan, I am Deputy Minister Abbas Hükümdar of the Turkish Ministry of the Interior. We are advised you have been running a treasonous anti-Turkish underground, aiding and abetting the escape of undesirable persons. I have a warrant issued by the Istanbul Court of First Instance, authorizing a complete search of your residence for all physical evidence that tends to prove you have been operating an illegal center for refugees, in direct violation of the Law of Neutrality."

He showed her the search warrant and introduced the four men who accompanied him. Three were high-ranking officers in the internal security forces. The fourth was a magistrate from the court. "You may have a lawyer attend if you wish."

"Come in, gentlemen," Halide said pleasantly. "I've nothing to hide and no need for legal counsel. You may look anywhere you want in the house, for whatever you'd like."

An hour later, Halide invited the five men to take tea. Four of the five were exceptionally courteous and most apologetic for having disturbed her. Obviously there'd been a dreadful error. The fifth man, Hükümdar, was ashen-faced and said nothing. As they took their departure, he muttered under his breath, "You bitch!"

"Why Mr. Haratürk – I'm sorry, I meant Deputy Minister Hükümdar," she replied softly. "I fear you mistake me for someone else. Surely we all make mistakes. Good evening to you."

6

At the beginning of 1943, Nadji, who'd steadfastly remained Turhan's only link to the outside world, came to speak with his friend. "Ah, I see the dead man still breathes."

"Yes," Turhan said wearily, "but only Allah knows why."

"Don't you think it's about time you stopped blaming Allah for your problems? Your grief's become tiresome."

"It's easy for you to say, Nadji. You never had a love like Rachela."

"I know, I know. No one ever loved like you. You can never love again. Listen, why don't you simply unearth the poor woman, jump into the ground with her, and tell her all these things?"

"Who in hell gives you the privilege to mock me?"

"Good! Good, Turhan! Shout, yell, scream! Does it bring your lady back? Did it stay her hand when she killed herself? Did I take her from you? Do you expect me to bring her back?"

"No," Turhan mumbled. "I'm sorry, Nadji. It's not you. It's just that I feel so empty."

"There, there, old comrade," Nadji softened instantly. He walked over to Turhan, held him in his arms, and rocked him gently. After several moments, Nadji said, "Do you want to talk about it?"

Turhan started speaking. Words poured out in a cascade. Through it all, Nadji listened patiently, sympathetically. Finally, Turhan felt drained of all emotion, empty. He collapsed into a deep sleep. Nadji spent the night at his friend's home. The healing had begun.

A month later, Nadji appeared at Turhan's home with a strikingly attractive middle-aged woman, just over five feet tall, with emerald green eyes, and dark hair, flecked with gray. The fawn-colored skin jarred Turhan's memory.

"I believe you knew one another in the past," Nadji said.

"That is quite correct, Colonel. Well over thirty years ago."

"Zari? Zari Ben David?" Turhan's eyes went wide in amazed recognition.

"It's been Zehavah Kohn for several years, but I'm the same girl you knew in Sinop. I kept *Yildiz* in good condition for years after you gave her to me. Her great, great, great grandsons and granddaughters still roam the fields near our home in Sinop."

"And your husband? Does he live in Sinop as well?"

"Jacob died five years ago. *Yengetch burju*, cancer. He was an engineer, a very good man."

"I'm sorry."

"We had eighteen loving years together and three fine sons. And you, Turhan? Whatever became of the boy who was so tongue-tied he couldn't find words to speak to me?" Turhan wondered how much Nadji had he told the woman "You can leave out the part about Rachela if you want. Nadji told me it would be very hard for you to talk about her. It was the same with me when Jacob died. At least I have my sons to keep me company, and my work keeps me occupied. I've followed the 'public' Turhan for years. I read *Isharet.* I listen to the Turkish radio, even the BBC from time to time. I really mean what ever became of the *little* boy I knew?"

"It's been a long road for me, Zari. I grew up, became friends with the *Gazi*, started several newspapers in villages in the southeast. I've managed to stay out of jail and keep my head on my shoulders. This last year has been very difficult. What about you?"

"Papa wanted me to be a lawyer from the first. He said I could argue better than anyone he knew. He teased me that anyone who could best him in an argument must pursue that career. I graduated from the university twenty years ago, then became an *avukat.*"

Allah, Turhan thought. *Have we all aged so quickly? I'm forty-six. Professor Ben David was only a few years older than that when I met him – and I thought he was an old man.* "What about your father?"

"Papa died a few years ago. Mama lives with us in Sinop."

"And your brother?"

"Avi emigrated to Palestine. He's been running refugees from Cyprus to Jaffa."

So here you are, a widow, and here I am, an eligible bachelor, and my friend Albay Akdemir just happens to bring you up to my hillside 'estate.' Rather a coincidence, Turhan thought. "What brings you here?" he said.

"I knew Nadji had connections with the Jewish underground. I asked him to seek you out. I need your help."

"Why me?"

"Because a newspaperman makes contacts in places a lawyer dares not go."

"I've been away from Istanbul for nearly a year."

"But you cemented your connections while you worked with the underground. Are you willing to help an old friend?"

"Tell me what you're talking about before I commit."

"Very well. You know the name Abbas Hükümdar?"

"Deputy Minister of the Interior. Not a nice man to tangle with." Nadji had told him about the attempt to trap Halide.

"He's been buttering his political bread for the post of Interior Minister. Yalniz announced he's stepping down at the end of the year. Hükümdar's the heir apparent, even though the Assembly's embarrassed by his politics. For months he's been searching for something that would bring him to the attention of the Turkish public. If it hurt the Jews, that would help. If he could somehow be cast in a sympathetic light, that would be best of all."

"I'm aware of his sympathies."

"It seems Hükümdar's found the cause he wanted," she said bitterly. "Right in his own backyard, so to speak."

"What do you mean?"

"Abbas has a twelve year old son, Kâzim. A month ago the boy disappeared, dropped out of sight. Hükümdar went crazy. No one ever saw him in such a rage. He threatened to bring the kidnappers to justice if it cost him his last *kurush*. He placed his villa and a reward of one hundred thousand lira as bond for anyone who could find his son's abductor and successfully bring the villain to justice, the bounty to be paid on conviction. Needless to say, Istanbul caught the fever, fueled largely by greed. Neighbor spied on neighbor, friend on friend. When Hükümdar hinted Jews were at the bottom of this contemptible act, there was public outcry for a bloodbath against the Istanbul synagogue. Ultimately, they found the child."

"Alive?"

"And unharmed."

"Where?"

"That's the problem, Turhan. In the home of Mose haLevy, the *Khakham* of the Jewish congregation."

"Quite convenient for Hükümdar."

"Worse than that, the boy refused to leave haLevy's home. When Hükümdar sent officers to the place to seize the boy, they found the home deserted. They razed it, for all the good it did them. Now, in his frustrated rage, Hükümdar has brought action against haLevy's three sons, claiming they must pay for their father's sins. He's demanding the sons be convicted as accessories to kidnap, that they be punished for the principal crime, and that all their property in Turkey be confiscated to the use of the Republic."

"Why have you come to me about this?"

"Because we need a reporter to insure that our side of the story is told, but mostly because I don't think there's anyone else in Turkey who could locate the boy. You've been able to dig up things no one in government ever found."

"Why don't you just ask the sons?"

"They've told me they have no idea where their father is. I'm convinced they're telling the truth."

"You're an *avukat*, Zari. You've got your own investigators."

"Hükümdar controls the interior ministry and internal security. No investigator will risk the cancellation of his license by crossing Hükümdar. You've taken on the government before."

"With the result that I spent an enforced vacation in England. Surely if you have enough money you can find someone?"

"Turhan, there is no money. I'm handling the case for expenses only."

"I need to think about it, Zari. I sympathize with you, but it's a bit strange when an old friend comes out of the woodwork after thirty years seeking a favor."

"Nadji said you'd respond that way. I don't take offense at all. I was only hoping you'd consider. As an advocate, I'd be remiss if I didn't knock on every door," she said sadly. "What if you do decide to help us?"

"Nadji knows how to get hold of me."

Less than two weeks later, Turhan was up early pulling weeds in the garden outside his residence, good humoredly cursing the unwanted vegetation. Spring had come to the coastal hills. It was a warm, sunny, cloudless morning. The only sound was the shrill chattering of jays, and the more musical courting sounds of smaller birds. Turhan paid scant attention to the sound of a motor vehicle climbing the hills below his home. More likely than not, the American Tobacco Company was sending a buyer to inspect his neighbor's first growth. As the sound grew louder, he became more attentive. A gray sedan pulled up outside his house. Nadji and Halide emerged from the automobile.

"Halide...?" he began.

"We don't need to talk about it, my friend. We need your help. I'm here to make sure that this time you don't refuse."

"What are you talking about?"

"Abbas Hükümdar."

"Rather desperate of Zari to send you."

"Do you want to talk out here, or are you going to offer your old friends some tea?"

Halide's face wore a pained expression as she recounted the events which had led her to Turhan's home. "We were fortunate that Nadji warned me just in time. Last week Hükümdar got his revenge. I'll never be able to prove it, of course, but I find it much more than a coincidence that just before dawn last Wednesday, a fire broke out and burned down the part of my home that had been used as our way station. I find it strange that after the fire department found oil-soaked rags in places where a blaze would ignite the fastest, the police did very little to investigate, and reported the fire as 'accidental.'"

"Allah!" Turhan said. "Did everything burn down?"

"The outside survived, charred but intact. Thank God, I'd worked late at the college that night and didn't feel like making the trip back to Belgrade Forest. Still, I felt so – violated."

"You're certain it was Hükümdar?"

"Turhan, my intuition has rarely been wrong. Less than two months before, I humiliated him in front of his subordinates, made him appear the buffoon after he'd sworn out a search warrant. Then this thing with his son. Why would the fire just 'happen' to start in the only area of the house I'd used to shield the Jews?"

"But you've only got suspicions."

"Turhan, my life was burned up in that fire! All my photographs, letters from my father, from Metin. A picture of Sezer taken the day Yujel Orhan Teachers' College opened. Whoever set the fire knew my house from the inside. Maybe a fire doesn't mean anything to you because you've never experienced one. Maybe you've never seen the memories of a friend taken away from you with no justification except the malicious spite of another human being!"

"*It's nothing but a wooden church. The damned Armenians can put up a new one when it's over,*" echoed in Turhan's brain.

"Would it help you to know, Turhan, that the *Khakham* of the Istanbul Jewish community, the man whom Hükümdar seeks to destroy, was the one human being in Turkey who unhesitatingly signed documents in 1938 agreeing to sponsor Bernhard and Rachela Friedman and bring them from Vienna to Istanbul?"

"What must I do?"'

"Find the boy, Turhan. Find the *Khakham*. Tell our side of the story to the world."

Turhan was shocked when he saw the damage done to Belgrade Palas. As he and Zehavah sat in Halide's living room, the advocate briefed him. Turhan scratched his head, then stroked his chin and glanced at his friend. "Hükümdar's the Deputy Minister of the Interior. He's got the entire police force at his command."

"That may well be, but nine out of every ten Turks live in villages. You know how villagers react to outside authority."

"Twenty million people live in Turkey. Just like that, I'm supposed to find a twelve year old boy who's dropped off the face of the earth. That's an insane request."

"And I'm asking it of you, Turhan," Zari said. "The only thanks I'll get for handling this case is that my house and everything I own will probably be watched by the police for years to come. I'm just as naïve as you in my hope that there's justice in this country and that the little people can make a difference. So what's your answer, my friend?"

"An insane request demands a suitably crazy answer. I believe you Jews have a word for it, *Meshuginah*. I guess that's what I am, because I'll help you. It is impossible, you know."

"Yes of course." Zari kissed him. "Welcome back to the land of the living, my friend."

7

Hükümdar retained special counsel, Romali Sonbahar, a senior Turkish senator, advocate to both Atatürk and Inönü, one of the most renowned lawyers in the republic, to prosecute the case. Sonbahar, a tall, broad shouldered man, wore his sixty years with elegance. He had a thick, stylish growth of iron gray hair, wide set cobalt eyes, and was clean shaven. His hands were manicured, his clothing of the finest tailoring, cut from superb materials. Abbas Hükümdar was staking his political, emotional, and monetary fortune on the outcome of this case. Only the finest would do, regardless of cost. It was reputed he'd paid Sonbahar one hundred thousand lira to take on this case.

When Sonbahar arrived from Ankara, his entourage included junior associates, legal consultants, and professors from the Istanbul and Ankara law faculties, secretaries, investigators, and clerks. They set up a luxurious suite of offices in Cumhüriyet Caddesi, the most prestigious address in Istanbul, to prepare a showpiece presentation.

Zehavah rented two small rooms on Okchumusa Caddesi, adjacent to the Neve Shalom synagogue, in the shadow of the Galata Tower. She could not boast any of the high-priced talent employed by Sonbahar. But she had Turhan Türkoğlu.

In May, 1943, the Judicial Council appointed Bilgili Ishchi as presiding judge of a three judge panel. Had the fates themselves intervened, a more curious selection could not have been found. Ishchi, thirty-five, had been a judge in Sivas for less than a year. He'd presided over small civil cases, never a major trial. His appointment to the judiciary had itself been a mystery. Very little was known of his private life. Within two days of his appointment, Turhan unearthed substantial information on Ishchi. "He was one of the most brilliant students who ever graduated from the Ankara University Law School. Served as a law professor in Adana for five years, then practiced for another five. His appointment was a political compromise. The Senate rejected two proposed appointees. The judicial appointments secretary had to scurry around to find the least controversial figure they knew, to avoid a complete deadlock. Senator Sonbahar did not participate in the debates or the nomination. Ishchi was appointed to the bench because he was a complete political cipher. As a junior judge, he was sent to Sivas. He's a relatively young man. I'm sure the Senator will try to bully him. From what I've learned so far, Ishchi may surprise him."

Within two weeks of his appointment, Judge Ishchi called for a preliminary meeting among counsel in the Istanbul courthouse. The *Mahkeme*, a high-ceilinged, decrepit old building, steeped in history and tradition, was in a state of terminal decline. Although there was gracefully-carved stonework on the outside, one had only to come within twenty feet to see that the cracking, chipping exterior was held together by the oily grease that concealed its original color.

As Turhan entered the edifice, he was assaulted by the smells of an emerging Turkey, strong cigarettes, sweat, the sour smell of fear. Garlic, onions, fried fish, broiled lamb. The sweet-milk aroma emanating from a peasant woman sitting on the floor outside a courtroom door, suckling her infant.

He looked about him and saw the same assortment of humanity he'd seen outside, the orange juice merchant, the shoeshine man, teen-aged boys, with huge wooden racks atop their heads, carrying *s'mits*, huge, warm, sesame-seed-covered pretzels. Women covered their faces with shawls whenever a man walked by, but didn't hesitate to nurse their babies in public view. Small, dark men with thick moustaches, dressed in dark pants, white shirts, dark sweaters and flat caps. Lawyers pompously parading through the halls of the courthouse, studiously ignoring the riffraff through whom they had to wade to get to their destination. And everywhere, boys of eight or nine carrying trays filled with glasses of tea.

Inside, the courtroom smelled musty. Turhan sat in one of the dark-stained wooden benches behind the bar and listened as Judge Ishchi addressed the lawyers. "Counsel, I am honored to preside over a trial of this magnitude. As I understand this case, the plaintiff, Abbas Hükümdar, asks the Court to declare there's been a felonious kidnap. He asks that this event be treated as treason because it involves the abduction of a high government official's child, and that the matter be tried as a civil action before the same court. In lieu of the incarceration of *Khakham* Mose haLevy, the alleged kidnapper, who appears to be in hiding, Mister Hükümdar requests that all property of the *Khakham* and his sons be confiscated, and that the Plaintiff recovers One Million Lira for his injury. Is that correct?"

"It is, your Honor."

"Avukat Kohn, your defense is there was no kidnapping. You claim the boy, Kâzim, exercised his own free will and chose to remain under the protective guardianship of Khakham haLevy. You ask for dismissal of all charges on the ground there is no proof sufficient to sustain them, and you are requesting reasonable fees and costs."

"That is correct, your honor."

"Very well. There's been an estimate of thirty days to try this case. I've found that when lawyers take an inordinate amount of time, they are speaking to impress rather than to express. To avoid such showmanship, I propose to limit your pre-evidentiary questioning of the judges. Each of you will prepare a written list of questions which I will ask."

"But Your Honor!" Senator Sonbahar responded. "That's completely untenable. The whole purpose of such questioning is for counsel to find out everything about the judges and to educate each judge what the case is about."

"Indeed, Avukat Sonbahar. I believe that's what the *trial* is all about. It would make no sense if someone had a preconceived view of the evidence."

"Your Honor, in my thirty-six years as an advocate, I've always used pre-evidentiary questioning for this purpose. The public has a right to know what we intend to prove. This practice has become so ingrained that it cannot be seriously questioned."

"Avukat Sonbahar," the Judge responded patiently. "That may well be your perception. My view is that pre-evidentiary statements are used as a tool to demonstrate rhetorical skills and curry favor with the media. Unfortunately, perhaps for us both, I am the judge. My choice of procedure will prevail over yours while I am presiding judge. If any question I ask, or any answer given, prompts you to ask another, please write it down and hand it to my court clerk, who will transmit it to me. If I find the inquiry relevant and valid, I will ask it, otherwise not."

"Your Honor," the prosecutor appealed. "Under the practice you propose, my client may not have the full time necessary properly to present his case."

"He might not at that, counselor. But that's your problem, not mine. This is a trial, not a political platform. If we assume a single percipient witness testifying each day, we could take a month to try this case. But from the witness list both counsel have handed me, I can't see either side presenting more than five witnesses before the evidence becomes cumulative, and, I might add, boring. Any objections to evidence will be clearly stated. No lectures will accompany them. Nor do I anticipate your objections will lead the witness to answer in a given manner. If this happens once, I will advise you at side bar. If this becomes a habit, I will let the other judges know my displeasure and will, perhaps, give other sanctions as well."

Sonbahar reddened. His world was one where trial advocates jousted with one another from beginning to end, often muddying the water with their excessive zeal. This child-in-judge's-robes would have to be taught the way of lawyers.

"Finally, counsel, I will expect you to ask relevant questions, proving material facts. If either of you wanders off the path too often, I will have the offender submit questions to me and I will ask them of the witness."

"Your Honor, with respect, Sir," Sonbahar said quietly, bottling his rage, "I respectfully tender a challenge for cause and ask you to remove yourself from presiding over this case."

"On what grounds, counsel?"

"First, Your Honor, I feel your experience in judicial matters is insufficient to allow you properly to judge a case of this magnitude. Second, Your Honor has set forth unique and unusual procedures that fly in the face of established precedent. Third, I believe Your Honor may be unconsciously prejudiced against my client's needs to fully express his feelings, resulting in my inability to properly and competently try this case. Finally, I object vehemently to the limitations you place on the freedom granted counsel. By these acts, you usurp the role of prosecutor and defender when you should remain neutral as judge."

The prosecutor sat down, glancing with apparent satisfaction at his client.

"Thank you, Senator Sonbahar," the judge responded. "Your motion is denied. With reference to my age and experience, I have been appointed trial judge by the Court of Cassation. I don't recall my appointment being limited to large matters or small ones, simple or complex. As it happens, I am no happier than you that I find myself presiding over this case. Nevertheless, a trial is a search for truth. That can best be accomplished through competent evidence, not vitriolic posturing. I believe the procedures I have set forth are well within my discretion. The law clearly states that the trial judge sets procedure within the confines of the code. If you can point out anything I do that in any way deters us from finding the truth through the development of evidence, I will be happy to reconsider my ruling. If you feel I am guilty of abuse of discretion, feel free to appeal my decision to the Court of Cassation."

"But, Your Honor, the Supreme Court of Appeals is presently in its current full session. That might take months, years."

"It might at that, counselor. And during that appeal, unless prohibited by special order of that court, I intend to carry on with the trial of this case. Now, Sir, if I might continue. My rulings are not intended to interfere with your client's right to prosecute his case vigorously, giving appropriate vent to his feelings in the context of admissible evidence. That means your client may comment precisely on what he feels to be his damages and show how he arrived at that conclusion. That does not mean your client will use this courtroom as a podium from which to promote his political interests. Neither I, nor my fellow judges, have any prejudice, conscious or otherwise, against either side in this case. We should be able to make our determination based on competent evidence, period. Finally, counsel, so long as the questions and answers are kept within the reasonable bounds of relevance, I will give you absolute freedom to try your case as you wish. I will take over the questioning only if I perceive an abuse of practice that is continuous and deliberate, after there has been ample warning.

"We will commence trial on September 20, 1943. Five days prior to that time each of you will present me with a series of proposed evidentiary exhibits, motions to limit testimony and citations to appropriate legal precedent. At the conclusion of the presentation of evidence, we will discuss them together. I bid you good day."

"You were right, Turhan," Zehavah said. "Ishchi certainly stood up to the Senator."

"Even so, we don't have much to work with. I've been able to find Jewish leaders, members of the Istanbul city council, even some members of the Grand National Assembly, who are willing to testify to the honesty and integrity of the haLevys, but we've no hard evidence. Just when I feel I'm hot on the trail, the path forks in two, three, even ten different directions. I've no doubt there's a network protecting Mose haLevy."

"We don't have a chance without the *khakham* or the boy. The haLevys will take the stand, admit the boy is missing, admit he was last seen in the company of their father – whose whereabouts they don't know – and tell the judges that it's in boy's best interests. Judge Ishchi will let me put on four, perhaps five witnesses to say what nice fellows Israel, Joshua and Daniel are, and I'll sit by and watch politely while the panel of judges calmly hands Hükümdar the brothers' heads

– their property – on a platter. Not the type of thing to inspire great confidence."

"I'll keep trying, Zari. That's all I can do."

In a far more luxurious suite of offices, across town in Taksim, Abbas Hükümdar was engaged in an entirely different kind of conversation with his lawyer. "That miserable young cur is going to keep the rein pretty tight, Senator. You heard him."

"Indeed I did, Your Excellency. I tried everything possible to have him removed from the case. My friend, Judge Gallus, told me he'd bent the Chief Justice's ear to get rid of Ishchi, but it didn't work. This case is such a political bombshell they're happy to give it to a junior member of their group. So we're stuck with Ishchi. Don't worry, my friend. Even if he holds us strictly to the evidence, we've got a sure winner. He can't stop you from making public statements outside the courtroom. The newspapers will publish what you tell them. You can still try your case in the marketplace."

"Yes, but that Jew-lover Türkoğlu is the most widely read journalist in the country, and the Ministry of Information refuses to muzzle him. The ultimate decision in this case rests with the judges. They don't care what the newspapers say. As soon as the trial's over they'll go back to their regular court calendars. I doubt they'll be influenced by what I say to the press."

"Is that what you're really worried about, Abbas? I thought you were so anxious to get your son back."

"Sonbahar, I left child-rearing pretty much to the servants. Mina's been in and out of clinics as long as I can remember. I can't even remember when I last saw the boy. The main thing about this trial is to show the world how rotten these Jews are. Put them all in a bag together, and watch the slime ooze out."

"Mr. Minister!" The advocate was shocked.

"Don't worry, my eminent counsel. You're being well paid and I won't embarrass you. I will be the weeping, pathetic, wretched father shedding his life's blood over the loss of his only son. Pity I won't be able to tell the judges and the audience how villainous all these Jewish vermin are."

8

Zehavah became more frustrated by the day. The haLevy financial coffers were hurting. Not only had Zehavah been paid only a portion of her costs, she was now finding that more costs would have to come out of her own pocket. Trial was two weeks away. She hadn't heard from Turhan for ten days. Perhaps Hükümdar's internal security forces had arrested Turhan and were holding him incommunicado. The next day, she received a curt, hand delivered note in Turhan's unmistakable handwriting. "The trail is warming up."

On September 20, the trial began. Judge Ishchi, true to his word, maintained a tight grip on proceedings. The courtroom filled to overflowing. The judge rejected Senator Sonbahar's initial motion that court be adjourned to one of the City's large meeting halls. "Your Honor," objected Sonbahar. "The law affords its citizens the right to a public trial."

"Indeed it does, counsel. Such members of the public as come early enough shall have the best seats in the chamber."

"But, Your Honor, that denies a large portion of the populace its right to be present when evidence is presented."

"When the time comes to present evidence, Senator Sonbahar, I will reconsider your motion. I believe that after the first few days, this large courtroom will be more than ample to house all who remain interested."

"Very well, Judge Ishchi." Sonbahar now addressed the full bench. "Good morning, Your Honors, Romali Sonbahar, of the city of Ankara, servant of the people and Senator in the Grand National Assembly, humbly appearing before you as counsel on behalf of the plaintiff. May I present the august Deputy Minister of the Interior, The Honorable Abbas Hükümdar." The plaintiff rose ponderously to his feet and nodded, as he'd been instructed to do.

"Good morning, Your Honors, I am Zehavah Kohn, a member of the bar of Sinop Villayet. I represent defendants Israel, Joshua and Daniel haLevy. My respects to you all." The brothers rose, nodded, and sat down.

The Presiding Judge addressed his two associates and advised them of the nature of the case concerning the disappearance of Kâzim Hükümdar, born May 1, 1930, then twelve years of age. "At this time, I will allow each counsel to make an opening statement," he concluded. "Counsel for the prosecution, you may proceed."

Sonbahar stepped easily to the rostrum. He knew his opening statement would carry no weight whatsoever with the judges, who heard such pleas every time they tried a case. However, members of the public, the press, and newscasters from the Turkish Radio, were present in the room. Those were his real target audience. "Your Honors. I speak to you today not as a Senator of the Grand Assembly, nor as an orator, but as a father and a human being. There is nothing in the world more precious than parenthood. It is the sons of our loins from whom we achieve our measure of eternity.

"From the beginning of the world, man has been told to be fruitful and multiply his kind. Through generations of sons we have achieved greatness. Can any of you ever forget the first time you laid eyes upon your first-born? Can you ever forget the certain knowledge at that moment, that you'd preserved your line beyond your own life? It is a cruel, vicious blow when any child is ripped from us through disease or the negligent act of another. But that loss, great as it is, cannot compare with the outrage one feels when a child is stolen – *stolen* – by another man. How can it fail to affect you when you hear that another man's son has been taken from him, hidden from him, for over a year?

"My client, Abbas Hükümdar, is well-known to the citizens of this republic. Through his efforts, his outstanding works, his love for his fellow man, he has achieved the position of Deputy Minister of the Interior. Beneath it all beats the heart of a man, one who, just like you and I, puts on his suit in the morning, works the day through, comes home to a loving wife, a handsome son, a beautiful, modest daughter. One day he comes home expecting to find, as always, this heartwarming tableau. But alas, something is missing. His loving wife is sick with grief. The sister pines for her brother. This pillar of his community is shocked, outraged to find his son has been forcibly ripped from the bosom of his household. Stolen from a circle of family love. Had the father been castrated, could his shock have been worse?

"As this loving father proceeded in his grief to reach into every corner of the nation to find his only son, he finally located the boy, in the clutches of a depraved monster who has the effrontery to call himself a religious leader." The advocate spat out the word with disgust.

"A religious hypocrite, who falsely professes to be among the gentlest beings on the face of the earth. Yet, when the loving father went to claim his child at last, he found that this 'holy man' had slunk away, like a beast in the night, taking the lad with him. Stealing away into hiding, shunning the light of day. His sons, who parade their innocence before you and claim adherence to the law of Moses, break their own Commandments. They steal, they dishonor a mother and father, they covet, they destroy a family. In the name of what?

"You will observe, Your Honors, the havoc this has wrought, the pain, anguish, and humiliation. You will see lives torn asunder. In the name of what? What is the role of this so-called 'gentle man of faith?' To mock the ties of familial devotion? To hide the sinner? To run from truth? The defense will tell you the boy went of his own volition. That he was free to come or go as he pleased. That he chose a religious leader over a father's love. Do you believe that? If this child exercises free will, I pose the simple question to you: 'Where's the boy? *Where's the boy? Where's the boy*?'"

As if on cue, a group in the audience took up the chant, "*Where's the boy? Where's the boy? Where's the boy*?" Large groups can always be churned to a mob's frenzy, and this was no exception. Sonbahar had made certain that a claque of well-paid supporters attended the Court session. Moved by a tidal wave of emotion, shouts of "*Where's the boy*?" thundered through the courtroom.

Judge Ishchi banged his gavel in vain. The roar did not abate. Finally in frustration, the jurist ordered the courtroom cleared and declared a one hour recess. He ordered both counsel into chambers during the break. The judge was seething as he sat down at his desk. "Mister Sonbahar, I find your cheap histrionics deplorable and disgusting. A courtroom is a place of order, not trashy theater. I cannot control what you say, provided it is within the scope of relevant comment. I cannot, as a matter of law, state that what you said out there was beyond the scope of proper introduction, however inflammatory. I have every suspicion the words were spoken to induce the reaction you got. If I see this occur again, I will declare the Court to be in closed session except for the presentation of evidence. *Is that clear*?"

"But Your Honor, can I be blamed for the emotions stirred by my words?"

"Yes, counsel, I *do* blame you. You are an officer of the Court, sworn to uphold the dignity of this tribunal. I don't know how you do things in Ankara. But in this city, at this moment, I am running this Court, a fact-finding means of resolving differences between people. If you cannot comport yourself with the propriety I exact, then perhaps you'd better practice elsewhere!"

"Judge Ishchi," the prosecutor began, fuming. "I insist all of these comments be reported for the record. I have practiced not simply 'in Ankara', as you say, but throughout the land. My reputation speaks for itself. Although I have every respect for the judicial robe, Your Honor, I am a member of the governing body that placed you on the bench. If I am an officer of the court, so are you. You, as well as I, are bound to uphold the law. If I am deprived of the right to try my case as I see fit, why bother to have trials in the first place? Why have lawyers if the judge is going to do everything? I resent being called to account for the impression my words make on others. I am deeply offended that this Court condemns me simply because I'm doing my job in the best way I know how. We are trying a serious, heinous claim, a claim so substantial that if successful, it will teach the haLevy family a financial lesson they won't soon forget. And you instruct me to temper my argument? Your Honor, you are sworn to uphold justice. Yet you do a grave injustice by shackling counsel who seeks only to emphasize the truth. Let that be reported."

Judge Ischi was keenly aware that the court reporter was duly transcribing everything. He chose his words carefully, to defend the record, but spoke them in icy tones so there would be no doubt as to his meaning. "*Senator* Sonbahar," he hissed the word to emphasize his disdain for the honorific. "No one is more aware than I of the great honor done me by the Senate, which voluntarily and with whole heart selecting me to be a Judge. Nor does anyone challenge the sanctity of the senate acting as an independent body, free from the intercession of anyone.

"As the judge in this case, I am vested with discretion to preside over the conduct of trials. If I abuse that discretion, that is a matter for the higher court on appeal. But in order to determine whether a case is properly tried, there must be a clean, orderly record. How can there be order if there is chaos in these proceedings? How can justice best be served? By rule of law or by rule of the mob? If I am removed as Presiding Judge of this court by act of a gang, then our Turkish experiment in human rights has failed. I am bound to uphold Atatürk's precious heritage. I intend to do so in the best way I know how. Prosecutor Sonbahar, you will please conduct yourself with decorum commensurate with the seriousness of this case, is that clear?"

"But, Your Honor …?"

"I repeat, *is that clear, counsel?* One cannot support a Court if one has contempt for it."

There was no pretense of indirection. Contempt of Court resulted in counsel being jailed, sometimes for months, until a proper appeal could be sent to Ankara. During that time, an advocate was barred from pursuing his practice. If the contempt citation was upheld, it cast a solid black mark on a lawyer's professional reputation. "Yes, of course, Your Honor," the prosecutor remarked with oily obsequiousness. "I would never think to do otherwise than honor this august tribunal."

"Very well, then. I expect you to do so."

When Court reconvened, the more unruly in the crowd were quickly ushered out of the Courtroom. Sonbahar briefly finished his opening statement. "My apologies, Your Honors, for the interruption caused by that outburst of very human emotion. I can sympathize with these feelings. I believe you, too, can understand them. It is through the presentation of evidence in this case that the plaintiff intends to place you in his shoes, to make you feel as he feels. To allow you to find facts to be true and act upon them. The charges involve the most serious of crimes and civil wrongs. You are bound to uphold the law, no matter how difficult the decision, no matter how grave the consequences. That is all we ask. Thank you."

The prosecutor sat down, avoiding Judge Ishchi's icy glare.

"Counselor Kohn?"

"Thank you, Your Honor. May it please the Court. You have heard the accusations made by my learned colleague. You hold in your hands the fortunes of three humble men whom no one – not even the prosecution – can show have a vicious thought in their collective heads.

"My clients do not deny that Kâzim Hükümdar is missing. The plaintiff claims his son was forcibly abducted by Khakham Mose haLevy, acting as my clients' representatives. My clients do not concede that the evidence will in any way demonstrate that the boy was kidnapped, nor can the Plaintiff hope to prove the haLevy sons sanctioned, ordered, or condoned these acts. Instead, we will hold the Plaintiff to his burden of proof – and it is the *Plaintiff*, not the Defendants, who must prove his case by a preponderance of the evidence. If the evidence is evenly divided – if you are in any way uncertain that the Plaintiff has sustained his burden to prove every element of his charges – then the law is such that you cannot rule in Plaintiff's favor.

"It is easy for the Plaintiff to point a finger, to allege a wrong, to demand absolutely outrageous amounts of money for his 'suffering.' But our system of law is such that a plaintiff must prove his case by a preponderance of the evidence. Unless that burden of proof is met, Your Honors – and we submit it cannot be – you prostitute the law of Atatürk if you award the plaintiff any relief whatsoever. Thank you."

A number of witnesses testified that Abbas Hükümdar, one of the most respected men in the republic, had started life in a low station. Ultimately, he'd been elevated by the Grand National Assembly to his present position. He had no known vices. He did not drink *rakı* immoderately, participated actively in Islamic rites, gave generously to charities. Two of Hükümdar's household servants testified how they'd discovered the boy missing and reported the news to their master. Under cross examination, they stated that Hükümdar was a stern father and devoted an extraordinary amount of time to political interests. Mina Hükümdar did not testify because, according to her physicians, she was undergoing extensive medical treatment in a private clinic for deep, chronic depression.

Finally, the prosecution called its last witness. Abbas looked gaunt, haggard, as he took the stand. His eyes were sunken, as if he'd been crying each evening of the trial. He began his testimony softly, reciting his joy at the birth of his first and only son. How the lad had been bright, intelligent, obedient. He condemned himself for his occasional sternness with the boy, humbly accepting blame that the interests of state kept him away from home much too often. Hükümdar related his shock at the discovery that his son was gone, the joy at knowing the boy had been found, only to be followed by a still greater loss when the youngster disappeared again. He detailed the deterioration of his family, starting with how much he missed seeing the youth's well-scrubbed face when he came home each evening. A wife thrown into an emotional chasm so deep she'd required medical care each day since the incident. A younger daughter now left without a brother.

Men and women in the audience started openly to weep. A bad sign, a very bad sign, Zehavah thought.

Hükümdar enumerated his staggering monetary damages. Since the kidnap of his son, he'd exhausted most of his fortune in fees, costs and medical treatment for his bereaved wife. He demanded justice, nothing more. He pleaded with the judges to give him not one cent, if only they would return his son to him. When he finished his testimony, the judges were in such a state of agitation that Zehavah requested a two day break to enable things to cool down. She was astute enough to realize that cross-examining Hükümdar at this point in the trial would be the most dangerous thing she could attempt. The Court, sensing it would be highly prejudicial not to grant such a continuance, consented.

9

Turhan's coat was off. He'd not bathed in two days. "It's hopeless, Halide," he said, sighing. "The Jews swear they don't know the old man's whereabouts. I believe he's in Thrace. That cuts out ninety-seven percent of Turkey, but it's still an incredible amount of area to cover. More important, time has about run out. Now you expect me to go running off to Keshan on an anonymous errand?"

"What have you got to lose?" Halide replied. Turhan noticed for the first time how much his friend had aged during the past year. She was bent over and walked with difficulty.

"All right," Turhan said wearily. "Tell me the story again."

"Five days ago a man showed up at the safe house in Keshan. He gave his name as Moishe Cohen and said he came from Vilna. He was accompanied by a boy who could be anywhere from ten to fifteen. He said the boy was a Lithuanian peasant whose parents had helped him escape, and that he'd promised he'd care for the lad. The boy hasn't uttered a word since they came to Keshan. The man who calls himself Moishe Cohen says it's because the lad was frightened into silence on his trip."

"Halide, more than ten thousand Jews have crossed the Maritza River into Turkey. Each has a different story. Do you want me to follow ten thousand leads in the time I've got left?"

"No, I don't. But the HIAS man told me that Hayam Burdur, the man who runs the safe house, is completely dependable, and unlike most Muslims, he's fluent in *Hebrew* as well as Yiddish."

West of Istanbul, the land flattened out. The wide, well-maintained road traversed dry, rocky terrain. Three hours from the city, Turhan arrived in Tekirdağ, halfway to the town where Moishe Cohen was staying. When he went to the address Halide had given him, a coffee house on the main thoroughfare, a middle-aged man with a huge belly, who'd been seated at an outside table, rose and lumbered toward his car.

"Hayam Effendim?"

"Turhan Türkoğlu? I've read your articles for years. Kovalevsky told me of your work at the Belgrade Palas. It's a great privilege to meet you."

"Is there some reason you wanted to meet in Tekirdağ? Another two hours and I could have been in Keshan."

"There is. Tea or coffee?"

"Coffee, thank you."

After the two men had ordered, Burdur began, "How well do you know Yiddish?"

"Barely. I learned a few words while I was at Belgrade Palas, the simplest kinds of greetings, requests for food, things like that."

"Do you speak German?"

"Quite well. A very special – friend – and I spoke in that language before she – went away."

"What about Hebrew?"

"I neither speak nor understand it at all. Why?"

"Because I was no more suspicious of Moishe Cohen than I was of anyone else until I heard him at Sabbath services last Friday night."

"What do you mean?"

"Cohen says he comes from a little town, a *shtetl*, outside Vilna, Lithuania. In Yiddish, they call anyone from that country a '*Litvak*.' Every town and village where Jews lived in Eastern Europe has its own peculiar Yiddish accent. There are so many different inflections that unless one man comes from precisely the same village as another, it's almost impossible to prove or disprove a Jew's home town. Yiddish is mostly German-based, with a smattering of Russian, Polish, Roumanian, and so forth. Anyone who speaks German can get along passably well in Yiddish."

"So?"

"Moishe Cohen's accent was not too much different from anyone else's when he came to Keshan. He said he came from Chavel. I put that down in the entry book and didn't think twice. One of my jobs is to help the Jews set up for their *Shabbat* service every Friday night. I usually attend because they're not allowed to do any work, not so much as turn a light on or off. But as a *goy*, I'm allowed to do that for them. Last Friday night, Cohen attended the service. He sat in the back of the room and was not conspicuous. One or two men looked at him oddly while he was praying. You're certain you don't know Hebrew at all?"

"I said I didn't."

"Very well. There are two major divisions among Jews, the *Sephardim* and the *Ashkenazim*. The *Sephardic* Jews came from Spain and Morocco. Many of them settled in Turkey nearly five hundred years ago. All the Jews who come from central and eastern Europe are *Ashkenazi*, 'German' Jews. *Ashkenazim* and *Sephardim* do not mix. They never have. Each sect considers the other a lesser grade of Jew. They practice their religion differently. The *sephardim* have a *khakham*, a prayer leader. The *ashkenazim* have a *rebbe* – sometimes they call him a *rabbi* – who is not only a prayer leader, but also judge, teacher, arbiter of disputes, and all-around wise man.

"In their native lands, it's easy to tell the *sephardi* from the *ashkenazi*. But these are difficult times. There's a mingling of many races, not only Jews, seeking to escape from Europe. Moishe Cohen looked like any of a hundred other Jews who've used the safe house in Keshan. There is, however, one inescapable way to tell a *sephardic* Jew from an *ashkenazi*. Their pronunciation of the *Hebrew* language."

"Go on," said Turhan.

"I'll give you an example. When an *ashkenazi* Jew greets his coreligionist on Friday night, he says, '*Shabbos shawlom*.' When a *sephardi* gives the same greeting, it comes out '*Shabbat shalom*.' In their opening prayer, the *sephardi* sings, '*L'chah dodi li-kraht kalah*,' while the *ashkenazi* chants '*L'choh dodi li-krahss kah-loh*.'"

"So?"

"I heard the man pray in Hebrew. When he prays, he uses the Sephardic accent of the *Turkish* Jew. I'm convinced Moishe Cohen is no more a native of Lithuania than I am. Do you have any photographs of the missing man?" Turhan pulled out two photos, one of the *Khakham* and one of the boy. "Unfortunately, these pictures could be of anyone," Hayam said. "The only thing Moishe Cohen and Khakham haLevy seem to have in common is that they're both in their late sixties, have thinning hair and beards."

"And the boy?"

"He's at the age of greatest change. Anyone can read whatever he wants into a photograph."

"I have an idea," Turhan replied. "The odds against it are very long, but I've never been known for not jumping into a situation as directly as possible. When is the next Sabbath service?"

"Friday night."

"I'll be there."

That Friday evening, Turhan made certain he was standing next to Moishe Cohen at evening services. As he'd been instructed, he wore a *yarmulke*, the Jewish skullcap, and a small *tallit*, the fringed shawl, inside his sweater. Burdur had earlier advised that the large prayer shawl worn over the shoulders was only used during daylight hours. He mumbled words tonelessly, his lips moving, and rocked back and forth as he saw most of the other men doing. At the conclusion of the Sabbath service, Cohen nodded to his neighbor in silent greeting.

Turhan responded, in a mixture of Hebrew and Turkish, *"Shabbat shalom, Khakham* haLevy. I need to talk with you. Urgently."

Turhan's trained reporter's eye caught the flicker of fear in the man's eyes and the sudden pallor in his face just before the other responded in Yiddish, "You must be mistaken *Reb Yiddene*. My name is Cohen."

"Whatever you want to call yourself is fine with me," Turhan said, in Turkish. "But we need to speak. And I won't leave your side until we've spoken."

He saw the resignation in the man's eyes and knew his gamble had paid off.

"Very well," haLevy said with a deep sigh. "The game has finally come to an end. I've been expecting it."

"Why didn't you come forward before?"

"I was sworn to secrecy. I would not break my sworn oath. Even now, I've not been given permission to do so."

"But you must, Khakham haLevy," Turhan said. "Slim as it may be, it's our only hope."

"I cannot."

"Even if it means the financial destruction of your family?"

"Even so, Turhan Effendim. The faith given another human being by a sworn promise is stronger even than family fortunes."

"When was the last time you saw the boy?"

"Yesterday. He's staying at the home of a friend between here and Medjidiye."

"We've got to talk to him. If he gives his consent for you to testify, will you do so?"

"Selim, how could you have let a thirteen year-old child out of your sight, particularly when you know they're looking everywhere for him?"

"Khakham, could you keep a bird on this farm if it wanted to fly away?"

"Did he say anything?"

"He was reading about the trial in one of the Istanbul newspapers. He seemed very upset. About noon today, he asked me for twenty lira. He said he wanted to give you a very special Sabbath gift."

"Anything else, Selim? Anything at all?"

"No, not that I can recall. Wait a moment. Yes, he did. He spoke the last words sort of under his breath. He said that justice must be done, even if he had to suffer."

"What do you think he meant?"

"God only knows," the khakham responded.

"I think I do, too," said Turhan, softly.

10

Zehavah had tried to prepare her closing argument all day yesterday and today. It was no good. Anything she said would dig the grave deeper. Waive closing argument? Worse yet. Her head pounded from exhaustion. Perhaps a little sleep. She had a small couch in her outer office. It would have to do. There was a knock at her door. Who could it be at this hour? Still dressed, she opened the door a crack. "Turhan? What are you doing here?"

"I've found the Khakham."

"What?" She brightened. "That's wonderful!"

"Whether it's good or bad, I don't know. The boy left Khakham haLevy four nights ago."

"Can I speak with haLevy? Perhaps put him on the stand tomorrow?" It was a chance. Very slim, very remote, but certainly better than nothing at all.

"Of course."

"Where is he now?"

"In hiding at a friend's home."

"Hükümdar's people have watched this building day and night since I rented the space. How will I be able to speak with him?"

Turhan bade Zehavah follow him. They descended a flight of stairs Zehavah hadn't known existed, then went through an ill-lit passageway. She counted two thousand paces before they climbed another flight of stairs. "A rather long tunnel," Turhan said. We Turks are masters of intrigue and have learned to cover our tracks when we want to." He smiled as they emerged into the street near a comfortable, middle-class house.

As they entered the house, Zehavah saw a small man, about sixty-five, wearing a dark kaftan, a leather hat, and the earlocks worn by pious Jews throughout the world. "Zehavah Kohn, may I present Khakham Mose haLevy," Turhan said. He excused himself, and left.

Zehavah was impressed with the honest simplicity of the plain, ascetic man. She listened with amazement, then shock, then outrage as the khakham recounted his story. When she returned to her office, it was an hour before dawn. Without the boy, the khakham's testimony was inadmissible hearsay. So near and yet so far from the single piece of evidence that would save her clients. Zehavah lay on her office couch. Sleep eluded her. She tossed and turned, to no avail. Well, she thought, when one thing goes wrong, everything goes wrong. She'd not even outlined her closing argument. To top it all off, she'd had no sleep in a day and a night. She'd be useless in the morning.

There was a soft, barely audible scratching at her door. "Yes?" she called out.

Another rasping sound. Zehavah arose, shivering, wrapped herself in a bed cloak, and opened the door. Turhan stood in the doorway with another person. "Avukat Hanım?" The voice came from the hooded figure. It could have been girl or boy. The voice was in-between.

"Yes, what is it?" Zehavah answered groggily.

"My name is Kâzim Hükümdar, Avukat Kohn. Might I speak with you for a little while?"

Zehavah appeared in Court that morning haggard and disheveled. Before the Court session, she asked to speak with the Presiding Judge and opposing counsel in chambers. "Counsel, you look absolutely dreadful," the Judge muttered to her. "Did you drown your sorrows in wine? You look as if you haven't slept in two days. How can you present yourself to a court looking as you do?"

"Your Honor, I'm on the verge of collapse, but not from drink. I've not slept in two nights. This morning, just before dawn, I located the boy. We spoke for more than an hour. He has requested to speak with you alone, Your Honor, out of the presence of both counsel."

"What say you, Senator?" the judge asked. "After all, your client is the boy's father. He has legal custody over the child."

"I'll have to take it up with my client," said the stunned advocate. "The father might well want to speak with his son beforehand."

"Your Honor, the boy wants to speak with the Court alone, outside the presence of anyone else. I've given him my word that I wouldn't divulge his whereabouts until he receives a response."

"You're aware I could order you to produce the lad and, if you did not do so, I could hold you in contempt of Court?"

"I am very much aware of that, Your Honor."

"And you'd risk that?"

"I would, Your Honor. You know I have nothing but the utmost respect for this Court. I would ask that were you to hold me in contempt, you suspend the imposition of sentence until you speak with the boy."

"I see. Counselor Sonbahar, would you speak with your client?"

"Yes, Your Honor. I'm certain Deputy Minister Hükümdar will be relieved and will give an appropriate response." Sonbahar left. He returned momentarily, pale, visibly shaken. "Your Honor, with all respect, my client demands to have his son returned to him forthwith. He says he wants to speak with the boy before the Court does."

"Romali Bey," the judge began wearily. "We've been taking evidence for nearly a week. We're at the very close of this trial. Zehavah has the boy available. If I deny his request, she tells me he'll bolt and run again. I can hold defense counsel in contempt. That would accomplish nothing. The whole purpose of this trial has been to return and restore the lad. Now he's back. Wouldn't it benefit your client simply to let the boy talk with me alone? I suppose I could order that, too."

"Your Honor, a father's right to see his son is superior to that of the Court, particularly when the lad is a legally incompetent child. A parent's control is absolute. The Court has no discretion but to order the boy returned to his father. Therefore, my client demands such an order forthwith."

"You are correct, counselor," the jurist began, "that a child under the age of thirteen years is legally incompetent to do other than the bidding of his parent. It's only when he achieves the age of thirteen that the Court may, in its discretion, take cognizance of anything a minor would say. Kâzim Hükümdar attained the age of thirteen more than a month ago. I am prepared to use my discretion in one of two ways. I will order the boy to appear before me *in camera*, out of the presence of both counsel, or I will order him to appear and give testimony in open court, if he can be found. I will leave the decision to your client."

"May I have a few moments to confer with my client."

"You may."

Sonbahar returned. "Your Honor, my client feels that if this Court elects to treat the lad as an adult, he must learn to testify as a man, in a public forum. Therefore, my client exercises his parental right to refuse the Court's request for private proceedings. He demands his son speak directly to the open court."

"Avukat Kohn?"

"Your Honor, I don't know what he'll say. He wanted to speak privately with you."

"Counselor, I will adjourn these proceedings until this afternoon."

"Your next witness, Avukat Kohn."

"Thank you, Your Honor. The defense calls as its next witness, pursuant to Court order and the plaintiff's demand, Master Kâzim Hükümdar."

There was an audible gasp from the audience. The prosecutor glanced at his client, who glared stonily at his son. The boy, slight, a little taller than Zehavah, straightened his back. Without looking at his father, he walked to the stand. The clerk administered the oath.

"Master Hükümdar," Zehavah began, "do you understand the seriousness of an oath?"

"I do, ma'am."

"What does it mean?"

"It means you promise to tell the truth."

"Do you know what happens if you don't tell the truth?"

"Yes, ma'am."

"What is that?"

"You can be put in jail, Ma'am. More important, Allah demands you tell the truth or your soul will suffer eternally."

"Do you promise to tell the truth today?"

"I do, ma'am."

"How old are you, Kâzim?"

"Thirteen years."

"Do you recognize the Plaintiff?"

"I do, Ma'am. That is Abbas Hükümdar, my father."

"Did you make a request of the Court earlier today?"

"I did, ma'am."

"What was that?"

"That I be able to speak with the Judge privately, so I would not have to speak before the open court."

"What was the result of that request?"

"The judge told me I would have to speak publicly or not at all, at my father's request."

"Have you spoken to your father before coming here today?"

"I have not, ma'am."

"Why is that?"

"I wanted to speak to the Judge alone."

"Move to strike the answer as non-responsive," Sonbahar jumped to his feet. "The question called for the reason he has not spoken with his own father."

"Motion granted. Answer the question."

"I have not spoken with my father because I fear the consequences of what I have to say."

"Master Hükümdar, early in 1943, did you leave your parents' home?"

"I did."

"Were you abducted by anyone?"

"No, ma'am."

"Where did you go?"

"To the home of a friend of mine, a Jew who introduced me to the Khakham haLevy. I was so mixed up I didn't know what to say or where I could seek help. My friend told me that the Khakham was a good man and a wise one, and that I had nothing to fear from talking to him. Besides, since he was not a member of the Muslim religion, I need not worry that word would get back to my father."

"Did anyone force you to go there?"

"Object, Your Honor," Sonbahar said. "At the time of the event, the boy was legally incompetent to make a voluntary decision on his own."

"Sustained."

"Did anyone force you to see Khakham haLevy?"

"Same objection, Your Honor."

"Sustained."

"Do you know Israel, Joshua or Daniel haLevy?"

"No, Ma'am."

"Was there a reason you left home?"

"Yes, Ma'am."

"What was that?"

The boy coughed. "Might I speak with the Judge privately?"

"Young man," the Presiding Judge said kindly. "We've been through this. Your father refused me the opportunity to speak with you out of his presence. If you wish to speak, you must do so in open court."

"Your Honor, I will speak." the boy said. For the first time, he was hesitant. He looked down at the floor, then began to talk very softly. "For as long as I can remember, my father would take me into a special room in our house, a servant's quarters. I was about four or five when it started. He would tell me I'd been a bad boy, a very bad boy indeed, and that I'd have to be punished. He said my mother would not want to see me punished, but he knew better, and he was master of the house.

"He would take me into this small room and make me take off my shorts. Then he would get a whip and hit me quite hard. It raised sores on my bottom. While I was crying, he would take his... his penis... out of his pants and would start rubbing it against my bottom..."

"Enough!" The enraged deputy minister leaped from his chair. "That's a lie!" he roared. "It is out-and-out slander! The boy has been brainwashed by the accursed Jews! Hypnotized to lie about his own father! I will kill them! I will kill them all!"

"Order! Order! Order!" the Judge shouted, banging his gavel furiously. "Bailiff, hold that man back! Shackle him if necessary! I will not have disorder in my courtroom!"

Pandemonium erupted. Newsmen escaped before they could be restrained. The news spread instantly throughout the city. The Presiding Judge abruptly adjourned the proceedings. He telephoned the clinic in Izmir and spoke directly with Mina Hükümdar.

Late that afternoon, the Judge called his colleagues and counsel together, still in closed session. Abbas Hükümdar was not present. "I understand the parties have reached a settlement of this case. Avukat

Kohn, Avukat Sonbahar, would you state your stipulation for the record."

"Yes, Your Honor," Zehavah said, smiling wearily. "All charges against the haLevy family, father and sons, are dismissed. The boy, Kâzim Hükümdar is remanded to the custody of Khakham Mose haLevy, who will act as guardian until a good Muslim family can be located. Abbas Hükümdar is to pay for the care, maintenance and education of the boy until he attains twenty-one years of age in such amount as shall be set by the Court. The Plaintiff is ordered to pay to the haLevy brothers the sum of one *kurush* as damages, and attorney's fees of fifty thousand lira, plus all costs incurred in bringing this case to trial. Finally, Abbas Hükümdar shall issue a formal public apology to the haLevy family and to the Jewish community of Istanbul, which apology shall be publicized at his expense throughout the republic."

"Do you join in that stipulation, Senator Sonbahar?"

There was the slightest hesitation. Then, quietly, "Yes."

"It is so ordered. This court stands adjourned *sine die*."

An exhausted Zehavah Kohn left the courtroom by a rear exit, to avoid the crush of people waiting in front of the courthouse to congratulate her. She didn't want the adulation of the crowds, nor a victory celebration. All she wanted was a hot bath and two days of uninterrupted sleep. As she left the building and felt the cooling twilight air on her face, a figure suddenly emerged at her side. "It's over, my friend," Turhan said. "You had faith, and the miracle occurred."

She squeezed his hand. "Without you, Turhan..." She looked away, reached into her purse, found a small handkerchief and blew her nose.

"Without *us*, Hanım Effendim," he said quietly. "Now, then, Zari," he said. "You recall that when you found me, I was living in a country home where it was so quiet the sound of my own mind was the loudest thing I could hear? I must remain in Istanbul for a month. It seems I'm *Isharet's* most popular reporter once again – even with my cowardly editor, Fahri Dikkat." He handed her a key ring. "The first key on the ring is to the black automobile you see parked across the street. The second is to the house. Rest well, my friend. Allah knows you deserve it."

11

At the beginning of 1945, when it became obvious that Germany was not going to win what was now being called World War II, Turkey declared war on the Reich, just in time to enable it to become a charter member of the newly formed United Nations.

One Sunday afternoon the following month, Nadji drove up to Turhan's hillside retreat. The two friends embraced warmly. Turhan poured rakı for both of them. "So you've settled down and become the gentleman farmer, eh? Don't you get bored?"

"No, I don't, Nadji. I send a few articles each month to *Isharet* and simpler ones to the Ministry of Information, which sends them out to the village newspapers. I grow all my own vegetables. A tenant farmer provides me with all the lamb I need. Money's no problem. I've hardly spent a *kurush* since I bought this place."

"You're fortunate you live without money, my friend. Food costs five times what it did at the start of the war, and income has dropped by a quarter. The average Turk makes a little over three hundred lira a year."

"Has anyone heard of Hükümdar since the trial?"

"Yes, indeed. He's been appointed Regional Administrator of Security in Kars."

"Ugh. That's truly the end of the world."

"Have you seen Zehavah since the trial?"

"Once."

"I always thought you and she would get together," Nadji said.

Turhan sighed. "I often thought the same myself, but somehow nothing ever happened. She knows I've never gotten over Rachela. What about you and Aysheh?" He saw his friend wince. "Still a sore spot?"

"Yes, but one I can't escape. We try to avoid each other as much as possible. I suppose one of these days we'll get around to filing divorce papers. That's one of the reasons I asked about you and Zehavah."

"Oh?"

"Aysheh and I haven't slept together in over four years. I thought that if you have no claim on Zehavah, I'd like to ask her to dinner."

"Nadji, if you can charm her better than I, by all means, feel free to try. Allah knows my attempts have certainly been fruitless."

"I don't have any great romance in mind, you understand. But it would be nice to have the occasional companionship of an attractive female."

Zehavah accepted Nadji's invitation to dinner the following week. For a month after that, they dined casually with one another. Twice, he escorted her to the newly-established national theater. He had no better luck than his friend in striking a spark of romantic interest. Zehavah was a delightful companion, warm, thoughtful in every way. But Nadji received nothing more than a polite squeeze of the hand, or, if he was truly fortunate, a peck on the cheek each time he dropped her at her Ankara apartment. At forty-three, he was classically handsome and knew he cut a dashing figure. Unlike most men he knew, he tried to divert conversation away from himself. Why, then, was his courtship going nowhere?

One night, as they dined at the Ankara Palas restaurant, he asked her point blank, "Zehavah, we're both mature people. We've known each other nearly three years. I can't pretend you're unattractive to me. Why is our relationship destined to remain platonic?"

"Nadji," she said, smiling and taking his hands in hers. "You are such a dear, sweet, innocent man. I'm not so naïve not to know you've been trying this past month to change our relationship from what it's been. You and Turhan are so very transparent and childlike. It's enough to make me love both of you."

"Yet nothing happens with either of us."

"Of course not. He'll go to his grave with the memory of Rachela impressed on his heart. No woman can compete with that. Besides, he's got another love. Turkey. The Motherland has been his mistress since I first met him, thirty-three years ago. He's very like Atatürk in that way. Turhan wants to see the system work, to make sure all citizens in Turkey, Ottomans, Jews, Greeks, Armenians or Kurds, are given a level playing field when they compete in the game of life. You've only to pick up *Isharet*, or his favorite means of communication, the one-page village journals, to see what I mean."

"What about me, Zehavah?"

"Nadji, you're in love as well."

"What do you mean?"

"You've never stopped loving Aysheh. Nor, my friend, has she ever stopped loving you."

"How can you say that? We've been separated for years."

"Nadji, listen to me. During the time you were in Vienna, was she starting to drink?"

"Yes, how did you know that?"

"In our small circle, word gets around. She reached out to you. Where were you?"

"I was always there for her."

"Were you? Did you return to Turkey with her when she begged you to request reassignment?"

"No. It would have been unseemly for me not to have finished out my tour. It's a question of duty, of loyalty to the Military that goes back for generations of my family. It would have resulted in a black mark on my record."

"Was there no one else available who could have done the job as well as you?"

"What are you getting at?"

"Nadji, no affair ever starts entirely due to the fault of one of the partners. You were reaching for your colonel's epaulets. Even now, your fondest wish is to pin on your Brigadier's star. Aysheh's a beautiful, sensitive woman who saw you slipping through her fingers. She felt that she was nothing more than a decoration, a toy you'd put back on the shelf because you had another, more sparkling trinket within your grasp. She was bored, frustrated, and terrified. I understand she had a miscarriage. She had no one to talk to."

"She could have told me those things."

"Think back, Nadji. Didn't she tell you those things? Not in so many words, or maybe even in so many words. I was never in your bedroom, so I wouldn't know."

Nadji looked down, averting her gaze. "How do you know so much?"

"You really want to know?"

"Yes."

"Promise me not to reveal the source. On your honor as a soldier and as a man."

"You have that."

"Very well. You believe Osman Etap, our transportation minister, is simply the 'other man,' the immoral villain who stole your wife from you. I've known Osman twenty years. He's a good man, a widower with grown children. He confided many things to me along the way."

"You've been talking with a man who would destroy me? How can you call yourself my friend?" he asked, angrily.

"Please be quiet until you've heard what I have to say," she snapped back. "You gave me your word of honor as an officer and a gentleman. I expect you to keep it. Aysheh and Etap haven't been together for more than a year. One reason is that she can't let go of you any more than you can release her."

"I can't believe I'm hearing this."

"Believe it. There's a very special bond between you and Aysheh. It goes beyond duty, beyond anger. Neither of you has allowed your circle to close. Neither of you wants it to close. Why do you think you never filed for divorce? Or that you've never received documents from her?"

"Go on."

"Osman told me he could not contest her love for you and didn't want to. For the past year, he's acted as a fatherly listener as she vents her unhappiness over your continued separation. She's not drinking anymore. Perhaps that's something you should know. But she's a very frightened, sad little girl inside, just as you are an insecure little boy, despite all the epaulets and ribbons you'll ever wear. She doesn't know what will become of the rest of her life. Nadji," she looked deeply, steadily into his eyes. "It's time for you to go home."

"I can't." He averted his gaze. "So much blood has flowed under the bridge..."

"Is it really so difficult? In our society, cruel as it may be, the woman is never allowed to make the first move."

"What if her pride doesn't let her return to me?"

"Nadji, I'm an *avukat*, I'm your friend, and I'm a woman. Trust me when I say I understand these things."

"But you and I...?"

"I think we should go back to my apartment now. There's someone I'd very much like you to meet."

The man was shorter than Nadji, rugged-looking with dark, curly hair and a clear, open face. His smile was engaging. Akdemir instantly liked him. "I'm pleased to meet you *Albay*, the man said, in thickly accented Turkish. Zehavah has, of course, told me about you and a few of her other close friends."

"You are?"

"Aharon Barak. You could call me an 'irregular' in the Haganah. Others might call me a smuggler, even a terrorist."

Nadji was charmed by the candor of the man who he guessed to be five years his junior. "You're not Turkish?"

"Israeli."

"From Palestine?"

"That's what it's called under the British mandate. Those of us who were born on the soil have always referred to it as Eretz Israel. That's one reason it's so important for us to help as many of our fellow Jews as possible escape from Europe. I heard of your work from Zehavah's brother, Avi. I liked you before I even met you, Colonel Akdemir."

Nadji looked from one to the other, bemused. Zehavah broke the silence. "Avi and Aharon have worked together, smuggling Jews from

Turkey to Cyprus, then to Palestine. I met Aharon a year ago, when I visited my brother in Anamur. After the police closed Antalya to the Israeli 'fleet,' they had to look for less obvious ports of embarkation. Aharon and I developed a strong attraction for one another."

"But you're Turkish, a successful *avukat*."

"And, you seem to forget, a Jew and a woman. Our people have never had a land of their own."

"What about your children?"

"They've met Aharon. So has my mother. The boys are almost old enough to go to the university. I hope you'll keep it under your *shapka*, my friend, but within the next few months, we hope to emigrate to Israel."

"But the English have shut off all entry into the land. You can't..."

"How many times have you believed in the word '*can't*,' Nadji? Would you have gotten as far as you have if that word ruled your life? I remember someone who encouraged me to take on the case against the deputy minister of the interior. Nadji, we Jews have lost six million people in the greatest holocaust in our history. More than one third of our entire population was extinguished. We've nothing more to lose and a world to gain."

"What can I do to help?"

"Wish us luck, my friend. And remove the word 'can't' from your vocabulary. Especially when it comes to Aysheh Akdemir."

It had been three months since he'd first called her. They'd had dinner, gone for walks, attended plays together. They'd spoken of friends, current events, small things, as though they were two remote acquaintances, not quite enemies, not quite friends. Nadji and Aysheh were courteous toward one another. Yet there was an underlying current of... discomfort? Hesitancy? Fear? Aysheh finally made the first attempt at a breakthrough.

"If we continue like this, nothing will ever be resolved."

"These things take time, Aysheh."

"I don't believe that, Nadji. It's a question of facing what happened in our past honestly, and deciding what we want to do."

"You can't make a decision like this in such a short time."

"Nadji, do you love me or not?"

"Don't make me answer that question now."

"Why not? Would your answer be any different now or in six months?"

"Would yours?"

"I don't know." She backed away from the precipice, unwilling to make a commitment before she knew what his feelings were.

"I've got to go down to Izmir for a month. The Americans are starting preliminary discussions about a joint military operation there. Perhaps a short time apart will give us time to think things through."

"Suppose I asked to go with you? After all, I am your wife."

"Do you want to come?"

"I'd have to think about it."

The mutual fears had dropped the curtain of politeness between their first attempt to really talk. It was disappointing. As Nadji said good night to her later that evening, he felt she was still the most beautiful woman he'd ever known. But such thoughts could not pierce the armor he'd built around his heart.

"What are you doing here?"

"One of us had to decide whether we'd spend time together in Izmir. Since you chose to leave without settling the matter, I determined to come."

She had come into his office unannounced. He looked frankly at her and felt a stirring he'd not felt in years. Aysheh was forty-two years old. She still had the firm body of the nineteen-year-old she'd been when he first met her. A trifle thicker in the waist, perhaps, but she still had those astonishing grey-violet eyes.

"So what happens now?"

"Nadji Akdemir, I don't give a damn if you're a captain or a colonel. You're going to take today off. For once in your life, you're going to tell your officers you are sick, or you are tired, or you need a holiday, but you're not going to work today. You are going to take me to Ephesus, just as you did that night twenty-three years ago when we promised each other …"

"Aysheh," he said, wearily. "Isn't that a bit forced? I have conferences..."

"I don't care if Ismet Inönü himself is coming to speak with you. I don't care if your presence here today makes the difference between your retiring as a colonel or becoming a general tomorrow. I've come hundreds of miles to be here. One of us had to risk it all, and it was me. You are not going to turn me down, do you understand?"

"All right, Aysheh. I can't see any reason why I have to stay here today. I suppose Major Tandoğan can handle any emergencies."

Within the hour, they were leisurely driving south on the new coast road, toward the Greek and Roman ruins. They said little on the way down, but the barrier of courtesy had dropped. Nadji started to marvel at the courage it had taken her to come to him.

"This is crazy. You really want to walk through Ephesus at night? We did that one night so many years ago, and look what happened."

"Why not, Nadji? It may bring back some fond memories."

Ephesus was different than he'd remembered. Teams of archaeologists had unearthed so much more. The city was vast. Still, there was a feeling of connection to forever, a timelessness that bound tonight to another night twenty-three years ago, and perhaps, for another man and woman, an evening twenty-three hundred years before that. "Do you remember, Nadji?" she said softly.

He turned and gazed in the direction of her voice. The magic was there. Standing atop a small rise, twenty feet away, his beautiful, exciting, nude goddess beckoned him as she had on a similar evening, half a lifetime ago. Aysheh was the most beautiful woman in the world, at any time, in any age. "This is crazy, Aysheh," his voice sounded unnatural, choked.

"Perhaps it is. But then again," she smiled at him, "perhaps it isn't. And I'll say the same words to you now that I said then. Years from now, when our children's children are grown, look at me then, and remember me as I am at this moment."

Slightly more than nine months later, Omer Seljuk Akdemir bellowed his arrival to the world. His radiant mother swore he'd been conceived on that very special, magic night. As newly-promoted Brigadier General Nadji Akdemir held the tiny hand of his son for the first time, all he could think of was, "Grey-violet eyes? How can a little boy have grey-violet eyes?"

PART SIX:

COMING OF AGE

1947–1960

1

After the Nazis' defeat, the Allies started squabbling among themselves. There were new alliances and new enmities. One thing was a constant. As long as Nadji could remember, Russia and Turkey had spread death and destruction along their several-hundred-mile border. Sometimes the Russian bear attacked directly. More often, Russia waged war against its neighbor in the guise of supporting a homeland for the Armenians. In spring, 1947, the United States perceived Russia as its enemy. President Truman asked the American congress for four hundred million dollars for aid to Turkey and Greece. In July, Washington and Ankara signed an accord that brought American money, military manpower and credit to the Turkish Republic to aid in the task of reconstruction from the war effort.

That summer, Nadji and Turhan were sitting in the café at the Park Hotel, overlooking the Bosphorous and reminiscing. Turhan was visiting Istanbul during one of his periodic trips from his rustic Aegean farm. Nadji was awaiting his next military assignment in the East – a major command, but not the best of all possible worlds for a new father.

"Mark my words, my esteemed general," Turhan said caustically, "the Americans aren't so altruistic they'd give something for nothing. What kind of 'reconstruction' do you think we need? Or do you know of refugees and physical damage I've never heard about?"

"Our neutrality cost us an enormous amount of money," Nadji replied. "Before the war our budget was always balanced. The lira's fallen. Inflation has wrecked the average Turk's earning power. I believe America's sincere in wanting to help us."

"It certainly doesn't hurt that our frontier cages the Russian bear. Do you see them sending massive funds to Romania or Bulgaria, who've sided with the Soviets? There's a reason the Yankees are granting us easy credit to buy *American*-made planes, tanks, and machine guns. When these toys need maintenance or spare parts, where do you think we'll have to go for replacements? And at what cost then?"

"Don't you trust anyone? Are you that cynical?"

"I prefer to call myself 'realistic.' The Americans plan to construct defense bases for the protection of *American* interests at Adana, Yalova and Izmir. They're setting up spy posts at Sinop, Samsun, Trabzon and Diyarbakır. All places where United States forces will be relatively safe. Meanwhile, our new allies are advancing millions of dollars to provide for *Turkish* forces to guard the really dangerous borders in the east. What I can't understand is why we must rely on yet another foreign power. Atatürk's Turkey wouldn't have been anyone's client state."

"It's been ten years since the *Gazi* died. Things are different now. No nation can go it alone anymore. Do you really think we could have kept the Russians out last year when they demanded control of the straits? Praise Allah we had American help to keep them out."

Nadji awakened to the mournful hoot of an owl. Aysheh, her back to him, snuggled closer. He reached his right arm over her body, cupped her breasts in his hand, and rocked her gently back and forth. Any moment, the sporadic gunfire from the nearby gunnery training range would begin. They'd finally become used to the sound. When the first rounds were fired, she'd stir, moan, and drift into the twilight state between sleep and wakefulness until Yavuz awakened. She'd stopped nursing their second son two months ago, which gave Nadji a few extra moments with her before the brothers demanded their morning meal.

He thought back to their difficult times in Vienna and afterward, and smiled to himself. He would not have wagered a single lira back then that their marriage would survive, let alone that in the spring of 1948 Aysheh and he would be more content, more secure than at any time since the earliest days. Omer had been a happy accident. Less than three months after his birth, Aysheh conceived again. Now, Nadji could proudly boast, "I have *iki erkekler* – two *sons*."

He hardened with desire for the woman lying beside him. Allah! This coming June they'd celebrate twenty-four years of marriage. Her still honey-colored hair was flecked with strands of gray, but that simply gave her a more womanly allure. He rolled over on his back, lest he awaken her, and thought, "How we've all changed in the past few years, Aysheh and me, Turkey and the world."

Nadji was drawn out of his reverie. He realized with a start that Aysheh's soft hand was idly playing with his erect member. She started kissing his chest.

"The boys," he whispered. "At least let me lock the door."

"Let the little boys wait," she replied mischievously. "I've got my own big boy to take care of."

It had not always been so pleasant. When Aysheh had come east four months earlier, things had been tense. The lovely, sophisticated woman, who'd been schooled in Italy, lived in Vienna, and never been east of Ankara, first saw her new home at the end of November 1947, when winter's full fury was upon the land. Erzurum was a somber, depressing city, whose inhabitants looked as though the city's long, bitter winters were permanently etched on their careworn faces. The city, more than six thousand feet above sea level, lay in the shadow of Mount Palandoken, a two-mile high, brooding sentinel. Erzurum's women dressed from head to toe in brown, shapeless sacks. Each man looked the same as every other: baggy, black trousers, threadbare coat, flat fisherman's hat.

Aysheh had endured a grueling seventy-two hour train ride from the capital to this outpost. Once in Erzurum, the babies contracted ear infections from the combination of bitter cold outside and dusty, soft coal fires within. Yavuz started teething. The normally placid Omer became moody as he saw attention diverted away from him. Turkish troops trained in fields and mountains so close to the garrison that even in their home it sounded as though a new war started each morning before the sun came up. Aysheh had been ill-at-ease from the first day she set foot in Erzurum. After a week, her frustration erupted in a screaming fit. For the next several days, she barely spoke to her husband. Nadji hired a full-time housekeeper-cook. Before the month was out, he'd arranged for Aysheh's sister, Talya, to visit from Istanbul.

By the time Talya left, so had the ear infections, the bulk of the teething, and Omer's tantrums. Despite the gray, frigid winter, Nadji made certain that Aysheh found a bouquet of fresh-cut flowers in the crystal vase she kept in their living room at least twice each week. At the end of March, there was a striking change. A bright, spring sun warmed the land. Palandoken's summit was clothed in white. The dry rust color, which started a third of the way down the mountain, provided a buffer zone, much like the two-hundred mile area between

Erzurum and the Russian border. Below that, red, orange, and yellow poppies, violets, and a hundred different kinds of flowers formed a stunning mosaic over green grass, as far as the eye could see.

"I almost forgot, Halide's coming today," Nadji said, as he disengaged himself from Aysheh after their sensual lovemaking. "We have to be at the station before noon."

"Isn't she a little old to be traveling?"

"Listen, woman, she's only five years my senior."

"But her arthritis has given her so much trouble."

"Halide said it was important that we talk."

"She could have used the telephone, darling."

"She said what she had to tell me could not be transmitted by phone."

As Halide stepped off the train, Nadji saw she was aging. Unquestionably, her unrelenting hard work and the arthritis had taken their toll. "Welcome to springtime in the east," Nadji greeted her. "Anywhere Halide Orhan appears, the sun shines."

"Flatterer," she chided. "I remember as many gray days as you."

"Sometimes they seemed black, didn't they?"

"Indeed. My God, Aysheh, are you *never* going to age? Are you keeping your husband in line?"

"Barely. The winter's been rugged. We're settled in now. It's not Belgrade Palas, but it's one of the best accommodations in the east."

Once they'd arrived at the house, and Halide unpacked, Nadji asked,

"What was so important that you needed to speak to me in person?"

Halide nodded toward the kitchen. "Later."

Aysheh picked up the message immediately. "Behiji," she addressed the housekeeper. "Why don't you take the rest of the day off? I'm sure between us, we can handle the boys."

"Very well, Madame. *Chok teshekkür ederim*, many thanks."

"Oh, and Behiji?"

"Yes?"

"General Akdemir, Halide and I will be leaving on our journey day-after-tomorrow. Are you certain you've been able to arrange for the nanny?"

"Indeed, Madame. I'll bring her by tomorrow, so you can meet her."

"Very good."

When they were alone, Halide said, "Distance yourself from Lieutenant Colonel Irvan."

"What??"

"Turhan told me to make sure I got that message to you immediately."

"But Yüksek's indispensable. He arranged for us to hire Behiji, looks after my car, and finds flowers in the middle of winter. I couldn't ask for a better aide."

"I'm simply telling you what Turhan told me."

"Halide, the man's a rising star. I don't mind that he's attached himself to me. It's always been that way in the military. If he looks good, so do I."

"And if he's arrested as a spy for the Russians?"

General Akdemir paled. "You can't be serious."

"I wish I were joking."

"How sure is Turhan about this information?"

"How many times have you known him to be wrong?"

"How did he find out?"

"Remember our friend Hükümdar?"

"That slimy devil?"

"Whatever you think of him, Hükümdar's a cagey survivor. A counterespionage coup would catapult him right back to Ankara."

"Hükümdar told Turhan?"

"Not bloody likely," Halide said. "But Turhan's eyes and ears are everywhere. He's always managed to stay friends with the 'little people,' the clerks, the typists, the cryptographers."

"How much do they have on Colonel Irvan?"

"Turhan told me Hükümdar's got enough to make it very ugly for you and that Hükümdar intends to go public with the information within the month. Names, dates, meetings, couriers."

"I see," Nadji said. "If Akdemir's aide is implicated, it looks very bad for General Akdemir and very good for Abbas Hükümdar."

"You can be certain the words, 'Brigadier General Nadji Akdemir's confidential aide' will be highly publicized."

"Everything's ready for your trip, General."

"Thank you, Yüksek. As always, I can depend on you for everything."

"It's my privilege, Brigadier Effendim," the young lieutenant colonel said, saluting smartly. Then he relaxed. "I see 'Turkey's resident angel' is going with you."

"So you've picked up what the papers are calling her?"

"Who hasn't? Ever since *Isharet* ran that series of articles last year, the average Turk views her as a saint. Gelibolu, a one-woman revolution in education, the safe house, the teachers' college."

"Yüksek, I wonder if we might talk confidentially."

"Of course, General."

As the door closed, Nadji bade Colonel Irvan be seated. "Why, Yüksek?" he asked, without preamble.

"General?"

"Why, Colonel?"

"What are you talking about, Effendim?"

"I've received disturbing information, Yüksek, from very high sources. It seems there are things you've hidden from me."

"What are you talking about, General Akdemir?" the colonel asked, sensing a change and reacting nervously to it. "I've been scrupulously honest, I've done my best to do everything you've wanted of me and more. Are you dissatisfied with my services?"

"No, Colonel Irvan," Nadji responded. "I am not in the least unhappy with your services. Neither are your other commanders."

"My other commanders? What in the world are you talking about? What kind of riddles are these?"

"The Russians, Colonel."

"What kind of insane...?"

"Do you want the details?" Nadji asked, hoping his aide would not call the bluff. The younger man crumpled. He dropped his head into his hands and covered his face. He said nothing for several moments. When he looked at General Akdemir again, his face was ashen. "Why?" Nadji repeated, very gently.

"What difference would it make?" Irvan replied bitterly. "You wouldn't understand."

Nadji sat quietly, his hands in his lap. Yüksek continued, "Isn't there a different story for everyone? Money, a woman... In my case, there was a boy – a Circassian. It was fourteen years ago. I was a junior in the academy. My parents would never have understood. They'd have died of shame. The fellow moved away. I got married, had a son. Everything was forgotten. It was a childish mistake. Three years ago, he surfaced again. This time he brought a friend, a Russian. They threatened to disclose everything if I didn't cooperate. By that time, I was a major. Our second child was on the way. They promised me it would only be for a few years."

"What information did you give them?"

"Troop movement orders, numbers," the colonel replied miserably. "Nothing strategic."

"Yüksek, I'm going to call in my chief of intelligence, Brigadier Gench, now. You can repeat your story for him."

"What will happen?"

"I don't know. That will be up to the authorities."

Not long afterward, Nadji was summoned to the office of the Third Army Commander-in-Chief, a four star general. Although he himself was a brigadier general, he'd only been in the Commander's office once before, on the day of his arrival. This is probably the most elegant office in all of Erzurum, he thought, as the man bade him sit.

"Wine, Nadji?"

"Sir?" Akdemir's surprise showed in his face.

"Don't worry, my friend," the commander chuckled. "I trust you're sophisticated enough to recognize that our command doesn't always honor *all* of the Prophet's injunctions." He winked. "Besides, this calls for a bit of a celebration. I suppose all I can say is thank you. You realize by keeping this within the military, we've avoided a major scandal."

"I do, *Pasha*," Nadji replied. "But it still doesn't make me feel better."

"It's his doing, not yours."

"What happens now?"

"There'll be an investigation. Turkish General Staff has ordered Hükümdar to turn over all his information. He wasn't thrilled, but he had no choice. Since Gench witnessed Colonel Irvan's confession, I don't think there'll be any need for your presence during the next couple of weeks. I understand you're thinking of taking Aysheh and your friend, Halide Orhan, on a two week 'inspection tour.' Combining business with pleasure?" the commandant remarked, smiling at his subordinate.

"By your leave, General. Could you think of a better time to visit Kars and Artvin?"

"Take a few extra days and visit Trabzon. You've certainly earned it."

East of Erzurum, the road climbed ever higher into the Allahuekber Mountains. Flowering fields gave way to dark forests of giant pines. The highway snaked through a wild, amazingly beautiful land. Anywhere the road straightened out, the travelers saw endless rows of abandoned old Russian barracks, a reminder that the area had been a Czarist stronghold until thirty years before. "I can't believe this is Turkey," Halide said. "I've always thought of it as an endless steppe."

"You won't find many Turks in this area. Mostly wolves and foxes. They're better able to deal with the cold than we are," Nadji replied. Aysheh shivered and moved closer to him.

Their driver maneuvered the large Chevrolet sedan well. They arrived in Kars by late afternoon. "My home, General, ladies," the driver said proudly. "Frontier capital of six empires, most recently the Russians."

"It looks like pictures I saw of turn-of-the-century Saint Petersburg," Aysheh said.

Nadji nodded, then asked the driver, "How come there are so many blond-haired people with light-colored skin?"

"At the end of the last century, the Russians brought in Germans and Estonians to build the railroad. Many laborers settled down in this part of Asia, particularly in the suburb of Karaja Oren, which has a Christian Protestant community."

The visitors' quarters were spartan, with one incongruous exception. Aysheh and Nadji found to their delight that their bed was a hand-carved work of art, made of sturdy oak, over a hundred years old. An old-fashioned brightly-covered featherbed and four huge, goose-down pillows completed the picture. "Oh, Nadji," Aysheh sighed. "If only we had a bed like this in Erzurum." She snuggled under the comforter. "I've often wondered what it would be like to sleep on a cloud. Now I know."

Despite Nadji's earnest attempts to purchase the bed next morning, he left empty-handed. The housing officer, a portly man, told him, "With respect, General Akdemir, I can neither give nor sell the piece to you. Marshals and ministers of state have made exorbitant offers for this masterpiece. It's been a legend at Kars fortress since it was delivered during the last century. It was once a fixture in St. Petersburg's Winter Palace. Kars was the farthest Russian frontier. Alexander II declared he wanted a bed with all the comforts of his home when he came to review the troops. Alexander III and Nicholas, the last Czar of all the Russias, slept in that same bed when they visited Kars. After Turkey recaptured this garrison in 1921, Atatürk ordered that the bed remain here, reserved always for the highest visiting dignitaries."

After breakfast, Halide asked, "Nadji, is there any way we can visit Anı, the famous Armenian ghost town?"

"Unfortunately not," he replied. "That's right on the Russian border. No one except military can get anywhere near it."

"Such a shame," she said sadly

"Don't worry, my friend. You'd really do well to preserve your mind's picture of the place. Today there are many ruins, but only about eight Georgian churches. Even they are in pretty bad repair."

"A hundred thousand people, a thousand fabled churches, at a time when Europe was in its darkest Middle Ages," she said, sighing. "Now there's nothing left. Where does it all go, Nadji? Will there be any hint of our own civilization seven hundred years from now?"

"Who knows? With the nuclear weapons America and Russia are developing, there may not be an inhabited world a hundred years from now."

The following day, as each turn in the road revealed another beautiful panorama, Halide remarked, "I haven't seen anything this magnificent since I was in the Swiss Alps, more years ago than I care to think about."

"It reminds me of Salzburg," Aysheh joined in. "You'd never believe we were in Turkey."

"Look!" Halide cried, "Swiss chalets!"

"Not Swiss, and I'd hardly call them chalets," Nadji said. "But unlike any place else in Turkey, there's still enough wood in these mountains to make all the log houses anyone would need."

Artvin was perched in an almost perpendicular position on a mountainside, two thousand feet above a narrow valley. A heavy cloud cover drifted below them, creating a kaleidoscope of change every minute. As the clouds parted, there were dark pine forests, walnut, apple, cherry and mulberry orchards. Soon, Nadji returned with good news. "We'll be staying in one of those chalets you saw on the way in. We'll have to get there by mule. The path to *Dağ Kaleh* can't accommodate automobiles."

After a ride that seemed to go straight up the side of a mountain, the mule train halted at a clearing, a hundred feet from a solid, plank-and-stone Alpine building, surrounded by a large deck. As they walked toward the residence, their guide explained, "*Dağ kaleh*, mountain castle, was built fifteen years ago, in anticipation of a visit from Atatürk. He never came. It's been reserved for state visitors ever since. How long will you be staying, General?"

"Two days."

"I'll wager you'll want to stay longer. Everyone does."

They were interrupted by an ecstatic squeal from Aysheh, who'd bounded up the stairs ahead of them. "Nadji! I want to stay here for ever and ever! Just look!"

Dağ kaleh was fifteen hundred feet above Artvin. Immediately above them, a high, narrow waterfall descended to a pool which, in turn, fed a swift-running river below them. To their left was a high meadow of the brightest green. The valley floor below was carpeted like a fairyland with wildflowers of many colors. To their right, the land was terraced. Blossoming fruit trees descended the mountain. At the bottom, there was a large tea plantation. In the distance, the perennially snow-capped peaks of the east rose in unconquered majesty. Alpine houses dotted the valleys, their natural log-brown bases, whitewashed sides, and red-tiled roofs blending perfectly, an incomparable bouquet for the senses. It was the most beautiful place Nadji had ever seen. The rooms were furnished in comfortable oak furniture. "How long can we stay, darling?" Aysheh asked.

"The commander gave me open leave. What's your schedule like, Halide?"

"Don't worry about me. I haven't taken a vacation for years. There's lots of reading I'd like to catch up on. I might even write some verse. I've always fancied myself a bit of a poet."

"Hanım Effendim," their guide said. "There is not only all the paper you'll need, but two of the new electric typewriters as well. There are four apartments in the chalet, two upstairs, two down. The kitchen, dining facilities and library are centrally located."

"The library?" Halide said. "They really didn't forget anything."

"Indeed not," he said, leading the three of them to a room filled floor-to-ceiling with books suitable for a wide variety of tastes, from philosophy and military science, to the latest European and American novels.

The next two days were the most relaxing Halide could remember. She read, walked in the woods, and wrote. Her spirit was at peace. Nadji and Aysheh celebrated a honeymoon. All the hardships of the past six months evaporated as they made love, at times passionately violent, at other times with disarming tenderness. They walked through meadows redolent with the sweet smells of spring. Occasionally, Nadji wondered aloud about the boys, but his wife reassured him, "They're in Behiji's care. What possible harm could come to them?"

"I 'm just concerned, darling. Yüksek Irvan found her for us. She's probably a relative. With his court-martial coming up..."

"She can't blame you, darling. After all, Yüksek confessed to the authorities."

"But only after I confronted him. Who knows what story he told his family? Even if he told them the truth, blood is thicker than water. His kinfolk would stand by him, help him in any way they could. I'm virtually certain he'll be hanged. What a tragedy! I know it's against every rule in the book to have pity on a spy, but he really was a decent chap. Perhaps I should testify as a character witness on his behalf."

"And put your career on the line? What if the scandal had burst like a bombshell over your head? Hükümdar remembers why he was sent east. He can't be delighted you've stolen the key to his return. Much as you'd like to help Yüksek, you're a brigadier general. Irvan's *quiet* conviction will enhance your own credentials."

On the afternoon of their third day at *Dağ kaleh*, Nadji saw five mules coming up the mountain toward their retreat. He recognized their guide from the way he slouched in the saddle, but he became curious when he saw that a second man rode on a mule behind the guide. As the sun momentarily cast a metallic glint off the man's shoulders, Nadji concluded he must be an officer, another dignitary coming to visit. He stifled his disappointment. Even though there were four separate suites, he'd have preferred not having to share the capacious quarters. "Aysheh, Halide!" he called. "If you're not dressed decently, you've got about fifteen minutes to do so. It looks like we're going to have company."

"General Akdemir," the man, a full colonel, saluted as he spoke. "May I have a word with you in private?"

"Is it a military secret?"

"No, Effendim."

"Very well then, Colonel. You may speak in the presence of us all. I accept full responsibility."

"General Akdemir," the man started, hesitating. Then, very quietly, "General, Hanımler Effendim...," his voice broke.

"What is it, man?" Nadji said. Sensing the colonel's intense discomfort, he said, more gently, "I absolve you of all responsibility for what you say. Please go on."

"Very well, Sir. It's Colonel Irvan. It seems that someone smuggled a gun into his cell last night."

"Allah! Is he dead?"

"He killed himself just before dawn, General."

"How horrible, Nadji," Aysheh said.

"May his soul rest in peace," Halide added.

"There's more, Effendim."

"Yes?"

"Your sons, General..."

"No!" Aysheh gasped.

"Continue, Colonel."

"They're missing, Pasha. No one has seen the boys or the women who were caring for them. When officials went to check this morning, the house was empty. We believe the boys were kidnapped."

As Aysheh broke down in tears, Nadji could only try helplessly to comfort her.

2

Halide took Aysheh home to Belgrade Palas with her. She made certain Aysheh was never left unattended. Nadji implemented her access to military phone lines from Istanbul to Erzurum at all hours. Every suspicious finger pointed to a connection between Irvan's death and the disappearance of Nadji's two children. Internal security police reported that Behiji was Irvan's second cousin, that the woman she'd retained to assist her in caring for the general's children was her niece, and that Behiji had voiced pro-Soviet sympathies on more than one occasion. The reports went on to state that the niece had dated a Russian student during World War II, and that the two women were bitter over Colonel Irvan's death. They felt he'd been unfairly trapped into a false confession.

"How come our own reports don't mention these things?" Nadji asked Brigadier General Gench, his military intelligence counterpart. "We should have pursued this line of questioning."

"We have, Nadji," the intelligence chief replied. "I'm almost as frustrated as you. Chief Hükümdar's security police are always one step ahead of us. When we talk to people who've given them statements, they have nothing more to say to us."

It had been nine days since Omer and Yavuz had disappeared. Nadji realized that unless he forced himself to keep calm, to use reason and logic, he'd only hinder the search. He telephoned Aysheh every night with what little news he had. Military police guarded both his quarters and Belgrade Palas twenty-four hours a day. As he digested General Gench's words, Nadji became suspicious. "Gütchlü," he addressed the brigadier in charge of the investigation, "you say Hükümdar's forces are always just ahead of yours?"

"Correct."

"You know my history with Hükümdar."

"We do. He swears he bears you no ill will. He himself told me he wanted to be involved in this investigation so he could somehow make up to you for the difficulties of some years back."

"Strange. He never attempted to talk to me after the boys' disappearance."

"They say he's working night and day. No one's ever seen him so obsessed by a case."

"Hükümdar's never been obsessed by anything but getting ahead and surviving once he's reached power. You say you've seen documentary evidence?"

"A letter purportedly written by Colonel Irvan to his wife the night before he died. Internal Security officers found it among his personal effects. The note implied you were to blame for his problems, and he wanted to see Behiji."

"Can I see the letter?"

"We have a typed transcript."

"No, General. My question is, 'Can I see the *letter itself*,' not a copy, not a transcript?"

"The commander-in-chief could order Internal Security to turn it over as evidence."

"Please have him do so."

A day later, Brigadier General Gench telephoned his friend. "Nadji, Chief Hükümdar has gone to Hakkarı. The acting chief says Hükümdar took the letter with him."

"I thought as much."

"The fellow claims he has a letter signed by Behiji, which might cast light on the subject."

"This gets more suspicious by the minute, Gütchlü. Unless she's the greatest actress Turkey has ever produced, which I doubt, I'd bet my general's stars Behiji's illiterate."

That evening, Nadji went into town. He was tired of the military investigators' daily reports of failure. He needed escape from the pitying looks of fellow officers in the open mess. He dressed in civilian clothes and went to one of his favorite restaurants, a plain *lokanta* on Cumhüriyet Caddesi, Erzurum's main street. His father had often told him that the Turkish villager always made sure his belly was well-filled, and that the quality of the food was more important than fancy surroundings. Since there was no menu in the place, Nadji walked back into the kitchen and pointed to something that looked appetizing. A waiter brought a bowl of hearty lamb stew to his table.

"Excuse me, General, may I join you?"

Nadji did not recognize the voice. When he looked up, he saw a large, husky man, with a wide, flat, unsmiling face. "Do I know you, Effendim?"

"You don't, *Tovarisch*," the man replied. "I asked permission to join you, and I am waiting for your reply."

"You're Russian."

"And your sworn enemy, yes?"

"So it would seem. How did you know me?"

"General Akdemir, you're not exactly invisible in these parts. Our intelligence knows the identity of every officer above the rank of captain who's stationed east of Ankara. Permit me, Effendim, to sympathize with you in your current loss."

"You know that, too?"

"*Da*, Tovarisch. That's the reason I sought you out. I want to help you."

"Like you helped Yüksek Irvan?"

"Silence!" the man roared. "I said *I* am here to help you, *tovarisch*," he said, in a much calmer voice.

"Look, Ivan, or whatever you call yourself."

"Mishkin. Aleksandr Davidovich Mishkin."

"Very well, Pan Mishkin. I love my children, but if you think I'd stoop to betraying my country to help the Russians, you're sadly mistaken."

"Listen, my friend," the big man held his hands up, palms toward Nadji. "I'm not seeking any favors. I don't want to interfere with either your country or your career."

"Then why would you want to help me?"

"May I sit down, at least?"

"All right."

"Thank you. You once knew a man named Samuel Kovalevsky?"

"Of what interest would that be to you?"

"You know him, then?"

"What if I do?"

"Let's not play games, General Akdemir. I am well aware of what you did for my people during the Great War of Liberation."

"Your people? I did nothing for the Russians, Pan Mishkin."

"I mean the Jews."

"You are...?"

"Minister of Customs assigned to Batum. I have other important duties as well."

"You're Jewish?"

"Yes."

"How have you attained such a position?"

"We Jews have always been adept at survival, the last war notwithstanding. I made it through the great purge in the late thirties. My brother Lev reached Israel because of the Belgrade Palas operation."

"I see."

"Before he died, your Colonel Irvan managed to get word to me about how you treated him. He said you were a decent human being."

"That's not what I've been led to believe."

"By whom?"

"Turkish Internal Security."

"Abbas Hükümdar?"

"You know him?"

"Of course. Not a nice man."

"I agree."

"Did you ever think he might want you to believe that Irvan hated you? Perhaps to divert your attention?"

"What do you mean?"

"I heard about your children being kidnapped the day after it happened. We have our own informants here. Since you saved part of my family, I feel it only right I save part of yours."

"Are my sons alive?"

"They are, General. Alive and well."

"*Mashallah*! You're certain?"

"I am."

"How can I ever thank you Pan Mishkin?"

"No thanks are due. The debt is repaid."

"For God's sake, man, where are they?"

"Machka. Five miles southeast of Sumela."

"You'll excuse me if I don't finish my dinner, Comrade Mishkin?"

"You've not even started it."

Within three hours, fifty specially trained military troops headed south from Trabzon. Shortly after midnight, they started a methodical sweep of every inhabited building within a five mile radius of the Sumela Monastery. Turkish officers questioned the muhtars of every village in the area whether they'd seen any new inhabitants, particularly in outlying areas, during the past month. Just before sunrise Nadji and General Gench arrived at Trabzon in one of the new Sikorsky helicopters the Americans used for Black Sea reconnaissance. They were driven to Sumela Monastery. Even in Nadji's agitated state, there was no way he could ignore the dramatic sight.

A seven story facade was built directly on a ledge, a thousand feet up a sheer rock face, above the forest valley. The monastery appeared to be part of the mountain itself. It was more imposing than pictures Nadji had seen of the Greek monasteries at Mount Athos. A morning mist rose from the valley, completing the surrealistic scene. What a shame Aysheh couldn't be here to see this. It was an El Greco painting come to life.

"So far, the troops have found nothing," Gench said. "The monastery's as good a place to wait as any. You'll have privacy, since there are nothing but ruins inside the façade. Go on ahead. I've got to make a couple of calls on the field telephone. I'll join you in a little while."

Nadji climbed for half an hour up a narrow, zigzag path, before he reached the final sixty-seven step ascent to the entrance gate, just south of the shrine. When he entered the spectacular walls, he saw demolished half-ruins, covered ledges and shallow rock caves. Otherwise the place was a shambles.

Suddenly he heard a familiar childish voice shout, "Papa, Papa!" in delighted surprise. As Nadji turned and looked up at a ledge, he saw his older son yanked back, and found himself looking into the malevolent eyes of Abbas Hükümdar, who was aiming a pistol at Omer's head. His other hand held the boy's shirt collar.

"Well, General Akdemir," Hükümdar spat the words out contemptuously. "We meet once again."

"Is this an example of your Brotherhood's courage, Abbas?" Nadji's tone was equally icy.

"Don't waste words with me, Akdemir. You stole from me twice. My own son, and my opportunity for revenge. Now I intend to even the score."

"You're insane. You'd take the lives of innocent children?"

"Your insults fall on deaf ears, General. Your seed means nothing to me."

"Where's Behiji and her cousin?"

"Those peasant cows? Dead, back at one of the houses where they stayed at my 'invitation.' The last thing I need are witnesses."

"Hold it right there, Hükümdar!" Nadji turned to see General Gench, pointing a handgun at the kidnapper. "One move and I'll shoot!"

Hükümdar did not change his position. "It appears we're at a stalemate," he said, smiling. The man was cool, still in control of the situation. "General Gench, do you really think the two of you could reach me before I killed this brat?"

"Where's Yavuz?"

"Your little darling's safe enough for now, Pasha. He's with friends."

"What do you propose, Hükümdar?" Gench asked.

"One life for two. I want safe passage to the Russian frontier, plus fifty thousand American dollars."

"How can we possibly trust your word?"

"No more than I trust yours, General Gench. I deliver this child to you when I receive the money. My insurance that I live to spend it is the younger lad. He crosses the border when I do. Those are my terms. Take them or leave them."

"Do we have a choice?" Gench asked Nadji.

"Spoken like reasonable, intelligent men." Hükümdar responded.

It took the better part of a day to make arrangements. Hükümdar insisted that Colonel Whitcomb, the senior American officer in Trabzon, handle the transfer of money, and accompany them to the border. The American counted out fifty thousand dollars. Hükümdar signed a receipt and turned over Nadji's eldest child. Nadji held the boy close to him. He felt a rash of conflicting emotions: relief, hate, love, bitterness, elation.

"Omer, you'll stay with Madame Gench until Papa comes back."

"I miss you, Papa."

"Don't worry, son, I won't be gone for long. When I return tomorrow, *Inshallah*, your brother will be with me."

It was dawn when they reached the frontier. No words were exchanged. Hükümdar flashed a prearranged signal with a pocket mirror. The gate on the Russian side was raised. A peasant woman walked toward them, carrying a baby. The Turkish gate went up. Hükümdar walked through it. Halfway between the guard posts, Hükümdar and the woman nodded at one another. Nadji saw that the child in her arms was indeed Yavuz. The woman handed him his son. Without a word, she turned and walked back across the border into Russia. Nadji was never certain, but the large man in a black greatcoat who greeted Hükümdar with a bear hug when he set foot on Soviet soil looked very much like Mishkin.

Gench, Whitcomb, Nadji and Yavuz rode back toward Trabzon in a single car. "I told you Hükümdar was a survivor," Nadji remarked bitterly. "Not only did he exact his revenge, but he ended up a wealthy man for life."

"Perhaps so," murmured the American colonel. "But, to use an American phrase, Hükümdar did not 'cover all his bases.'"

"What do you mean?"

"He may indeed be a survivor. He'll have to be when he starts to spend any part of the fifty thousand *counterfeit* American dollars he took with him across the border."

"And that's how it ended," Nadji said, as he embraced his beautiful wife. They were seated in the parlor at Belgrade Palas and Halide, always thoughtful, had provided small toys and cookies for the boys when they arrived in Istanbul.

"Nadji, we're so very lucky," she said, burying her head in the crook of his shoulder. "I can't think of two – make that four – more fortunate people in all the world."

"Perhaps it was another test, my love," he said, inhaling the entrancing fragrance of her hair. "Another test from Allah that we passed."

"Papa, Papa!" Their reverie was interrupted as Omer and Yavuz burst into the room. "Aunt Halide said she would take Yavuz and me on a walk to the Sea if you and mama would let us go. Can we, Papa? Can we? Can we?" Their younger son, Yavuz, started echoing his brother's cry.

"Well, now," Nadji grinned at his two sons. "That depends on what your mother says."

Aysheh had been rubbing the small of Nadji's back, eager to celebrate the safe return of her men. "I don't see why not. You take care of Aunt Halide, though. She'll need two big, strong boys to make sure she's safe."

"Oh, we will, Mama," Omer said seriously. With a whoop, the boys were gone.

"Well, Mama," Nadji said to his wife. "Your two little birds have returned to the nest safely. What do you suggest we do now?"

"We've got at least an hour," she said throatily. "I think you'll find something to keep us suitably entertained."

3

Turhan was bored with the peaceful, bucolic life in the hills above Izmir. Every two weeks *Isharet's* publisher, who realized the name Türkoğlu was money in the bank when it came to selling newspapers, called and asked when he'd finally come back to Istanbul as editor-in-chief. Turhan knew he was surviving on his reputation alone. If he did not produce fresh writing, if he did not come into the modern, postwar world, the self-styled "conscience of the nation" would become "the tired old man of Turkish journalism," before his fifty-first birthday.

Another two weeks went by before he telephoned Istanbul and told his publisher he would be returning to Istanbul within the month. The following year, Turhan shuttled between Istanbul and Ankara twice a month. He was one of the very few who urged caution as the courtship between Ankara and Washington heated up. He renewed his correspondence with Ed Baumueller, and spoke with his friend by international telephone several times a month. During one of their conversations, Baumueller said, "You won't believe it, Turhan, but I've got an old friend of yours here who wants to say a few words."

Turhan knew of no American friends except Baumueller. The voice came on the phone, and Turhan grinned. "Hello, *Tovarisch*. Are you still waiting tables at the restaurant?"

"No more than you're still playing piano at a whorehouse, Sascha, you old dog," Turhan said affectionately. "It's been more than thirty years! Are you still making it with the ladies?"

"I am, indeed. Four marriages, I can't tell you how many liaisons, and I've managed to stay friends with every one of them. But I have to work almost every night to support them in the manner to which they've become accustomed."

"Serves you right, you rake! Did anything ever come of your violin playing?"

"I'll say!" Baumueller, who'd been listening on a second phone, interrupted them. "He's the most famous concert violinist in the U.S. He travels back and forth across the Atlantic like you travel across the Bosphorous, Turhan. He was guest concertmaster when Toscanini started the Israel Philharmonic, and he's had a lucrative contract with RCA Victor records for the past fifteen years."

"All well and good," Turhan said, delighted. "But is there any reason, Mister Brotsky, that you never bothered to stay in touch with your old friend?"

"Sure. First off, who knew where you were? Second, it wasn't particularly safe for a Jew in Europe during the past several years. Third, as a Russian, I wouldn't be too popular in Turkey today. And finally, I'd be afraid to come to your country because who knows how many little Turks that I've fathered would seek financial support from me?"

"One excuse for each of your four wives," Turhan responded. "Listen, Sascha, enough of this foolishness. You'll stay in touch?"

"When you least expect it, my friend. Sayonara!"

"What?"

"I'm off to Tokyo next week. There's a buildup of American troops there. The State Department thought they'd enjoy a little culture."

When Turhan learned the outcome of the Hükümdar incident, his article "The Counterfeit Defector," evoked derisive laughter throughout the nation. In the summer of 1949, Halide telephoned him. "I need an escort for a Democrat Party dinner next week. You're the only available bachelor I know who's worthy of my company."

"You're not afraid I'll try to seduce you?"

"Not even remotely. You missed your chance in '15, '25, '35 and '45. You only get an opportunity with a lady like me once every ten years. Seriously, I think you should attend. There'll be people there you should get to know."

"When did you get involved in party politics? I thought Turkey's legendary teacher of teachers stayed out of such things."

"I try to. But the Sherifiks have been my neighbors for three years and they insisted I come. I've heard it said that happiness is much more joyful when it's shared, and the burden of boredom is lighter if it's carried by two people. Come with me. You'll have a chance to find out whether the old saying is true."

"I've had my share of black-tie dinners. I can't help but think back to that Turkish Embassy fiasco Sezer and I attended in Berlin back in 1933."

"My, aren't you showing your age?" Halide twitted him. "When you start to talk about things that happened more than sixteen years ago, it's time to freshen up your thinking. It's not formal, by the way. Open shirt collar and slacks."

"An informal political dinner? The times certainly are changing."

"These are the Democrats. They want to show how much they're in tune with the common man."

That evening, Halide's neighbor Sherifik greeted Turhan effusively. "Turhan Effendim, I can't tell you how pleased I am to finally meet Turkey's spokesman to the world. Tonight we're having a genuine, U.S.A.-style barbecue!"

"Wonderful!" Turhan muttered under his breath to Halide. "We've grilled meat over coals for a thousand years, and our host gloats that we're borrowing this manner of cooking from a country that wasn't even in existence two centuries ago."

"Are you always so gracious?" Halide asked, grinning at him.

As the evening wore on, Turhan found himself deep in conversation with two men, Jalal Bayar, whom he'd known since the Atatürk days, and Adnan Menderes, a strikingly personable man of forty-five. "You really believe you can upset Atatürk's Republican People's Party two years from now?" Turhan asked Bayar. "You're attacking Allah's appointed, you know."

"Don't forget, I was also one of Atatürk's new faces when I was Prime Minister during your absence from the country."

"But Ismet Inönü's led us through the minefield of the last war, and he was a hero of the War of Independence. You're fighting an uphill battle."

"We may surprise you, Turhan," Menderes said easily. "The *Gazi* made enemies. Inönü's policies haven't healed the breach. It's time to improve on some of Kemal's ideas, bring Turkey into modern times, cement new alliances."

"That's a contradiction in terms, isn't it, Adnan? The *Gazi's* political foes were Islamic fundamentalists, the most conservative force in our society. You say you want to appeal to them. At the same time, you befriend the most progressive western society in the world. How do you propose to satisfy everyone?"

"By emulating the United States," Menderes said. "The Americans are the most diverse group of people who've ever lived. Their citizens are immigrants from every country in the world. Look what they've accomplished. Two hundred years ago, we ruled most of the civilized world. We lost that leadership because we failed to adjust to the times."

"That's a politician's answer. The example's irrelevant. Never mind the diverse groups in the United States. How are you going to appeal to a diverse group of *Turks*?"

"Confidentially?" Menderes winked. "No press coverage?"

"If you say so."

"By learning from the American politicians. Promise the voters what we must, deliver whatever we can, and pray they forget most of what we said as soon as the election results are in."

"Allah! An honest politician at last!"

"Don't forget, I said those last words in confidence."

"Seriously, Adnan, how are you going to get around the RPP's control of the electoral machinery?"

"Our main goal during the next two years is to force the Grand National Assembly to pass a new law. As long as the voting takes place out in the open and the ballot counting is secret, Inönü's party can rig the election. I believe it's only fair that this situation be reversed: the secret ballot and open, public counting of the votes. The Americans are starting to pour money and aid into Turkey. Sooner or later they'll insist we become a 'democracy' like they claim to be. We simply try to speed the process along."

"You think Inönü will let Turkey have a real opposition party any more than the *Gazi* did?"

"Times were different then. Atatürk believed in an opposition only so long as it was a *loyal* opposition. There was no way he was going to give up a shred of his power. Ismet's not Mustafa. There aren't many giants left. Hitler and Mussolini are gone, Roosevelt's dead, Churchill was voted out of office."

"You really think you can pull it off?"

"Give us an election with secret voting and open ballot counting and you'll see."

June 1, 1950

Istanbul

Edwin Baumueller II, Publisher

New York World

The New York World Building

New York City, New York, U.S.A.

Dear Ed:

Remember what I told you last year about my dinner with the Democrats? Adnan Menderes' words proved prophetic. In February, the Assembly enacted a new electoral law that restricted the RPP's power to stifle opposition. Atatürk's party found itself bitterly contesting an election for the first time in twenty-seven years.

Inönü promised to stimulate private enterprise, increase agricultural credit, and limit inflation. The RPP said they'd give more credit, build schools, houses, and roads, and provide farm machinery, telephones, and electricity. The Democrats pitched their campaign to everyone who was dissatisfied with RPP rule, even if their promises were conflicting. Peasants wanted more land, landowners wanted fewer restrictions. Workers wanted more benefits and higher wages. Employers wanted freedom from government control. The Democrats stressed that they wanted to end the monopoly of power in the Grand National Assembly, and provide what your government calls "checks and balances."

On May 14, 1950, the highest percentage of voters in Turkey's history, almost ninety percent of the electorate, gave the Democrats a stunning victory. What it boiled down to in the end was that the people simply felt Atatürk's party had been in power too long. The Democrats got more than eight out of every ten seats in the Grand National Assembly. Inönü turned the reins of government over to the Democrats three days ago. For the first time since the republic was founded, the RPP became the opposition party. The cagey old war horse didn't have much choice. If he'd created problems, there may have been a revolution. Now Jalal Bayar is President, Menderes is Prime Minister, and Köprülü is foreign minister. These three are as diverse as their constituency. Bayar's an old guard civil servant, who was prime minister under Inönü from 1937 to 1939. Köprülü's an Ottoman historian who taught at Istanbul University. He appeals to the intellectuals. The foreign ministry's the right place for him. The real power is Adnan Menderes, a spellbinding campaigner, who claims to represent the emerging middle class. It will be interesting to see how they handle such an overwhelming mandate from the people.

In spite of their optimism, it won't be easy. Menderes is shrewd enough to know that every "have-not" in Turkey voted ***against*** *twenty-seven years of RPP rule, and the Democrats just happened to be the beneficiary of that* *dissatisfaction. No matter how adept the Democrats are, I doubt they can force a happy marriage between the Imams and the Comrades.*

Percy Phillips, an old English journalist friend of mine, wrote me from London. He says you Americans haven't had enough of war. He's hinted something's about to break in Cho'sun – I believe they're calling it 'Korea' now. If you have any information you can spill to your old friend and brother-in-the-trade, I'd appreciate it. ***Hürriyet*** *and* ***Cumhüriyet*** *have been getting all the best stories – 'scoops' as you say – lately. It's time* ***Isharet*** *uncovered a major story. I'll write more as our political situation becomes clearer. If you see Brotsky, give him my best. My love to the family. Stay well.*

Sincerely, Turhan

4

"What would you say about my going to Korea, Turhan?"

"I'd say your fifty-five years have taught you nothing whatsoever. Haven't you done enough for Turkey already? I suppose you want me to be your medical corpsman again?"

"No. I'm a little too old and much too arthritic to spend my days carrying bedpans and scrubbing floors."

"Praise Allah, the woman finally talks with some intelligence. You're serious about going there?"

"I am. Our new *Tümgeneral* – isn't it wonderful that Nadji got his second star? – called from Ankara and told me our boys have nothing to relieve the monotony. The Americans send their movie stars to put on shows for their forces. Their soldiers are able to take holidays in Tokyo. Our troops have neither the money nor the social graces to do those things. For the most part, they're simple villagers, frightened and far away from home."

"Don't blame me. I'm the one who said, 'Don't cozy up too close to the Americans.' Now our government feels they have to repay our allies by providing them with a fighting force, in a place that has no meaning whatsoever to the average Turk. The only reason the Democrats brought us into this war is that they're eager to be accepted into the North Atlantic Treaty Organization."

"We've only got one brigade there," Halide said.

"True, but for the first time in this century, Turkish forces are fighting on foreign soil, and our interests aren't at stake."

"All the more reason they need someone from home to let them know they're not forgotten."

"What about Yujel Orhan Teacher's College?"

"I've become little more than a symbol in the past year. The school is in good hands, and I'll have the feeling I'm contributing something of value again, rather than just sitting on my throne at the college."

"Who am I to stop you? Go with Allah, my friend."

Early in September, 1951, an American Air Force C-54 put down at Pusan after two grueling days of choppy air and bone-jarring landings at Diyarbakır, Karachi, New Delhi, Rangoon, Manila, and Tokyo. The military version of the Douglas DC-4 carried fifty Turkish combat troops, two officers, and a small, grandmotherly-looking woman.

When Halide stepped off the plane, Colonel Firat Kayaburch, commander of the Turkish brigade, greeted her with a bouquet of summer flowers, which did little to mask the pungent odor that assaulted her nostrils. Kayaburch smiled indulgently. "It's *gübre*, Hanım Effendim, both animal and human manure, which they use to fertilize the surrounding hills. You'll get used to the smell. In about a week you won't even notice it."

"Will I be in Pusan the whole time, *Albay* Kayaburch?" she asked.

"If you stayed here, you'd only see Turks as they came into Korea at the beginning of their duty, and as they went home after six months. Our destination is Inch'on, southwest of the capital."

As they drove through the countryside, Halide saw tired, rounded hills, some as barren as Turkey's unending steppes, others verdant with trees. Villagers toiled by hand in green rice paddies. Although there was evidence of destruction everywhere, peasants appeared to ignore the burned-out huts and bomb-rutted roads. Every so often, Halide noticed incongruous stands selling American cigarettes, nylon hosiery, or Coca Cola, on the outskirts of small towns. At one such stop, a small man about Halide's age addressed the Colonel in broken English, "You want to buy American M-1? Bazooka perhaps, Mister Officer? I make you very good deal, OK? You finished fighting Commies, you take home, OK?"

Kayaburch politely refused. When they started driving again, he said, "The Americans occupy almost every square foot of this country not inhabited by Koreans. The Yanks are very rich, and they bring their lifestyle with them. Somehow, almost everything that's not nailed down, and many things that are, disappear from American posts all over this country."

"That seems almost impossible, after all the guard towers, fences and barricades I've seen at every American installation we've passed," Halide replied.

"That may be, but the Americans are soft. They're easy touches for anyone with a sad face and a story of a lost home or a relative injured in the war. They think everyone is as straightforward and honest as they. We Turks know better. Not one item has disappeared from the Turkish compound during the entire war. And we don't need watchtowers, guards or anything else."

"Why is that, *Albay*?"

"You'll see when we get to our camp."

An hour later, they pulled up to a large American base, with guard houses, imposing buildings and military police. "Our post is about a mile down the road." They continued beyond the United States fortress, until Halide saw a group of low, box-like buildings and several hundred tents. They pulled up to the gate which bore a simple sign, "Armed Forces of the Republic of Turkey, F. Kayaburch, Albay, Commandant," and a short flagpole bearing a drooping red star-and-crescent flag. A single gate guard raised the barrier, saluted, and waved them in.

"There's nothing guarding this camp but a single strand of barbed wire, Colonel," Halide said. "It would be the easiest thing in the world to take anything from here."

In reply, Kayaburch pointed to a blurred spot about a hundred feet from the entry gate. "There's no better sentry than that anywhere in Korea."

They walked toward where the Colonel had signaled. As they came within twenty feet, Halide said, "Albay, you'll please excuse me. I think I may be sick." Suspended in plain sight from the strand of barbed wire was a pair of human ears.

"We have forty-five hundred men serving in Korea at bases scattered throughout the country, clear up to the thirty-eighth parallel. They serve for six months, then return to Turkey. Inch'on is headquarters. We've got seven hundred here."

"Are all the bases as grim as this one, Colonel?"

"Worse, I'm afraid. Most of those assigned here are too young and inexperienced to have seen anything of the world. You'd be surprised how primitive some of them are. One in every three can read and write. We teach some of them how to use a knife and fork at the same time we train them to operate modern weapons. The way most of them drive a motor vehicle, you'd swear they're *almost* ready to deal with the invention of the wheel. Yet, these youngsters are the best soldiers fighting in this entire war! They're absolutely fearless. They do exactly as they're told. The Turks have the highest casualty rate of any forces in Korea. One out of every ten is seriously wounded. Of those, every third man is 'transferred to the Fourth Army.'" The colonel used the delicate euphemism for "killed in action."

"Have they nothing to keep them entertained?"

"Occasionally a man shows up in camp with a *saz* or a *tanbur*, but that's soon put away and forgotten. A Turkish soldier's usually too shy to make the effort to meet a man who'll either be dead or out of his life in six months. Once in a while, there's a fight in the barracks, and the fellows set up an impromptu wager on the outcome, but that's it."

"Colonel Kayaburch, would you mind terribly if I called my friend, Tümgeneral Akdemir, in Ankara via the radiotelephone?"

"By all means, Hanım Effendim. I'll contact the American commander and arrange for him to put you through, immediately."

"Are you serious?"

"Never more serious in my life."

"But your shopping list will fill most of the aircraft."

"Nadji, do you want me to help these boys or not?"

"Of course, but they may resist your pushing so hard."

"I learned way back in the twenties that you need patience, a sense of humor, and a willingness to look failure straight in the eye and defeat it. Can you arrange it, or do I have to go higher than a two-star general?"

"As usual, your wish is my command, Halide. I'll even get my most dependable *Bashchavush* – the best master sergeant in the Turkish army – to personally make sure everything is delivered to you in first class condition.

The following evening, as Halide was preparing for bed, she felt a mild pain in her lower abdomen. She attributed it to the excitement of the trip and exhaustion. Two hours later, she awoke drenched in sweat. She'd never experienced such severe pain in her life. Colonel Kayaburch's bedroom was just down the hall. She struggled to get up. The pain was so intense she thought she'd faint. She forced herself somehow to make it to the commander's door. "Colonel," she croaked. "Colonel Kayaburch, please help me!" She banged on his door with all her strength, then crumpled in a heap.

Inside, the commander was asleep. He heard Halide's voice, followed by a very slight bump. He was awake in an instant, opened his bedroom door and saw Halide lying on the floor. "Allah!" he swore, under his breath. Then he banged sharply at the entryway of a bedroom four down from his. "Doctor Üyan," he said, his voice as calm as his emotions would allow. "Please come quickly down the hall. I think Halide's had a heart attack."

The brigade medical officer, thirty-two years old and an excellent surgeon, moved swiftly. He listened to Halide's heartbeat and took her pulse. If she'd suffered a coronary attack, it had probably passed. Her breathing was rapid and shallow, her skin an unnatural greenish-white. "Colonel," he said, "it could be one of several things. My initial impression is that it's not a coronary." He gently prodded her abdominal area. Halide moaned in pain. "It's tender just about everywhere from the rib cage down. How soon can you arrange to get her over to the American hospital?"

"Immediately."

"Good, Albay. Then do so."

"Kidney stones," the American field hospital commander said, even before the test results came back.

"I thought that's something only men got," Colonel Kayaburch said, surprised.

"Both sexes. You hear about it more in men. We've given her medication to try to soften the stones and help her pass them. We may have to operate if she's not out of pain in a day or so."

"Thank you for taking her so quickly."

"No problem, Colonel. We're here to help any hour, night or day. It's been a while since I've had a female patient. The change will do me good."

"Will she be all right?"

"In your words, Colonel, '*Mashallah*' we got her here in plenty of time, and '*Inshallah*' she'll be just fine in a few days."

The American doctor was right. Within twenty-four hours, Halide had passed the kidney stone, a large one, with several smaller adjuncts. Except for the memory of the excruciating pain, she felt almost back to her old self. "Thank you, Doctor Jordan," she said, reading his name tag and smiling weakly.

"My pleasure, Miss Orhan. Please call me Phil."

"Only if I'm 'Halide' to you."

"Fine, Halide. For the next few days you'll be taking a holiday all right, while you recover fully. You'll be happy to know half-a-planeload full of crates arrived this afternoon from Ankara. The man who accompanied the shipment asked if he could visit you in the hospital. It's fine with me if you feel up to it. He's waiting in the hall."

"That must be the sergeant General Akdemir said he was sending. By all means allow him in."

"Fine. Sergeant Suvarli," the doctor called, "you may come in now."

"Good evening, Halide Hanım. I'm pleased you're feeling better. I'm honored you allowed me to visit you." The speaker was in his late thirties or early forties, with a quiet, intelligent demeanor and an open, handsome face. There was something vaguely familiar about him. He smiled and handed her a bouquet of flowers.

"Thank you, Sergeant," she said. "That's very thoughtful of you. Did the shipment arrive safely?"

"Indeed." He looked at her in a strange way. He blushed, and seemed at a loss for words.

Poor fellow, she thought. Another one of these shy Turkish men who don't know what to do when confronted with a recuperating woman. She tried to put him at ease. "Your last name is Suvarli, Sergeant. That's an interesting coincidence. Many years ago my first teaching assignment was in a village called Suvarli. It was a difficult time. I had a lot to learn about how villagers think. Two of those villagers in particular were very special to me, one girl, one boy. The girl was my first and greatest triumph. She went on to marry my closest friend, and became a wonderful teacher. *Mashallah*, she perished in the Erzinjan tragedy twelve years ago. The other student, the boy, was a bitter defeat for me. His mind was sharp and I predicted great things for him. Through him, I learned that loyalty to family and to the old ways are a great magnet. One of the saddest days in my life was when he told me he couldn't continue. Sad in the sense that I lost him as a potential teacher and friend. Sadder still, when I saw the look in his eyes as he spoke to me. Those, and a bittersweet memory of an unhappy hodja, who saw his world coming to an end, are my memories of Suvarli."

"Halide Hanım, was the boy's name by any chance Yurtash?"

"You know him?" Her eyes widened in excitement. "Can you tell me what ever happened to him?"

"His father passed on a few years after he stopped lessons. The boy enrolled in the primary school in the nearest town. He was twenty-two then. Sitting in a classroom with seven and eight-year-olds was embarrassing to him, so he joined the military service and vowed never to return to his village."

"Is that where you met him?"

"No, Halide."

The woman looked at him again, searchingly, carefully. She shivered involuntarily. "Merciful Allah be praised!" she said softly. "It's you, Yurtash."

"It's me, Hanım Effendim. I'm ready to continue my studies if you're willing to help me. I'm older and a little slower, but I'm willing to work as hard with my mind as I ever did in the field."

"So I didn't lose you after all," she murmured. Then, turning to him, she smiled broadly and said, "Yurtash Effendim, *Hosh geldiniz*, welcome home. When I get out of here, day after tomorrow, we'll begin our lessons again."

Halide marveled at the treasure trove Nadji had sent. Twenty-five *karagöz* puppets, fifty copies of plays by Turkish authors, three hundred books, everything from basic grammar to modern novels, musical instruments sufficient to start a large band. Twelve *keman* and another dozen *kemenjes* – Near Eastern-style violins and violas, twenty *tanburs*, long-necked lutes with eight double strings, thirty sets of drums, and fifty *neys*, the oblique wooden flutes that the whirling dervishes had used in Konya for the last five hundred years. She opened boxes that contained costumes of every sort. Finally, there was a large consignment of olive oil. It took her two days to catalogue everything Nadji had sent. She was like a child opening an entire store full of new toys. The greatest gift would be the one she'd give the Turkish troops in days to come.

Colonel Kayaburch assigned Halide one of the largest rooms on post. She borrowed seventy-five folding chairs from the American military base. Three weeks after her arrival in Korea, on orders of the Post Commander, the first troops were ushered into the makeshift auditorium. They sat stiffly. None of the soldiers appeared older than twenty-two. Many were still in their teens. Their heads were closely shaved. Each had a blank, resigned look. Their presence here was simply a response to another command.

Halide had placed flowers around her lectern to give the place a festive air. The decor seemed to have no effect on the young men. She walked to the front of the room and stood before them. "*Günaydin arkadashlar, hosh geldiniz*," she said, smiling. "Good morning my friends, welcome. We are about to start a great adventure." There was a shuffling and milling about in the seats. "How many of you can play a *saz*?" One or two hands slowly went up. "How many of you enjoy the sound of a drum and *tanbur*?" Twenty hands were raised in ragtag fashion. After a few moments, another twenty soldiers lethargically lifted their hands as well.

"Men," she continued, "we're going to start our own Janissary band." A few of the men snickered. Most sat silent. "Do you think we can't do it?" she asked, still smiling. "Let me tell you about a time when my father's father's father glued wool back on every sheep in his flock..." The village boys realized this grandmotherly woman was about to tell them an old Anatolian folk tale, and they perked up.

"In those fine old days, the villagers of Sivrihisar found Nasrettin Hodja pouring yogurt culture into a nearby lake. When they asked him what he was doing, he replied he was trying to turn the lake into yogurt. 'Impossible!' said the villagers. The Hodja replied, 'Suppose it works? Then...?'" The recruits burst into laughter at this timeless, but ever-popular, yarn of their far-off homeland.

When the laughter stopped, Halide continued, "We are all the children of Nasrettin Hodja. Each of you must stay in this Allah-forsaken place six months, obeying orders, fighting, suffering, sometimes dying. The Americans bring beautiful Hollywood movie stars to entertain their troops. You don't get to see Rita Hayworth. You get to see me. For some reason I find it difficult to explain, no one ever asked me to star in a Hollywood motion picture." There was good-natured, hearty laughter and applause. "But we have one another. We Turks have always created our own entertainment. Thanks to Colonel Kayaburch and a friend of mine in Ankara, three days ago we received everything necessary to give us pleasure except women." There was loud hooting, followed by more appreciative laughter. "We have musical instruments, costumes, *karagöz* puppets, even olive oil so we can set up grease wrestling contests." Now the noise turned to excited cheers. "I understand your regular duty hours are from six each morning until six each evening. Tomorrow night, from seven to nine, I'd like all of you who even *think* you can play an instrument to report to this room. If any of you have worked with *karagöz* puppets and can help us put on plays, please come. Within a month, each of you will have something worthwhile to occupy your spare time.

"One final question. How many of you can read?" There was an embarrassed silence. Ten men looked around, then raised their hands. "There's no need to feel ashamed. While some of us are preparing to entertain, Sergeant Suvarli will be teaching basic reading and writing to those of you who want to learn. Colonel Kayaburch has given us another large room for that purpose. Now if you'll excuse me, my fine, handsome young men, I must pass this news along to everyone on post. *Inshallah*, we'll show the world we're not only the best fighting force in Korea, but we also know how to have fun! *Tamam*, finished. *Güle güle*."

When she'd started teaching in 1928, Halide's success was slow in coming, because she was impatient to change hundreds of years of tradition within a very few years. In the fall of 1951, in a small nation halfway around the world from Turkey, her success was immediate and legendary. She brought the old culture – the songs, the dances, the *karagöz* shadow-puppet shows, even grease wrestling – to Turkish villagers thousands of miles from home. Within a month of her arrival, nine out of every ten men on the base were participating in some form or other in her programs. Sullen, homesick village boys made new friends. They'd found common ground at last.

5

In mid-November, the weather turned cold and bleak. Under ordinary circumstances, the troops would have succumbed to boredom, fights, or the stupor of their miserable existence. This year, with the eager concurrence of Colonel Kayaburch, Halide and Yurtash were busily working on what they hoped would be a history-making performance. "We've got the best of the best, Halide," Yurtash said proudly. "The forty men who won our talent contest last month have been rehearsing for two weeks."

"How many weeks to go before the show?"

"Two."

"How are they doing?"

"Truthfully?"

"Of course."

"Terrible. There's no direction. The men do anything you tell them, but I don't know how to organize a show."

"I have an idea. Perhaps my American doctor friend can help."

Later that day, she spoke with Colonel Jordan.

"Let me get this straight, Halide," he said. "You want me to find you a U.S.O. director. In exchange you'll put on an all-Turkish show for our boys. You'll charge a dollar admission and split the proceeds with the USO?"

"That's correct, Colonel Jordan. It won't be Marilyn Monroe, but how many times can your troops listen to the same Bob Hope jokes? It'll be something totally new and different, and it'll show that men of good will, who share neither language nor culture, can bridge the gap by playing as well as fighting together."

"To use an American phrase, Halide, 'you've got a deal.'"

"You're going to be presenting something completely alien to Americans, Miss Orhan. The music's different, the humor's different. The show can run an hour-and-a-half, two at the most. Even then you'll need an intermission." The speaker, Max Sharp, born Sidney Finkelstein in Brooklyn, twenty-eight years before, was one of those magicians who made United Services Organization shows come alive for American troops during the Korean conflict. He was in Korea as a volunteer. He had one goal in mind, to bring the best entertainment possible to the greatest number of people, using whatever resources were available. He was as dedicated to his profession as Halide was to hers. The two of them hit it off immediately.

"I see your point, Mister Sharp. As an American, you'd know your countrymen's tastes better than we would. Let's go over the songs, the jokes, the skits, and see what we can come up with."

"Great! Listen, Miss Orhan, I've been told you have an influential friend with the press corps in Istanbul. Many American troops in Korea are Negroes. I understand there's a particularly talented, beautiful young American Negress singing in a small nightclub in Istanbul. If the USO could raise the money to bring her here, do you think your friend could convince her to come?"

"It'll make a wonderful story, Turhan. Halide called over the military radio-telephone. They've got two weeks 'til show time. The woman's a professional and an American. It can't hurt her career. Not only would the change of scenery do her good, she'd probably have the most appreciative audience she's ever had."

"Where did you say she was appearing, Nadji?"

"Teksas Külüp."

"I'll ring you back within six hours."

A week before the scheduled show, the American entertainer arrived at the military base. Eartha Kitt was one of the most stunningly beautiful women Halide had ever seen. Her voice was unique, her presentation striking. She was a consummate professional, who could act as well as sing. Her stage presence was commanding. When the Turkish troupers met her, they redoubled their efforts, so that they might impress this astonishing female. The first performance was scheduled for December 15. The show was to run once each evening for a week, in the USO auditorium just outside Inch'on. Modest handbills were printed and distributed. The real advertising came by word of mouth. Max Sharp's budget allowed him a "slush fund," which he used generously to insure that several influential American soldiers spread the word to their buddies that this show was a "must see," a Christmas present from the Turks, and that it would be decidedly unpatriotic not to spend the buck to attend the show.

Colonel Kayaburch and Colonel Jordan arranged for a special ninth performance to take place in the American hospital auditorium. No one said a word about the American singer who'd come from Istanbul the week before. She was to be the *piece de resistance.*

"Yurtash, are you certain you've got to go to Pusan this week?"

"I've no choice, Halide. Turkish General Staff has ordered me to report back to Ankara the week after our final performance. I wanted to make sure I could arrange a special gift for our soldiers after all the hard work they've put in – the show touring throughout Korea. Colonel Kayaburch agreed to it immediately. He said it would increase the morale of Turkish forces a hundredfold. Would you believe it, for the first time ever, some of the troops – our performers – have asked to extend their tour of duty in Korea?"

Halide's face fell. "That's wonderful for you, Yurtash. You'll be going home."

He smiled broadly. "I'm doubly thankful to you, Halide. Coming here was the greatest blessing of my life. We've progressed farther than I ever would have done with any other teacher. And," he blushed, "I just received word today that I've been promoted to *Kidemli Bashchavush*, Senior Master Sergeant, the highest noncommissioned rank in the Turkish army. I promise I'll make it back by opening night. When I do, I'll be wearing five chevrons with a star on top!"

There were seven hundred fifty seats in the American auditorium. One hundred had been reserved for Turkish troops each night. The

Turks entered the hall an hour before tickets went on sale to the Americans. The show was to begin promptly at 7:30 p.m. An hour before curtain, it was clear it was going to be more than a sellout. A queue extended around the block from the theater. "Two *thousand* Americans in line," Sharp told Halide. "That's more than three times the number of seats we've got available. What should I do?"

"We can probably get fifty, even a hundred more in if they're willing to stand. After we've done that, why don't we start selling tickets to tomorrow's performance? When we run out of those, sell tickets to the following night's performance."

Half an hour later, Max Sharp was back, grinning broadly. "We've sold out the entire run! Almost seven thousand dollars!" he exulted. "When the men saw how fast tickets were going, they bought up blocks of four and five apiece for their friends."

"Let's hope tonight's show fulfills the promise. Otherwise, we'll be facing a rather angry group demanding their money back."

"Do you have any doubt we'll amaze them?" Max asked, squeezing her hand.

"Of course not. We're Turks. We'll – how do you Americans put it? – 'knock their socks off!'"

Just before show time, Halide addressed her Turkish cast. "Men," she said, "a few minutes ago, Max Sharp told me that every seat for the entire run of the show has been sold out. The Americans have a term they use before their entertainments, 'Break a leg.' I won't ask you to do that. I just want to let you know how proud I am of each of you. Each of your mothers has given birth to a lion. Tonight you are goodwill ambassadors from our nation to the world. One more thing. Sergeant Suvarli has not been with us for the past four days. As we speak, he's on his way back from Seoul. He should be here some time this evening. He called me this afternoon to say he's just completed arrangements for us to present this show to American and Turkish military installations all over South Korea for the next three months." There was a delighted gasp, followed by spontaneous applause. "Of course, that means you'll have to be absent from your regular duties during that time, but I'm sure you'll learn to live with that." Halide's last words were drowned out by whoops and cheers.

As the noise died down, Halide heard a knocking at the backstage door, and sang out, "Come in."

Colonel Kayaburch entered. The men ceased their cheering and snapped to attention. "At ease, men," the commandant smiled. "I just came to tell you that the heart of the motherland is bursting with pride at what you're doing tonight. You've made the front page of *Isharet*. Special souvenir copies of that newspaper are being sent to your families, and copies are being flown here for each of you. *Inshallah*, may your lives be filled with glory such as you bring the Turkish nation tonight! *Bol shanslar*! Good luck, and may Allah reward your efforts."

No sooner were the doors of the auditorium closed and the American troops seated than a modern Janissary band, twenty-four men dressed in warrior costumes dating back hundreds of years, exploded onto the stage, kettledrums booming, snare drums pounding, horns and bagpipes blaring, cymbals clashing, to the three-hundred-year-old battle song, *Sheyh Shamil*. They were in such thunderous accord that within the first few bars every man in the audience rose to his feet, clapping his hands and stamping in rhythm. When the song came to its abrupt end, the audience shouted, "More! More! More!" in continuous cadence, until the band erupted into a follow-up number, then another and another, until its members were exhausted.

Then came the *karagöz* puppet theater. Its Punch-and-Judy slapstick was so broad and obvious, that no translation was necessary. The house rocked with laughter, and demanded encores. Two giants performed a grease wrestling exhibition, which was supposed to last fifteen minutes. Such was the violent cheering and shouting that the last throw occurred forty-five minutes after it started. Once the floor mat pulled backstage, a Turkish folk ensemble came out. Soon the house was clapping in time to "Üsküdar," a perennial favorite of tourists who came to Istanbul.

The band had been playing for about two minutes when there was a sudden crash offstage. In the silence that followed, the audience could have heard a pin drop. There was an ominous pounding of two tympanis. One of the giants, still attired in his wrestling trunks, olive oil, and nothing else, lumbered up to the leader of the band, a slender fellow who barely reached the wrestler's chest. In broad pantomime, the giant indicated he wanted the band to play a certain number. The bandleader vigorously shook his head and wagged his finger at the wrestler. The two engaged in a furious, wordless, exchange. The huge man gestured to the rest of the ensemble. They shook their heads "no," to indicate they sided with their leader, and started to walk off stage. The wrestler hauled back and delivered a mock punch to the bandleader's nose. The musician, who'd been trained as an acrobat, rolled over and somersaulted completely offstage. The greased man now looked at the band members, who'd very quickly returned to their positions on stage and appeared to be quaking. This time, its members vigorously nodded their assent, and launched into a sinuous number. The giant grinned, and proceeded to perform a belly dance with all the grace of an ape. The audience nearly fell out of their seats with laughter. On and on the show went. By the time the audience finally allowed the cast to take an intermission, it was 10:30, fully two hours after the scheduled break.

By midnight, the audience was aroused to such a frenzy that anyone stepping onto the stage was destined for success. Max Sharp came out and stood quietly until there was silence in the theater. "Gentlemen," he said. "We are pleased and honored to have with us tonight a young lady, an American..." His voice was completely drowned out by thunderous applause and shouts. He waited for the tumult to die down, then continued, "an American who's been performing in Istanbul for the past few months, and who, I've just been informed, will be appearing in a Musical Revue on Broadway, 'New Faces of 1952' this coming year. I will say no more. My Turkish and American friends, may I present Miss Eartha Kitt."

When the singer walked onstage, dressed in a low-cut black dress, there was pandemonium. She waited for the sounds to die down. Then, accompanied by two guitarists, a bass player and a drummer, she electrified the audience as no other performer had done that night. She'd been scheduled to perform a single long set. At 1:30 in the morning, she was still onstage. The audience was hoarse from screaming its approval when she reprised her opening number, "*C'est Si Bon*," blew them a goodnight kiss, and made her exit.

Backstage, the cast was high on *rakı* and the intoxicating knowledge they had a smash hit on their hands. "Three months?" Max Sharp was shouting. "Three months, my Aunt Sophie's garters! This show will go on forever! We'll take it all the way to Broadway!"

6

By September, 1952, the war in Korea was winding down. Turkey was a full-fledged member of the North Atlantic Treaty Organization. Colonel Kayaburch had been promoted to brigadier general, and was rotated home to serve under Major General Akdemir at the new NATO Landsoutheast headquarters at Izmir. Senior Master Sergeant Yurtash Suvarli was still attached to Nadji as his *aide de camp*. Doctor Jordan wrote Halide a letter, urging her to visit him in Boston. The Turkish presence in Korea was coming to an end. Halide was delighted to hear that the giant grease wrestler and the bandleader had formed their own performing troupe, which was already enjoying modest success traveling throughout Anatolia.

At the end of that month, Halide received a long distance radio-telephone call from the administrator she'd left in charge of Yujel Orhan Teacher's College. "Halide Hanım, ordinarily I wouldn't call you in Korea, but there's a very insistent young man here looking for a job. He's barely twenty years old and just graduated Istanbul University. I told him to leave his application with us and we'll get back to him in due time, but he refused to accept that for an answer. He told me to call you. He deposited one hundred lira to reimburse me for the expense. He said it was his entire life savings, but the call to you would be worth that and more. He says you know his father and that you'd accept the call. His name is Ozal Suvarli, and..."

"Nurettin, listen to me. Give the boy his hundred lira back, and a hundred more besides. Make sure he stays at Belgrade Palas. Tell him to wait in my office every day if it takes two weeks. *Mashallah*, it's time for me to come home. I want the honor of hiring him myself!"

During the early days of the Democrat Party's administration, Turhan's star was at its zenith. He was fêted by the Foreign Press Club and awarded Turkey's highest prize for journalistic excellence. His pen had nothing but praise, both for Adnan Menders' Democrats and for Ismet Inönü's Republican People's Party, which had accepted defeat with dignity. Turkey's military showing in Korea brought glory to the land. There were record-breaking harvests. Private investment resulted both in increased production and rising per capita income. New schools were opening throughout the republic. There were signs of progress everywhere, improved roads, modern farming equipment, electric generators. Atatürk's dream of a Turkey able to hold its head high in the modern world seemed to be coming true.

But there was another face to the Democrat Party and some ominous clouds on the political horizon, and Turhan was among the first to spot them. In mid-1953, he wrote an article entitled, "Can Democracy Work? The flags of danger are flying," in which he pointed out, "Neither the RPP nor the Democrats really understand how to oppose responsibly or accept opposition in a civil manner. The RPP is irresponsible when it unfairly criticizes the government's economic and religious policies. The Democrats are no better when they suppress the opposition by unnecessarily restrictive laws that stifle their opposition."

Within three days, Abdullah Heper, the young publisher of *Isharet* who'd replaced Dikkat, summoned Turhan to his office. Heper introduced him to an assistant in the Ministry of Public Information, who had the nervous look and habits that Turhan had come to associate with a harried bureaucrat. He folded and unfolded his hands and began to speak in a high, whiny voice. "Gentlemen, the Ministry is concerned, most concerned, with what it feels to be a deliberate attempt by *Isharet* to undermine the Turkish political system."

"What do you mean?" the publisher asked.

"This article," he said, holding up Turhan's writing, "is demeaning to the Democrat Party."

"What are you talking about?" Heper shot back, angrily. "It's an even-handed, truthful statement of the way things are. On July 12, the government banned the Nation Party on the grounds it was trying to use religion to subvert the republic. Nine days later, the Assembly amended the University Law to restrict the universities' control of their own budgets. Is that responsible democracy?" Turhan smiled to himself. Unlike his predecessor, Heper was proving to be a courageous ally, an independent-minded man of principle.

"Nevertheless, Heper Effendim," the mousy bureaucrat continued, "I have been instructed to deliver you this notice. By order of the Ministry, the publication of *Isharet* is suspended for seven days and the paper is fined five hundred lira."

"That's preposterous!" Heper exploded. "I will seek the protection of the courts."

"By the time you do, the seven days will be over, Effendim," the ministry's representative replied.

In the fall of 1953, with national elections less than a year away, the campaign became vitriolic. It soon degenerated into name-calling, the tossing of tomatoes and manure at candidates, and the wholesale destruction of voter lists. On December 14, the Assembly confiscated all RPP property for "past misappropriation of public funds." The Republican party newspaper, *Ulus*, was suspended. Turhan blasted the Democrats. "Whatever the excesses of the opposition party, the government had neither cause nor the constitutional authority to do what they did. Regardless of the good they have done, the Democrat Party's present stance is unconscionable and reprehensible!" he said in a front page editorial.

At 10:00 P.M., the night Turhan's article was published, there was a knock on his door. When he answered, he was immediately grabbed by two husky police officers. "What is going on?" he demanded.

"You're going to headquarters is what's going on," one of them said. "Now shut up, and get in the car if you know what's good for you." Turhan's hands were forced behind his back. He was tightly shackled. The officers shoved him into the back seat of an unmarked black car, where a third man pointed a revolver at him.

During the ride, Turhan complained that the handcuffs were too tight and were hurting his wrists. There was no verbal response, but the driver malevolently maneuvered the automobile so it jerked from side to side, made tight turns, and forced the cuffs to dig further into Turhan's wrists. When they arrived at a police station far from his home, the shackles were removed. Turhan was shoved into a six-by-eight-foot detention cell. There was a small iron cot with no mattress and a single hole in the floor, for him to perform his excretory bodily functions. No toilet paper, no sink.

"I demand to speak to my publisher immediately!" he shouted after the departing policemen. They ignored him and continued walking.

Moments later, he heard the clank of a heavy door and the sharp click of a lock. Turhan's wristwatch had not been taken from him. He calculated he'd arrived at the station shortly after midnight. He slept fitfully on the iron cot. At five in the morning, he awoke when a burly guard shoved a tin bowl of thin gruel, a crust of day-old bread, a cup of watery brown liquid, and a six-inch square of wet cloth under the opening beneath his cell.

"Please," he said. "I want to see *Isharet's* lawyer. I'm Turhan Türkoğlu."

"I don't care if you're Mehmet the Conqueror," the guard responded. The rag is to wash yourself off after you take a shit."

Frustrated, Turhan tried to eat the 'breakfast.' The gruel was flour-and-water paste. A slight, greenish mold covered the edges of the bread. The lukewarm liquid tasted like brown-colored sewer water. He was constipated and felt a grabbing pain in his stomach. He shouted for the guard. There was no response. He lay down on the cot, moaning in agony, and tried to get some sleep. It was impossible. The metal springs dug into every soft place in his body. His neck and back were stiff from tension.

Shortly after noon, the guard reappeared. When he saw that Turhan had barely touched his morning meal, he said, "I'm happy you want to save the state money. There'll be no need to give you a different meal. We'll wait 'til you finish the one you have."

There were no windows in the cell. At seven that evening, he heard muffled sounds of shouting, followed by the clank of the security door being opened, and at least two pairs of footsteps coming toward him. He was weak from exhaustion and want of food, and he offered no resistance when two policemen lifted him to his feet and dragged him down a hall and up a flight of stairs. When he reached the lighted area, he recognized Mahmut Mardin, *Isharet's* legal counsel. The lawyer's face was red and he was berating the police sergeant mercilessly. "I will have your supervisor's head on a platter! There is no way my client will tolerate this abuse of the law. I demand to see the charges against Türkoğlu immediately, do you hear?"

"Avukat Effendim," the sergeant said apologetically, "there are no charges."

"No charges? Then you must release him this instant!"

"I can't, Avukat Effendim."

"What do you mean?"

"The man has no identification. He was seized as a derelict last night."

"That's insane. I told you he's Turhan Türkoğlu, the editor-in-chief of *Isharet*. No doubt he's told you the same thing."

"Ah, but he lacked identification on his person when he was detained, and he's not been able to produce any since then."

"When has he had a chance to do so, you idiot?" the lawyer asked. "Was he arrested on the street?"

"Not exactly."

"What do you mean 'not exactly?' Where was he arrested?"

"The report says number five Kurdele Sokak in Beyoğlu."

"That's his residence. There's a police station three blocks away. Why in Allah's name was he brought clear over to Eyüp District Police headquarters?"

"Any unidentified persons are brought here."

"This is getting us nowhere. I demand to see your captain immediately."

"But he won't be back until nine o'clock tomorrow morning."

"Listen, Sergeant. I am about to leave this place. As soon as I do, I will telephone my friend, the Minister of Justice in Ankara. I will be back here within half an hour. If, at that time, Turhan Türkoğlu, for whom I can personally vouch, is not released, or if a warrant for his arrest had not been processed, I will personally insure that your next assignment will be in Alijan on the Russian border. Do I make myself clear?"

"But Avukat Effendim, I'm only doing my job."

"And you have less than half an hour to do it properly!"

When Mardin returned to headquarters, he had Heper and a press photographer in tow. The captain had miraculously returned to the station. The police commissioner who accompanied him was oily obsequiousness and smiles. "Avukat Mardin, please accept our most humble apologies. There's been a dreadful mistake, dreadful. Apparently my constables acted on an anonymous tip that an unknown person was dealing in hashish in Beyoğlu District. We take such information very seriously. We simply didn't have time to investigate, or we would certainly have known that detaining someone of Türkoğlu's stature was clearly in error. We can do nothing but beg you to forgive us. Of course, since he was never prosecuted for any crime, or even arrested, praise Allah, the law unfortunately does not allow for restitution."

Within a day after his release, the front page of *Isharet* was plastered with gruesome photographs of Turhan Türkoğlu as a prisoner. The commissioner's words were prominently featured in large, bold print. *Isharet* hinted the "mistake" was deliberate and demanded justice. "Justice" was swift in coming. Isharet was suspended from publication for twenty days and fined ten thousand lira.

On May 2, 1954, the Democrats won the national elections with an increased majority. They captured ninety-three percent of the seats in the Assembly. The RPP became more acid in its criticism than ever. The new parliament responded by passing a law that all government officials and employees, including university professors and judges, were made subject to retirement as soon as they completed twenty-five years of government service or became sixty years of age. Naturally, the law was enforced against all but Democrat party appointees. Late in summer, 1954, the government declared open war on the press. By the end of the year, seven newspapermen were serving jail sentences for insurrection to riot.

In 1955, RPP general secretary Kâzim Gülek was jailed for insulting the government in a political speech. Five newspapers were closed down altogether. The universities became RPP centers of dissent. The Democrat Party responded with suspensions, restrictions and imprisonments. As old parties were outlawed, new ones, which espoused the same ideas as their banned predecessors, sprang up to take their places.

In 1956, Turhan wrote, "We are now at a crisis. The once unified Turkish nation is a fragile mirror, about to crack into a thousand slivers, with each piece trying to slice away the heart of the other. The new Election Law which prohibits party coalitions is a mandate for the Democrats to stay in power until the coming of Allah. The intellectuals and the Democrats grow farther apart by the day. But the RPP is so busy attacking the ruling Democrats it ignores the reality that, as repressive as this government might be, the Turkish masses continue to support it. Our villages and towns enjoy the benefits of new roads, irrigation, electricity, buildings, schools and hospitals, while the big cities are becoming ever more unmanageable. The Democrats distribute fifty thousand new tractors each year. There is a tremendous expansion of credit cooperatives. Even in the cities, most of the workers, shopkeepers, factory owners and providers of services never had it so good. The RPP should be asking the more important question: '*Who is going to pay the bill for all this development*?' At the end of the War in 1945, Turkey had a balanced budget. I predict that by the end of this decade we will have a national debt approaching one billion lira. Where is the money going to come from to pay it?"

Heper and *Isharet* displayed amazing courage by publishing the article. This time, not even the Minister of Justice could help. *Isharet* was suspended from publication for ninety days and fined fifty thousand lira, which brought the proud daily to the brink of bankruptcy. Turhan was formally arrested and charged with "Acts Damaging to Public Confidence in the Government."

Avukat Mardin convinced the three judges who tried the case that unless they supported the rule of law rather than the rule of man, anarchy would result. The judges were sympathetic. While they had no choice but to convict Turhan of the charges, they sentenced him to the minimum possible time in jail, three weeks in the honoree's section, and fined him fifty lira. Within two months of Turhan's trial and sentencing, the presiding judge retired. The other two were reassigned to the most inhospitable areas of Turkey. Each resigned when he learned of his new judicial duties.

In June, 1957, the Assembly amended the Press Law and placed severe restrictions on public assembly. A new law allowed police to fire openly at crowds engaged in "unlawful political activities," which were never defined. Deputies were limited to the number and scope of questions they could ask cabinet ministers. When the Democrats won the national elections again, this time only by a plurality instead of a majority, Turhan could remain silent no longer.

At the beginning of November, 1957, he publicly announced his retirement from *Isharet*, despite Abdullah Heper's entreaties to stay on. "Turhan," he said, "you're barely sixty years old, a mere infant. You're the most respected, astute journalist in the country, the Conscience of the Nation. We're the largest selling newspaper in the country because people want to hear the truth. I'm willing to risk the losses. So are our backers. Please stay on, if only until we've seen where these insane laws will lead."

"Thank you, Abdullah, but no. *Isharet* has been my home for almost forty years. I cannot risk killing the newspaper Ihsan Selimiye worked so hard to make successful. I tell you in confidence, my friend, that my voice will not be stilled. When this is all over, I'll be back as editor-in-chief, if you'll still have me. But I do have a final favor to ask."

"Anything, Turhan."

"Can you loan me newsprint and your press facilities in Istanbul, Ankara, Izmir and Adana during hours they're not being used? I want to print one hundred thousand copies of a single page, two-sided newspaper of my own."

"I knew you had something up your sleeve!" Heper said, grinning. "Since we're shut down for another week, why not start tonight?"

On December 3, 1957, there appeared all over Turkey a single-page newspaper, *Yeni Gerchek, The New Truth*. That single page was read by more Turks than any document in the history of the Republic. Abdullah Heper had secretly arranged for the printing of one million, five hundred thousand copies, fifteen times the number Turhan had requested. Every major newspaper in Turkey carried it as an insert. The press had finally reached the limit of its patience, and reacted to what it considered the most infamous and restrictive law since the Democrats had taken office, by declaring its independence from the government. The publishers knew if they stood together it would be impossible for the government to close all the newspapers down. The banner, which Turhan had approved in advance, was printed in red and blue, and emphasized, "This newspaper is published entirely by me, Turhan Türkoğlu, formerly of *Isharet*. I assume full responsibility for all of its contents. If there is a penalty for truth, let it fall on my head and mine alone. *Mashallah*!"

Underneath the banner was something that Turhan had never anticipated. In bold type, surrounded by a black border, were the words, "This newspaper insert is endorsed and supported *by Hürriyet, Isharet, Günaydin, Tercuman, Milliyet, Cumhüriyet, Son Havadis, Hergün, Aksham, Adalet, Yeni Ulus, Bügün, Zafer, Yeni Ashir, Izmir Ticaret*, and most assuredly by *Dorutay Dünya* and by every inhabitant of the proud village of Dorutay, Turkey." The newspaper contained a single editorial article.

TOWARD POLITICAL SUICIDE - AND INTERNATIONAL DISGRACE

by Turhan Türkoğlu -- The Conscience of the Nation

In 1945, our nation subscribed to the United Nations Declaration of Human Rights. In 1950 I cheered both the Democrats and the Republican Peoples' Party when we had the first completely open, democratic election in the history of our motherland.

In the years immediately following the Democrat victory, my skepticism turned to admiration as our nation progressed beyond Atatürk's dreams. We were truly entering the twentieth century at last, a proud people, respected in the world's eyes. Our performance in Korea was legendary. Everywhere one looked, there were signs of material, educational, cultural progress. What I perceived to be the Gazi's one mistake, over-reliance on government involvement in business and industry, was replaced by private investment. The Grand National Assembly was truly a constituent parliament, the judiciary was independent and responsible only to the rule of law, not the vagaries of politicians.

Why couldn't we be satisfied with what we had? A philosopher once said, "Power corrupts. Absolutely power corrupts absolutely." Another said, "The fine art of politics is to disagree without becoming disagreeable." Our motherland now sheds tears of shame and sadness for the political turmoil that has come to pass.

Less than a dozen years ago, I met a brilliant young politician, one of the few who was able to laugh at himself and his profession, who told me, I'm certain in jest, that the secret of political success is to promise what you must, deliver the minimum you can, and pray that the voters forget what you promised as soon as possible after the election. Here, I thought, was an honest, balanced man, and the nation would be blessed if he came to power. That man was elected by the widest majority in recent political history. But, alas, Adnan Menderes allowed his popularity to corrupt him. His need to retain power prevailed over his common sense.

Was it necessary to pass the most restrictive election laws in recent history? Was the University Law necessary? Could the independence of the judiciary have been maintained at the same time the Menderes regime stayed in office? Of course. The 1954 elections proved the Assembly's new "laws" were completely unnecessary, for the party of Menderes and Bayar swept into power with a greater majority than it had in 1950.

Had the Democrats ignored the juvenile attacks mounted against them by hotheaded radicals in the university community, had they simply gone to the people and said, "Look at our positive accomplishments! What does the opposition promise that will improve the progress we've made?" the minority would have become a national laughingstock. Instead, like the owner of an animal who rules that beast by fear rather than by love, our government dignified the criticisms of the RPP by "legally" raiding that party's treasury and attempting to silence its press. Our government, in the name of "civil order" passed laws that have not been matched since the days of the Nazis.

While all this was going on, inflation and the national debt increased beyond anything in our history. We were like children having a wild party on raki and wine. The party cannot go on forever. Soon, besotted, we will be vomiting in the streets as our creditors demand payment. Our country teeters on the verge of bankruptcy.

I call for an end to repressive laws! I call for the Democrats to act responsibly, as a properly constituted government should act. I call for the Republican Peoples' Party to return to the dignity afforded it by Mustafa Kemal and to stop acting like a small child whose toy has been taken away. The opposition must be a ***loyal*** *opposition and must act as responsibly as the party in power.*

Laws limiting assembly and censoring a free press are absurd! They are an insult to civilized society, a direct blow to the principles of the United Nations charter, and, most of all, a national disgrace to the Turkish people. I call upon the government to revoke these embarrassing and humiliating pronouncements, or, if it chooses not to do so, to be honest enough to impose a dictatorship in name as well as in practice.

A year ago, after I published an article critical of our government, I was "detained by mistake" as a "vagrant who might be dealing in hashish" for nearly a full day. The treatment I received was savage. At the end of my incarceration, I was told that the government was sorry for the "mistake," but since I'd never been formally charged, I had no recourse against those who "detained" me.

I have little doubt that when this newspaper is published, I will be inside the walls of a prison once again, no doubt carefully chosen for maximum secrecy. This time there will be no "mistake." Whether I live to see the outside of those walls again is highly uncertain. I do not expect to be called before the Grand National Assembly and showered with honor for what I say.

In Hitler's Germany, the Reverend Martin Niemoller said, "When they started to take the Jews away, I did not protest, because I was not a Jew and it did not affect me. When they started to take the Gypsies away, I did not protest, because it did not affect me. When they started to take the laborers away, I did not protest, because it did not affect me. And ultimately, when they came to take me away, there was no one left to protest on my behalf."

I cannot sit silent. I protest. I cry "Shame!" And I call for an end to what, ultimately, can only be political suicide and international disgrace. Long live Atatürk! Long live democracy! Long live Truth! - by Turhan Türkoğlu, The Conscience of the Nation

7

For five days after *Yeni Gerchek's* publication, the government seemed paralyzed by shock, both at the audacity of the challenge and at the fact it was so widely sponsored and distributed. In that time, "Orfez Halip" could have used his still-valid diplomatic passport to escape Turkey. No doubt the government would have been spared embarrassment had he done just that. But Turhan refused to go underground. He walked the streets of Istanbul each day and returned to his apartment in Beyoğlu each night. He did not expect kind treatment. Ultimately, he was not disappointed.

On the morning of the sixth day, the internal security police seized Turhan on the government's instructions. Although no formal charges were pressed, there was no "mistake," for Türkoğlu was fingerprinted and the paperwork to book him took the better part of three hours. Early in their history, the Turks developed a most barbaric and vicious punishment. Ottoman warriors would take cane-sized sticks and beat their victim on the bottom of his feet for hours at a time. The captive would not show a mark on his body, but by the conclusion of the beatings, which lasted several days, the victim's mother would not have recognized him, for he would have been rendered physically crippled and mentally insane.

On the day after his arrest, Turhan was moved to a prison on an island in the Sea of Marmara. There, he was subjected to three hours of such beatings, which were done in absolute silence. During the first few minutes, he never believed he would survive the pain. Shortly thereafter, he lost consciousness. The following day, he was tied to an upright, wooden chair, and left to sit for several hours. Eventually the warden, a barrel-chested middle-aged man dressed in clothing several sizes too small for him, paid Turhan a visit. "Ah, if I'm not mistaken, it is Turhan Türkoğlu, the self-proclaimed conscience of Turkey. Would you like a bit of *rakı*, Effendim?"

"Thank you, yes."

The man poured a tumbler of the anise liquor and tossed it into Turhan's face.

"Very civil of you," Turhan said acidly. "Was that drink another courtesy of our government toward an honored guest?"

The warden slapped him across his face, hard. "Listen, scum, you're not here to write your fancy articles, and you're not dining with the Grand National Assembly. You are my prisoner. I'll thank you to conduct yourself appropriately."

"If I don't, what will you do? Beat my feet some more? Place sticks under my fingernails? Question me about my alleged 'crimes' against our government?"

The warden bottled his rising anger. He'd been told in advance this prisoner was not an ordinary criminal, and that he was one who could be taunted and humiliated. He'd also been warned by his superiors that although Türkoğlu was to receive "mild" punishment, he was to be treated very carefully, for he had several friends in very high places.

"Tell me," the warden said, "Why does a man like you, who has things an ordinary Turk only dreams about, risk it all?"

"Ah, the questioning starts."

"No. I just wanted to know for my own information. Frankly, you won't be here long enough that my inquiries will have any effect on what ultimately happens to you."

"I'll answer if you tell me why your first act was to throw *rakı* in my face when you knew I couldn't even reach out to wipe it off."

"Instinct, I suppose. I have to let prisoners know who's in charge."

"Have you any doubt every prisoner knows you're in command?"

"Not really."

"Then why is it necessary for you to emphasize your authority in a needlessly brutal manner?"

"It's expected."

"What if you were to exercise humane treatment toward your wards?"

"I'd be replaced, of course."

"How do you know that?"

The warden did not respond. Turhan pressed his point. "What do you fear would happen if you were replaced?"

"I've never given it much thought."

"Do you think you'd starve?"

"No. I could always work for my brother-in-law in Polatlı. He's a tractor mechanic. But I'd be humiliated in front of my family if I lost my job."

"Did you actually read the article I wrote, Warden Effendim?"

"No."

"I'm surprised, because you perceptively answered the very questions I raised when I wrote it. For all I know, you might have written it yourself."

"How dare you say such a thing!"

"Warden Effendim, the only difference between us is that when you speak your friends in the *kahve evi* listen. Perhaps, on occasion, your wife may even listen." The remark was broken by the warden's hearty laughter. "I'm in jail because when I speak, I have a platform from which all Turkey can listen if it so chooses. What I said in my article was no different from what you said. Our government throws *rakı* in the face of the opposition party. The RPP can't fight back because it has only a few seats in the Grand National Assembly. The RPP's insults have no more force than I have when I sit here, bound to a chair, and talk back to you. Yet, the government worries about losing its power if it allows the RPP to express an honest difference of opinion, just as you worry about losing your job if you don't overreact. Will the Democrats die if they lose an election? No more than you'd starve if you had to go to work for your brother-in-law. It would be embarrassing, but it would not be fatal."

The warden said nothing for several moments. Then he stood and said, "There's no reason for you to be bound. You won't try to escape." He untied Turhan. He poured two glasses of rakı and handed one to his prisoner. "*Sherefinize*! Whatever happens, Turhan Effendim, I wish you *bol shanslar*! Allah's blessing and courage."

Aksaray, just south of *Tuz Golu*, the great salt lake in the center of Turkey, was indistinguishable from any other market town on the

Anatolian steppe. It was not far from Ankara. Rather, its remoteness was occasioned by its nondescript nature. It was by no means a secret place, nor even one that was out of the way. It was just off E-5, the London to Teheran international highway. Few travelers stopped at Aksaray, for aside from a crumbling Sixteenth Century fortress, an old wood-and-brick *hamam*, and a regional market day that took place every Thursday, there was little to interest the tourist.

The fortress was not bad as Turkish prisons went, Turhan thought. This morning, when he voided his bowels, he noticed there'd been a six-inch worm in his stool. If that were the worst thing that happened in this place, he could live with it. He'd arrived at Aksaray fortress with a reasonable amount of money, which the Turkish security kept in a trust account for his use. With it, he could purchase cigarettes, rakı, lamb, rice, and vegetables to supplement the standard prison fare of pasty gruel, weak tea, and ekmek. Turhan had been sent to Aksaray five weeks after he'd been arrested. Charges still had not been preferred. He began to surmise he'd been purposely forgotten, left to languish in the obscurity of the endless steppe until he died or turned to dust. His newsman's instinct told him that unless someone heard from him within ninety days, he'd be as stale as three-day-old toast.

Ten days after he arrived at Aksaray, an American military officer came to visit a young United States citizen accused of attempting to smuggle hashish out of Turkey. Security at the fortress was such that by paying a guard a few lira a month a prisoner could have as many visitors as he wanted. Over the years, Turhan had learned how clearly money speaks. Now he decided to gamble. "Guard Effendim," he called out. "Please. I'm having terrible stomach cramps. I need to see you immediately."

The guard strolled over casually. "Prison doctor comes tomorrow. Can't it wait 'til then?"

"No, it can't." Under his breath, he said, "There's fifty lira in it for you if you can convince the American officer to speak with me for a few moments."

"Where's the lira?" the guard, who earned less than that in a month, asked with interest. Turhan fished in his shoe, took out a crumpled bill, and passed it surreptitiously to the guard, who smiled and walked away as slowly as he'd come. Turhan calculated he'd have at least a half-hour wait before he saw the American officer. During that time, he wrote three identical messages, which read, "I am being held at Aksaray fortress prison. I believe the government intends to do nothing about it, since I've never been charged. They've made certain no one knows where I am. I was shipped out of Marmara prison late at night. I believe if anyone learns where I am, I'll be transferred from here when no one is expected to be watching. Help me. T.T." He folded the letters and placed them in blank, unsealed envelopes. Although he was allowed mail privileges, he did not for a moment doubt that anything he sent out would not only be censored, but would subject the addressee to difficulties as well.

Five minutes after Turhan finished the letters, the American officer came by his cell. "I understand you wanted to see me. Do you speak English?" The man was in his late twenties, of medium height, wore glasses and had an alert, intelligent look.

"Yes, Captain," Turhan said, noticing the silver tracks on the man's shoulders. "I'm fluent in your language. I see from your chest insignia you're a member of the Judge Advocate General's corps?"

"Correct." The officer was apparently impressed, both by the fluency with which Turhan spoke English and by the prisoner's perceptiveness. Then, Turhan saw the man's eyes narrow with suspicion.

"Don't worry," he said. "I'm not a Russian spy. I won't ask you to buy or sell anything on the black market. My name's Turhan Türkoğlu.

You can check my credentials with your embassy by having them contact Mr. Edwin Baumueller at the New York *World.* If they need more immediate verification, they can contact Abdullah Heper, the publisher of *Isharet,* Turkey's biggest newspaper. I trust you're stationed with JUSMMAT, the Joint US Military Mission to Turkey?"

"Correct again. If you aren't a spy, a black marketer, or a smuggler, what are you doing in Aksaray prison?"

"I'll tell you if you insist, but I think it best for your own interests that you know as little as possible. I very much doubt an American military officer wants to get involved in Turkish politics."

"Darn right. Why did you want to see me?"

"I've written three identical letters, which I've placed in unsealed envelopes. The chances of these letters being delivered in the regular course of Turkish mail are nonexistent. I ask that you take these letters to your staff judge advocate or your commander, so that one copy may be delivered to Major General Nadji Akdemir at Landsoutheast headquarters in Izmir, one be delivered to Miss Halide Orhan, director of Yujel Orhan Teacher's College in Istanbul, and the third copy be delivered to Abdullah Heper, *Isharet's* publisher, in Istanbul."

"How do I know you're not planting contraband on me?"

"I thought you'd ask that." He handed the officer the three envelopes. "These are unsealed, and they're written in English, which each of my friends understands perfectly. You may test the paper for hidden messages if you desire. I'm sure you'd agree I'd have to be an incredible cryptographer to manage something like that in this place."

The captain laughed appreciatively. The shadow of suspicion disappeared from his eyes. "Sounds to me like you've got all the right answers, Mr. Türkoğlu. I make no promises. I'll check with my superiors and see what they say."

"That's all I ask."

The captain, Richard Murchison, had majored in political science before taking his law degree at Georgetown. He was an independent sort, not a career officer, and he was close to finishing his two year assignment in Ankara. Unlike most Americans stationed in Turkey, he loved the land. One day he intended to return, perhaps even to do business in this fascinating country. The Turkish prisoner who spoke English so well had given him three names. Each appeared to occupy a position of responsibility and success in Turkish society. He had ten days' accrued leave time. His colonel probably wouldn't hesitate to let him take five of those days after he got back to Ankara. If he gave his boss the letters, it would probably be a month before anything happened. In that time, the prisoner could be dead. A couple of days in Istanbul and two more in Izmir would not be a bad way to spend some time off, he thought.

"Can you describe him to me, Captain Murchison?"

"About sixty, Mr. Heper. Wispy, thinning hair. Roughly as tall as me but not quite so heavy. Brown eyes, gray-black moustache. He asked me to contact you, Major General Nadji Akdemir and Halide Orhan and give each of you a copy of the letter. He also mentioned he was friends with Edwin Baumueller of the New York *World*."

"That's him, all right. Captain Murchison, you've done a greater service for Turkey than you'll ever know. I'll give Halide Orhan a call this minute. I'm sure she'd be glad to join us for lunch at Liman Restaurant, where you'll find the best fish in Istanbul. You do have time for lunch?"

"Absolutely, sir," the captain said, a slight red flush coming to his cheeks. "It would be my privilege, *Effendim*."

"Ah, you speak Turkish?"

"*Biraz.* A little. I hope to learn more in years to come."

"Your accent is very good, *Yuzbashi*. Now, let me call Miss Orhan and a taxi to Liman. While we're dining, Halide and I will have many things to tell you about the man whose life you've probably saved."

8

A week later, Turhan was in the fortress yard, doing his daily twenty-lap walk around the inside perimeter, when he was summoned by the warden. "Türkoğlu, there's a visitor who wants to see you alone, without me being there. I trust you'll not try to escape."

When he was ushered into the warden's office, he found himself face-to-face with the Prime Minister. Menderes waited for Turhan to say something. The journalist, sensing the politician's acute discomfort, said nothing, but took a seat directly opposite his visitor. Forced to speak first, Menderes said, "Just tell me how you did it."

"What do you mean, Adnan?" Turhan refused to use the honorific "Effendim," the title "Your Excellency," or anything else that would indicate respect for the Democrat leader.

"Don't play games with me. I don't need to tolerate your journalistic diarrhea."

"Then why are you here?"

"You really don't know?"

"You may not be aware of it, Adnan, but this is neither Istanbul nor Ankara. Not much except wind and rain filter through the leaky walls of this old fortress."

"You suspected you'd remain here a while, out of the public eye?"

"I had reason to believe that was your plan."

Menderes said nothing. He opened a large briefcase and pulled out half a dozen newspapers. He tossed them at Turhan. The six largest Turkish dailies. Each carried the same message, in slightly different words, "Turhan Türkoğlu, Turkey's leading journalist, is being held incommunicado in Aksaray fortress prison, without charges being pressed, without bail being set, in absolute violation of Atatürk's Constitution. Türkoğlu was arrested over a month ago at his home in Beyoğlu. He was secretly taken to Marmara prison, then transferred to Aksaray under cover of night. We, the editors of each major newspaper in Turkey, plan to post reporters outside Aksaray prison every hour of every day, to insure that Turhan Türkoğlu is neither forgotten nor whisked away again. We will carry Turhan Türkoğlu's story on our front pages in every edition. We demand justice under law! If charges are not preferred, we demand Türkoğlu's release. If he is charged with any cognizable crime, we demand that reasonable bail be set! No matter what party is in power, no man and no government can be above the law!"

Praise Allah, Turhan thought. *The American got through!* He sat calmly, waiting for Menderes to speak. The Prime Minister shifted uncomfortably in his chair for several moments. Beads of perspiration formed on his forehead.

"All right, now you know what I'm talking about. There may as well be giant searchlights aimed at this prison night and day, and, of course, those same spotlights are trained on the government as well." Turhan placed one leg over the other, and crossed his arms across his chest. "Well?" Menderes said at last, exasperated. "What do you have to say about this?"

"What do you want me to say, Adnan?"

"I want you to retract your statement in that rag you published, supposedly 'with no help from anyone else,' which somehow managed to be distributed with every newspaper of consequence sold that day throughout Turkey."

"You seriously believe I'd withdraw the truth?"

"Perhaps we might reach an accommodation."

"An 'arrangement' where I trade my integrity for physical freedom, is that what you mean, Adnan?" Menderes and Turhan sat for the better part of a minute, glaring at one another. Finally, Turhan broke the silence. "Adnan, when I first met you, you were a reasonably honest man and a good politician. You succumbed to a weakness as old as man's desire to rule other men. When you came to power, it was a strong drug. You became addicted to it, as if it were hashish or opium. You lost your perspective. You're not the only good man that's ever happened to. When your party first won control of the Assembly, it passed just laws and demonstrated ambitious policies. But then Inönü's minority locked horns with the Democrats. Does it really matter who started the fight? The result is what's important. Today you silence me, tomorrow you silence another editor. Do you really believe you can cut the tongue out of every speaker in Turkey?

"Adnan, look at the history of our country. Look at the history of our German ally of the First World War. Search the record of every nation that ever called itself 'civilized,' and you'll see the same thing. Each time a government starts down the road of repression, the same thing happens. There are restrictive laws, arrests, show trials. Responsible opposition leaders are silenced. They're replaced by more radical leaders who are harder to control. Ultimately, the governed realize what is happening, and they throw off the yoke of oppression, often with devastatingly violent results. Adnan, you're going down that road. It's almost too late to turn back."

"And who do you think you are, the Prophet Muhammad?"

"No, Adnan. Your government may survive a year or two. Hitler said his would last a thousand years. Your party may even survive one crotchety sixty-year-old journalist who'll never back away from the truth. But it cannot survive as it is much longer. The Turkish people can only be governed as long as they consent to that government. You didn't even win a majority during the last election. It took your 'plurality' law to keep you in power."

"Enough! I've come to offer you a bargain which will allow you to keep your so-called 'integrity.'"

"What if I refuse the bargain?"

"Then you'll be formally charged. You'll be afforded every civil right existing by whatever law then controls. I can't tell you how long it might take to get to trial. There's a considerable backlog in the court system. It might take five years, it might take ten, who knows?"

"You think the press will stand for it?"

"The media will have no choice. The press will be subject to censorship. Those that violate the laws of peaceful good taste will find themselves permanently suspended. The sale of newspapers generates a very substantial income for Turkish publishers. There will always be those whose lust for material wealth will overcome their moral need to speak out against the duly-elected government. And whether or not you think so, Turhan, the most important news of the day is not whether the government has passed a law against debate in the Assembly. People want to read about sex, scandals, explicitly described rapes, gruesome, gory crimes, and football scores. If and when you are tried, it will merit, at most, a single column buried on a back page, and will attract less attention than that day's comic pages."

Turhan thought about what Menderes said. The man was a consummate politician and he'd kept his finger on the pulse of his constituency. "What's your offer?" he asked, quietly.

"The government will press charges against you for treasonous statements against the public good. Bail will be set at five hundred thousand lira. I've no doubt the newspapers will underwrite that bail figure. 'Orfez Halip' will quietly depart Turkey." Turhan's eyebrows raised in surprise. "You think I don't know about the Atatürk incident back in the thirties? I trust you still have the passport?"

"I do."

"It's still valid?"

"Of course."

"In any event, Turhan Türkoğlu will be convicted *in absentia*, with imposition of sentence suspended pending his return to Turkey. The government will quietly arrange to return the five hundred thousand lira to those who stood bond."

"You think you can keep me from distributing underground articles?"

"That's the chance we take, isn't it?"

"What if I don't accept your offer?"

"I've already told you. Rot in jail if you want. If you still feel you must attack the government, would you rather do it from outside the country, where you might still have an audience, or would you rather prattle on from inside a jail cell where people will soon lose interest in you?"

"One thing remains true about you, Adnan. I once said you were a great politician. That's still an accurate statement."

The newspaper publishers were not stupid. While they could afford the five hundred thousand lira bail, with its guaranteed return, they no longer trusted the government's economic policies. Inflation was rampant. The lira was rapidly losing convertibility in world financial centers. They refused to post bond. Early in March, 1958, a very private meeting took place in New York City between Edwin Baumueller and a man virtually unknown outside the highest circles of Menderes' advisors.

"This is my deal," Baumueller said. "I will pay you five hundred thousand Turkish lira. No later than six months from today, on September 10, 1958, your government will repay me two hundred fifty thousand American dollars, based on the official rate at which the lira is pegged to the dollar today. I will not insist on interest."

"But Mr. Baumueller, what if the Turkish lira is devalued by that time?"

"That's precisely what I'm betting will happen. I'm not a Turk. I have no interest in your government's economic policies. I can make better investments right here in America."

"I thought Türkoğlu was your friend."

"Friendship has nothing to do with it. You're blackmailing him. Don't talk to me about honorable treatment."

"Those are your final terms?"

"Yes. The Turkish Democrat Party will execute a promissory note, which will be kept in my safe deposit box. If the two hundred fifty thousand dollars are returned to me, in cash, within the time provided, the note will be returned."

"What if it's not repaid? What if we say it was fraudulent?"

"I'll take my chances in the World Court and the world press."

"I must talk to the Prime Minister."

"There's a private telephone in my inner conference room. Feel free to use it as my personal contribution to the everlasting friendship between the United States of America and the Republic of Turkey. And tell Adnan I will need one week to raise the money."

❧

"He bought the deal, Mr. Baumueller?" Abdullah Heper asked.

"He had no choice, Mister Heper. Remember, no publicity."

"Turhan agreed to it?"

"Only after I told him that the B.B.C. had agreed to rehire him. Voice of America said it was too sensitive, with Turkey being such a close ally and all. Were you able to get the money?"

"Of course."

"At what rate?"

"Ten to the dollar."

Baumueller whistled. "The black market's giving that much already?"

"There's speculation it'll go to twelve in another couple of months. Are you sure you don't want to wait?"

"No. I'm not sure this government will last too much longer. I've cut my deal. Besides, I'm getting paid back in *dollars*, based on the official two-for-one rate."

"Not a bad bargain, Baumueller. You pay fifty thousand, you get back five times that much in six months. My only regret is that the Turkish press isn't allowed to deal in foreign currency. We'd have been able to recoup the losses from our fines."

"*Mashallah*, Abdullah."

9

For the next two years, Turhan used the world service of the British Broadcasting Corporation as a platform from which to broadcast his appeals that the Turkish government and the opposition try to reconcile their differences. The B.B.C.'s director was surprised by Turhan's moderate approach, given the circumstances under which he'd been forced to leave Turkey. When he mentioned this one day, Turhan responded, "I'm not really bitter, Sir William. I'm greatly saddened by what's happening in my country, but if I sacrifice truth for my personal animosity I'm no better than those who exiled me."

The events unfolding in Turkey wrote their own headlines, without the need for editorial comment from "the conscience of the nation." Violence escalated throughout the country. Verbal abuses in the Grand National Assembly led to physical fistfights outside its halls. A year after Turhan's arrival in London, former President Ismet Inönü, Mustafa Kemal's closest associate, was attacked twice by pro-Democrat mobs. The government imposed stiff fines and suspensions on the publishers of any newspaper that dared print news of the incident. By year's end, Turkey was nearly bankrupt. The official exchange rate for the Turkish lira had climbed to four to the dollar, but no one was exchanging, even at the black market rate of thirteen to one. In February, 1960, Menderes' finance minister was forced to accept severe restrictions on deficit financing, official devaluation of the lira, and a complete restructuring of the public debt in exchange for an International Monetary Fund bailout. Although inflation, which had been running at thirty percent per year was reduced, and the budget was balanced for the time being, the move choked off the very expansion on which the Democrats had wagered their political future. By the end of February, the government was under intense fire from the press, the universities, and the Republican Peoples' Party. Menderes called out the army and the police to maintain order.

On May 3, 1960, Turhan was scheduled to give an evening broadcast over *Deutsche Welle*, the West German short-wave radio world service. He took an early morning flight to Frankfurt, half a day before he was to meet with his German hosts. As he disembarked and went into the passenger arrival area, he barely nodded to a tall, exceedingly handsome man, with close-cropped, iron gray hair, dressed in a well-tailored sharkskin suit. After retrieving his single suitcase in the baggage claim area, Turhan caught the terminal bus and sat toward the rear. Within a minute, he was joined by the tall man. "*Guten tag*. Herr Jünglich?" the man addressed Turhan in German.

"I'm afraid you must be mistaken, sir," Turhan replied in English. "My name is William Potter."

"*Ach*, I'm so sorry," the tall man responded, switching his language. "I must have caused you deep embarrassment. May I offer my apologies? You looked like a business acquaintance of my partner. Please don't think all Germans are so rude. Might I invite you to coffee at my club."

"I'm sorry. I don't believe I caught your name."

"Fruchtmann. Heinrich Fruchtmann, Mr. Potter."

"I believe I can spare thirty minutes for coffee."

Ten minutes later, the bus pulled up at the Frankfurt Hauptbahnhof. The two men walked in silence to a shabby apartment building in the Königsberggasse, four blocks away. The tall man said nothing until they entered a second story flat, and he'd locked the door.

"All right, Nadji, what is going on?"

"Three weeks, four at the most."

"You're serious?"

"I am. The Democrats lost the support of the military two weeks ago, after the RPP walked out of the Assembly. Menderes appointed an investigation committee of his cronies which had the absolute right to arrest any citizen, close any newspaper, or suspend any law that interfered with its work."

"Then the rumors were true. Why didn't I hear about this?"

"Anything concerning the troubles has been officially blocked. Three days ago, the government closed the universities."

"Allah! Have the Democrats gone insane?"

"There's more, Turhan. Most newspapers have now been suspended and foreign periodicals reporting the situation have been refused entry into the country."

"All I heard in London was that there was student unrest, and that the police and army had it all under control."

"Turhan, I'll tell you anything you want to know, but promise on our friendship you'll keep it confidential until I give you the word."

"After almost forty-two years, do you even have to ask, Nadji?"

"*Korgeneral* to you, exiled enemy of the state," Akdemir grinned, playfully punching his old companion on the shoulder.

"Three stars! Nadji, your father would have been so proud! You'd outrank him! *Mashallah*! When do you pin the third star on?"

"The day after I tell you that your bond of secrecy is ended."

"That could be forever!"

"May 27."

"Twenty-four days? Who's in charge?"

"Gürsel."

"The Army Commander? I knew Jemal before I met you. He served at Gelibolu under Mustafa Kemal. He's as radical and political as you, Nadji," Turhan said, his voice gently mocking. Akdemir was completely apolitical, a conservative whose loyalty to the Turkish military was unquestioned. "Things must be in a horrible state to move Jemal Gürsel off his duff."

"They are. The country's on fire, and those who are supposed to be putting it out are sitting around, calling each other names."

"Allah! The last time the military became involved in politics was fifty-one years ago, when they deposed the Sultan!"

"As I recall," Akdemir said, "your life took a rather different direction after that."

"What will happen to Menderes?"

"It may be best not to ask."

On May 27, 1960, as violence in the streets reached a new peak, a group of officers led by General Jemal Gürsel, backed by key military units in Istanbul and Ankara, arrested President Bayar, Prime Minister Menderes, most members of the cabinet, and virtually all Democrat members of the Assembly. The new rulers instantly imposed martial law. The Turkish populace accepted the coup with virtually no opposition.

During the next few days, Gürsel and thirty-eight officers, newly promoted Lieutenant General Nadji Akdemir among them, organized themselves into the *Milli Birlik Komitesi* – the National Unity Committee – to operate the country. Gürsel stated publicly that he had no intention of ruling the nation beyond the time needed to bring to justice those responsible for betraying Turkish democracy, and the time required to draft a new constitution better able to protect the nation from abuses in the future. True to his word, the National Unity Committee held power for little more than a year. One of its first acts was to pardon Turhan and urge him to return to Turkey with full legal rights, a public apology, and honors. The Democrat Party was abolished. Its property was confiscated. Two weeks later, the Committee announced that the new government intended to try most of the deposed leaders on charges ranging from illegal entry onto university grounds, to corruption in office, to high treason.

On October 15, 1960, the day after the provisional government announced the start of the trials, Turhan, in a front page article in *Isharet*, begged the new leaders to temper justice with mercy.

DO NOT LET DEMOCRACY DIE WITH THE DEMOCRATS!

by Turhan Türkoğlu

I am not a political favorite, neither of the late, apparently unlamented Democrat Party, nor of the Republican Peoples' Party. At the 'invitation' of the fallen government, I spent the last two years in exile from my country for the second time in two decades. Now, Menderes and his associates have been removed from office. This does not trouble me in the least. Any government that rules solely by force, and that tramples the rights of those who oppose it, deserves to fall.

My concern, however, is that democracy – with a small "d" – must not die with the Democrat Party. The government that rules best is one that subjects itself to the freely-given consent of the governed. I have come to believe that the democratic system best fulfills those goals. Yesterday, our National Unity Committee announced it would try virtually every Democrat of consequence on one charge or another. That, in and of itself, seems to me to be unconstitutional, since whatever the Menderes regime did was done after it was legally voted into office, as part of the exercise of its government power. In this opinion, I am clearly in the minority.

I urge the High Court to consider competent evidence, free from the influence of the National Unity Committee, which is presently functioning as the executive branch of government, and to remember that it is trying legislators, thus interfering with a third branch of government and upsetting the delicate system of checks and balances. It is easy to say that the executive and legislative bodies under Menderes abused discretion in a way that was both despicable and illegal. This does not give the judiciary and the new holders of executive power license to hold themselves above the same law they claim was violated by the Democrats.

If there must be trials, let there be appropriate sentences. Fines, reasonable imprisonment, perhaps a bar from participation in electoral politics for a reasonable period. The rumors I hear of potential death sentences fly in the teeth of modern justice. Did any Democrat specifically condemn another man to death, simply because of political disagreement? I find no evidence of such a practice.

The world watched in shocked frustration as Turkey fell into anarchy. Our allies applauded when the National Unity Committee announced it was a caretaker government, in deed as well as name. Let us not foul the new nest we have built by using the blood of the vanquished to cement its parts. I urge the High Court and the Committee to temper justice with mercy.

The Gürsel government chafed under Turhan's admonitions, and several like them, but took no punitive action against him or any other member of the press. Ultimately, of the five hundred ninety-two defendants who were tried, fifteen were sentenced to death. Of these, only Menderes was hanged. Twelve, including President Bayar, had their sentences commuted to life imprisonment by the Committee. Within five years, Bayar was pardoned altogether, and the old campaigner was back on the political trail.

The leaders of the principal political parties and most of the prominent newspaper editors, including Turhan Türkoğlu, signed a pledge not to use the trials, which had taken place on the island of Yassiada, outside Istanbul, for partisan argument in the electoral campaign. These pledges of restraint were honored and, as promised, the Committee of National Unity returned power to civilian authorities after the general election of October, 1961.

In the election, a new party, the Justice Party which, oddly enough, was made up of most surviving Democrats, did remarkably well in the election. It finished so close to the Republican Peoples' Party that when Jemal Gürsel, who'd been elected President on a non-party ballot, asked Ismet Inönü to form the first civilian government, Atatürk's old comrade was forced to choose an equal number of ministers from each party. Within five years of the military coup, the "new" Justice Party secured a sufficient number of votes to once again command the Grand National Assembly. The people had spoken.

PART SEVEN:

IMMORTALS 1969–1983

1

On May 19, 1969, fifty years to the day after he'd written his first article for *Isharet,* Turhan entered Abdullah Heper's office. The publisher embraced his editor warmly and, after serving them both tea, said, "Congratulations, *arkadash*! Your name is on every front page in the city. It's your golden anniversary. We've been deluged with requests for today's edition. Would you believe we've sold over a million copies?"

"That's wonderful, Abdullah. I've always wondered where I'd be on the day I chose to retire. We're both pleased I'm still at the top."

"What do you mean? Surely you wouldn't step down now?"

"It's time, my friend. Times have changed. I've changed. The reins should be handed over to a new horseman."

"But Turhan, you *are Isharet.*"

"No, Abdullah. I've *been Isharet.* And if I remain *Isharet,* the paper won't continue to flourish. Praise Allah, I've still got enough sense left to know that. For the past eight-and-a-half years, neither the RPP nor the Justice Party has been able to win a majority of the popular vote. I've lost interest in the politics of oatmeal and pablum. Our prime minister, Süleyman Demirel, is smooth and competent – he ought to be, he was trained in America as an engineer – but he's a 'starlet,' not an old-time politician. Compared to Menderes, he's as exciting as fried eggs. Ever since our democracy was cleansed back in sixty-one no one's been able to win a clear mandate. It's been coalition and stagnation. Even Ismet Inönü's been relegated to the status of 'the grand old man of Turkish politics.'"

"Why not turn the political desk over to someone else? Try a different area."

"Abdullah, I'm seventy-two years old, not a good time to learn something new. When I was in Aksaray fortress prison back in fifty-eight, Menderes and I, who didn't agree on very much toward the end, debated the future of newspapers in Turkey. I'm sad to admit Adnan was right. Look what's selling papers today. Once the front pages of Turkey's journals featured serious, responsible comment by Ahmet Yalman and, I flatter myself, Turhan Türkoğlu. Now that same space is dominated by pictures of semi-nude young women, stories of sex, gore and violence. Even *Hürriyet* had to go that route, simply to compete. If *Isharet* wants to stay in business it'll have to go with what sells in the marketplace."

"Might I propose something that would interest you?"

"Such as?"

"Turhan Türkoğlu has become synonymous with *Isharet* and vice versa. As long as your name remains associated with the paper, it's good for us both. Might I suggest you assume the position of Senior Editor-in-Chief Emeritus, with no real responsibility, at full pension?"

"What would you expect me to do?"

"Write an occasional piece. Tour the world, do what you will. Mention *Isharet* from time to time."

Turhan thought for a few moments, then grinned. "Abdullah," he said, "old Selimiye would have loved the way you're taking care of both his children – *Isharet* and me. Let's drink a toast to the new relationship."

"Better yet, why don't you and I have dinner at the Tarabya?"

"You couldn't think of any place closer? That's halfway to the Black Sea."

"So? You don't have to be anywhere early tomorrow. You can sleep in without feeling guilty. I hear the *göbek* dancers they've got there to lure the tourists are the most attractive in Turkey."

"What would an old man like me want with a belly dancer?"

"Surely your eyes and your imagination aren't dead yet."

The Büyük Tarabya was fifteen miles up the Bosphorous. The modern, sand-colored eight-story resort hotel sat directly on the water, at the north end of a small, semicircular bay. The sheltered harbor to the south housed the yachts of Istanbul's very wealthy, which jostled for position among wooden fishing caiques. A colorful village climbed the hills immediately behind the harbor. The hotel complex stood removed from the village, a foreign element which could not disguise itself and didn't try. It was nearly sunset when Turhan and Heper arrived at the Büyük Tarabya. They sat at one corner of the virtually empty hotel terrace, overlooking the village and the Bosphorous. The weather was clear. There was a pleasant springtime breeze. "Tell me, Turhan, what was it like to work under Selimiye? I mean at the very beginning."

"Now, *there* was a newspaperman," Turhan began. Before long, he was so deeply engrossed in reliving the past he was in another world.

Forty-five minutes later, Turhan had reached the point where Ihsan had taken him to the secret rendezvous with Atatürk, when he was interrupted by a burly, balding man with a large, round face. "Excuse me, I have an important message for Turhan Türkoğlu."

Turhan stopped in mid-sentence. "That's me, sir, how can I help you?" His eyes widened. "Süleyman Effendim, aren't you quite a way from the capital?"

Prime Minister Demirel grinned. "Yes, but it's not every day one can celebrate fifty years of employment with the same master. Would that I'd be able to say the same thing!" He laughed good naturedly.

Turhan looked around the room, then glanced sharply at Heper. "So that's why you wanted me to come all the way up here. Who else is here?"

"Certainly you wouldn't expect me to let this be a Justice Party affair," Ismet Inönü said, as he took Turhan's hand.

"Ismet Pasha! Allah! In a moment I'd expect you to produce the Gazi," Turhan said, overwhelmed that Mustafa Kemal's old comrade-in-arms would be among the first to greet him.

Soon the terrace was filled with faces he'd known for years. Political and personal differences were put aside for the evening as two hundred people toasted Turhan. No matter how they felt toward one another on any given day, the guests realized that fifty years of such days passed in an instant, and that they, too, would arrive at the same destination. Turhan moved to the head table, flanked by his two oldest, closest friends, Nadji Akdemir and Halide Orhan. He marveled at how wonderful Ayshch looked. *Can this beautiful woman be sixty-five*? he thought. Next to her sat two handsome, erect young lieutenants in their early twenties, one wearing an Army uniform, the other an Air Force uniform. "Omer? Yavuz?"

"Indeed," Nadji replied. "The torch is being passed to another generation."

The words stung Turhan. His mind raced back in time and place, to his first mentor, Ibrahim, a man on a white stallion who'd been responsible for taking him out of Diyarbakır and across the spine of Turkey in 1915, and to Alkimi, the power behind Ibrahim, the old woman who'd died nearly forty years ago. "The torch is being passed."

After dinner, speakers vied with one another to glorify the "legendary" journalist's exploits. "I'd be more moved if I thought they were speaking to express rather than to impress," Turhan muttered to Halide.

"Shush! Be gracious if you think you can."

"Turhan Türkoğlu gracious?" Nadji said, so that only the three of them could hear it. "Might as well try to teach a bear to wipe himself with toilet paper after he shits in the woods." Turhan was barely able to swallow the *rakı* in his mouth without choking or spitting it out.

Finally, Turhan himself was called on to speak. He rose and said, "These wonderful eulogies may not yet be deserved. The man still breathes!" There was laughter. "Let's see if we're all around to do this on my hundredth anniversary at *Isharet*! To all of you, *Sherefinize* and *Inshallah*, you should each live to a hundred and twenty!" He sat down to loud applause, no doubt, because he'd been so mercifully brief.

The entertainment began. It was a celebration of everything Turkish, *karagöz* shadow puppet shows, folk dancing, belly dancing. Durul Genje stormed onstage with his modern Janissary band and stayed on, leading a smaller combo. Zeki Muren, Turkey's most popular recording star, sang Turkish renditions of the latest disco music from Western Europe as well as modern Turkish tunes. Just before intermission, *Görkemli Meydan*, Turkey's celebrated circus, put on their most popular routine, the grease wrestler-turned-belly dancer routine. The sophisticated audience went wild with laughter, just as villagers stationed in Korea had done almost two decades before. During intermission, Turhan groaned as the management played Tom Jones' recording of "Delilah," which had swept Turkey by storm the year before. "If I hear that piece of noise one more time..."

His voice was drowned out, as the room full of politicians and dignitaries, echoing the tuneful lament of taxi drivers and teen-aged boys with transistor radios in every major city in the country, joined in the chorus:

"*Why, Why, Why, De-li-lah? My, my, my De-li-lah.*

So, before, they come to break down the door,

Forgive me, Delilah, I just couldn't take any more."

"I didn't like it the first time I heard it either." Turhan turned and found himself looking into the brown eyes of a beautiful, dark-haired young woman. "I guess you learn to adjust to the new music. Eventually you find it's rather catchy."

"Don't get me wrong," Turhan replied. "I was in England when Elvis Presley was popular there. Even now, I find some of the Beatles' music quite appealing, but when you get to be my age..."

"A young man like you? Nonsense! You'll never get old. I'm so glad I can be here with you tonight. It's a great honor for me." She squeezed his hand, kissed him on the cheek and disappeared, leaving a faint trace of perfume in her wake.

"Thank you Miss...?" he said, but she was gone.

"Still able to charm the young girls off their feet, eh, scoundrel?" Halide said, grinning.

"But I didn't say a thing. She just came and left."

"I saw you kissing her," Nadji teased.

"Well, if you insist that I kissed her …" Turhan said, straightening his tie.

Their conversation was interrupted as the master of ceremonies announced, "And now, we're proud to call upon one of Turkey's newest up-and-coming young singers, Miss Ajda Pekkan, whose most recent claim to fame is that she was recently seen in public – this evening in fact – kissing someone who's already made *his* lasting impression on Turkish society, Türkoğlu the Magnificent."

Turhan blushed as the lovely woman, who'd spoken to him moments before, came on stage, blew a kiss and winked at him. She said, in a soft, husky voice, "My friends, earlier this evening our guest of honor said he had difficulty adjusting to Tom Jones. I hope he has less of a problem with this number, which I dedicate to him." The modern five-piece band, flute, guitar, bass, drum and piano, eased into the simple, beautiful ballad, *Yağmur* – "Rain." At the conclusion, Turhan stepped up to the small stage, bowed, and kissed the singer's hand. Immediately afterward, they were joined onstage by Erol Büyükburch, who was riding the crest of the hugely successful Russian ballad, "Those Were the Days." As everyone joined in the "La la la la, la-la" of the chorus, each man or woman, regardless of age, felt the kiss of mortality.

Edwin Baumueller stepped to the rostrum, accompanied by a short, balding man who held a violin and bow in his left hand. "My friends," he said. "Few of you were with our Turhan when he started his professional life as a waiter in a wonderful old Istanbul nightclub. I'm sure some of you may have been happier had he stayed a waiter. Back then, Turhan helped a young Russian emigrant get a job at *Rouge et Noir*. Unlike Turhan, this man didn't change careers. He still plays his violin. Ladies and gentleman, I give you the internationally beloved – in fact, since he's been married six times, a little bit *too* internationally beloved – soloist, Maestro Sascha Brotsky.

2

In March of 1972, Halide, now seventy-four and walking with the aid of a cane, said to Turhan, "Some of us can hold a job for fifty years. Others only last forty."

"What do you mean?"

"For the past few months, I've been thinking about how cold and wet it gets each winter at Belgrade Palas. Most of my neighbors have died or moved. When I first came to Turkey in 1915, we stopped at Kuşadası. I think I'd like to spend some time in the sun."

"You mean you'd leave Yujel Orhan Teacher's College?"

"Did you leave *Isharet*?"

"Of course not!" he said, huffily. "I'm Senior Editor emeritus."

"And you do a lot if you write one article a month. That, my friend, is retirement."

"Have you discussed this with anyone?"

"Yes. Ozal Suvarli. No one's more dedicated than he. I couldn't leave the college in more capable hands. What a miracle to have him take over. Both our lives and Sezer's are perpetuated through that fine young man."

"When do you plan to retire?"

"The school year ends June first. That would be a lovely afternoon to say '*à bientôt* to my friends."

Turhan and Nadji traveled to Kuşadası and found Halide a two-bedroom, waterfront apartment built the year before, that featured all the modern conveniences. Most important, it was all on one floor, which meant Halide would not have to negotiate stairs. It was on Ladies' Beach, close to town, yet secluded enough to afford her privacy. When they flew her down, she was delighted, both at the bright, airy apartment and at the amazingly low price. Neither told her they'd each paid ten thousand lira to the owner, so that he'd quote her the bargain rate. They arranged one other piece of business. "Remember, there must be no publicity of any kind, no newspapers, no announcements, nothing. She's a very private person. She'd never countenance what we're doing."

The next month was a busy one for Turhan and Nadji. It involved tracing down graduates of Yujel Orhan Teachers College from thirty-five years ago, combing the entire country to get the word to those people who'd be meaningful, and trying to keep word of what they were doing from their closest friend. Abdullah Heper placed the facilities and staff of *Isharet* at their disposal.

June 1, 1972 was the balmiest day of the year. Turhan and Nadji arrived at Belgrade Palas early to spend some time with Halide before the retirement ceremony began. "When will you be moving?" Nadji asked.

"At the end of the month. It's difficult deciding what to take. I'll probably leave most of the heavy furniture here."

"I'm glad you decided not to sell Belgrade Palas," Turhan said. "It's been such an integral part of our lives, not to mention the lives of so many others'."

"At the price I paid for the new apartment, there was no need to sell it. I'm glad you took my advice to move up here and take care of the place, Turhan."

"You made me an offer I couldn't refuse," he replied, grinning. "For the same rent I'm paying in Beyoğlu I get Belgrade Palas. Who knows? I may open the first brothel in the neighborhood."

"You do and I get half the commissions!" Halide snapped.

"And I'll provide security," Nadji broke in.

Beneath their surface gaiety, the three friends realized this might be one of the last times during their lives they'd all be together. Only Nadji was still employed full time. He'd be seventy in a couple of months, mandatory retirement age. He hoped to use his connections to move that retirement back another year or two. As their limousine headed south along the shores of the Bosphorous, they passed through suburban villages. "I remember when I first came to Belgrade Forest," Halide said. "It took most of the day to go into Istanbul because of the dirt roads and isolation of each of these small towns. Now it still takes the better part of a day, because of traffic congestion."

As they continued south from Arnavutköy, the old "Albanian Village," Nadji said, "Progress doesn't always mean things get faster or better, but there's one example of where it does." He pointed ahead to graceful twin spires rising on each side of the strait. "The Bosphorous Bridge. When it's opened, Europe and Asia will finally be joined by motor road."

"I agree it'll make things easier," Halide said. "Anyone who's spent two hours waiting for the ferry will bless the day the government decided to spend the money on the project. But there's something sad about it, too. The straits have always physically separated Europe from Asia. When the bridge opens, something unique will be destroyed. It won't really be that much different than crossing from the right bank to the left bank of the Seine."

Soon, they pulled into the circular driveway in front of Yujel Orhan Teachers College. When it was founded, the school had occupied three single-story wooden buildings, more than sufficient for its thirty-two students. Now there were more than twenty-five hundred students and a staff of one hundred fifty from all over Turkey, most of whom resided in college dormitories. The original building, now the school's museum, stood proudly to the east of the campus quadrangle, surrounded by three story brick structures.

Özal Suvarli was waiting on the front steps, a huge bouquet of roses in his hand. "We've planned a small retirement ceremony for you in the quadrangle at noon. Before that, I want to show you something."

She glanced at her two friends, who remained impassive, then followed her successor into the entry hall. There, she saw a bronze statue that showed her helping an old man write his name with a stick in the ground. He was just completing the final "h" in "Nasrullah."

"My God!" she said. "The first day in Suvarli. How could you have known?"

"A story handed down from father to son," he said quietly.

Ten minutes before noon, people started to arrive. Halide took a seat near the edge of the platform, so she might greet each person who came. By noon, the seats were filled. As she rose to speak, Halide heard a dull rumbling. More people were coming from all directions. For the next hour, a steady stream of men and women continued to arrive. By one o'clock, more than ten thousand people – students, former students, political leaders, and admirers from every walk of life – filled the quadrangle and spilled out onto the campus. The original two hundred had left their seats to make room for the visitors. Everyone stood in respectful silence.

The small, stoop-backed woman stood. Although she was overwhelmed by the amazing spectacle, she remembered that first and foremost she was a teacher and she must always display dignity and control. She stepped to the microphone and addressed the crowd in a strong, clear voice. "Good afternoon. Thank you so much for coming to bid me '*Bon Voyage*.' My friends, look around you. All of you who are here today are a testimony, not to Halide Orhan, not to Yujel Orhan Teachers' College, but to the power of the Turkish spirit. I was at Gelibolu when the supposedly dying 'Sick Man of Europe' fought in the trenches and pushed back the vaunted British Empire. I was in Istanbul in the darkest hours, when the nations tried to crush us like so much dust under their feet. Now look at us. *Look at us*! We hold our heads high with pride at what we have done. Had we been a large nation, a rich nation, like the United States of America, had we been possessed of centuries of universal education, of technology, and of strong alliances, such as Britain, Germany, or my native France, what we accomplished in less than fifty years would have been dramatic. Given none of those advantages, given nothing but our own spirit, what we have achieved is a miracle. If I stand as a symbol of that miracle, it is only as a single flower in a vast meadow. I was one of hundreds, then one of thousands, who came to teach. But who worked harder? The teacher, who already possessed the knowledge and brought it to the village, or the villager who, at an age when most were established with farms and homes and children, risked ostracism by the *imam*, frustration in having to become a student at the most elementary level, and fear of failure, so that he or she could learn? Brick by brick the building was constructed. Grain by grain the wheat field was planted, tended, and harvested. Look to the skies when you see birds flying south. There will always be one in the lead. But without others to follow, to risk that journey of thousands of miles, to trust in a course of action, the flock would wither and die in the cold, and shortly there'd be none left to bring their songs to the world.

"This morning, Özal Suvarli, the son of one of my earliest students, showed me the statue that now graces the rotunda. I am thankful that the statue is not only of me, but shows an elderly man as well. When we met, he was the same age as I am now. It was a day I've often remembered, for he was the very first of my students. The man came to an open field where I'd set up a small row of chairs. He was honest enough to tell me the only reason he was there was that he was tired, and it was a place to sit. But by the end of that day, Nasrullah had learned to write his name in the earth. He was perhaps prouder of his accomplishment, even than I. Nasrullah, you and those like you helped push us into the twentieth century. We are here because of you. *Mashallah!* May the blessings of Allah be on all your heads."

She sat down. There was absolute silence, except for the persistent chirping of a songbird in a nearby tree. Then a very soft voice started to say "Ha-li-deh, Ha-li-deh, Ha-li-deh." A moment later a second voice joined in, then another. Within a minute, the chant picked up throughout the audience. It never rose to a shout. Rather, it had the quiet force of an ocean wave surging along a coast. As Halide rose and, with the aid of her cane, walked silently through the crowd, it parted to let her through. At the end of the quadrangle, she paused for a moment and looked skyward. "We did it, Metin," she said softly. "We made our dream come true."

Turhan approached her quietly. "Hanım Effendim," he said, "would you accept a small token of affection from an old friend?" Before she could speak, he handed her a small package. When she opened it, she looked at him for a long time.

"Aren't you going to wind it?" he asked.

She remembered a day seventy years ago – a day when her father had calmed her tears by telling her the Hans Christian Andersen story of "The Ugly Duckling" and had given her that very music box. She had thought that very special gift had been lost forever on that terrible day in 1943 when the Nazi sympathizers had burned down that part of her home that had served as a way station for fleeing Jews. Her eyes never left Turhan's as she heard the ancient wooden music box play the strains of "Le Cygne." And the tears came.

On October 29, 1973, the Turkish Republic celebrated its fiftieth anniversary. In Ankara, cascades of fireworks turned night into day. In Istanbul, the Bosphorous Bridge opened to international fanfare. Turk embraced Greek, Armenian, Jew and Arab alike. It was a time of celebration the likes of which had not been seen in hundreds of years.

That day, two of Turkey's foremost citizens, its most honored journalist and a man who, ten months before, had been permanently promoted to the rank of *Orgeneral* – four star general – did not join the masses in the streets of Turkey. They'd flown to Kuşadası that morning to mourn the passing of their friend, "the angel of modern Turkey," who had passed quietly in her sleep the night before.

3

On July 20, 1974, Nadji, who'd retired to his home in the Chankaya section of Ankara was writing a letter to Turhan, when Aysheh interrupted him. "Darling, there's a young man in Army uniform who insists on speaking to General Akdemir. I told him you'd retired six months ago, but he said he needed to see you."

"It's nice to know someone remembers I was once a man of some influence." He smiled. "Show him in."

The man was thirty-five, rather old for a messenger boy, and wore major's insignia. "General Akdemir?"

"*Retired* General, Major."

"Sir, I've been asked to deliver this to you." He handed Nadji a white envelope bearing the General Staff seal.

Nadji opened it at once. "Aysheh," he called out. "You'll never believe this. I've been recalled to active duty! I'm to report to Headquarters immediately!"

When he got there, Nadji was surprised to see many of his contemporaries. "Officers," the Chief of General Staff said. "Please sit down. As you see, there are fifty of us in this room. This is a time of crisis. We need every senior military mind we have, no matter what age. What is said in this room this afternoon is top secret, a matter of utmost national security. I have asked General Kenan Evren, who most of you know, to brief us."

The man who stepped to the podium had white hair and a handsome, open, engaging face. He was a man who instilled such confidence that many referred to him as "Baba Evren," Father Evren. He was Nadji's equivalent in rank, four stars. "Gentlemen," Evren began. "We've been aware that since 1955 the Greek majority on Kibris – Cyprus – has systematically tried to force union with Greece and exclude the Turkish minority from its economic and political life. We believed the problem was solved when Kibris became an independent republic in August, 1960. Alas, this was not to pass. The key government positions were still held by Greeks, the worst lands left to Turks.

"When the Greek Cypriots called for *enosis* again, there was civil war in 1964. We would have intervened, but the United States threatened to blockade our landing by using its Sixth Fleet. We were compelled against our better judgment to call off our liberation forces. Since then, we've barred the U.S. Sixth Fleet from visiting Turkey, cancelled the U.S. Navy's home base in Izmir, and phased down American military presence on Turkish soil. Although peace returned to Kibris in 1965, Archbishop President Makarios was powerless to stop the anti-Turkish pressures on the island. Again, the Americans stopped us from going in, and again the Turkish people reacted against our American ally.

"Four days ago, Greek army officers assigned to the Cyprus National Guard deposed Makarios and installed Nikos Sampson, who's made it clear he intends to force union with Greece and no one will stop him. Within the past hour we've learned that wholesale slaughter of Turks is occurring on Kibris, under the guise of 'protecting the security of Greek citizens.'

"Gentlemen, at three o'clock this afternoon, a Turkish expeditionary force, six thousand troops, including armored and airborne units, will land at Girne – Kyrenia – on Kibris' northern coast. Within forty-eight hours, twenty-five thousand reinforcements, supported by air and naval cover, will move onto the island. We will not be deterred by the United States, nor anyone else, until we've secured the safety of every Turk on Kibris.

"We must prepare for condemnation from many corners, including the United States, which has not proved to be our staunchest friend in recent years. While we are all members of the Turkish Armed Forces, we are independent in our thoughts and deeds. Are there any of you who disagree with the proposed landing of forces on Kibris?"

No one raised an objection.

"Very well then, it's unanimous. You retirees who are returned to active duty will receive full pay and allowances and additional credit toward retirement." There was the comradely laughter of old friends. Each knew this was the last thing on anyone's mind.

Within two days, the northern third of Cyprus was in Turkish hands. Despite the cease-fire, a UN Security Council resolution calling for mutual troop withdrawal, and the exchange of prisoners of war, negotiations broke down. The Turks landed additional reinforcements, pushed Greek forces to the western extremity of the Kyrenia mountains, and secured a fist like grip around Nicosia. When the second cease-fire came, the Turkish army was in permanent control of the northern third of the island. Within one month of fighting, there were two hundred thousand Greek and Turkish refugees trapped in each other's territories, out of a total population of six hundred thousand on Cyprus.

Turkey demanded the creation of an independent Turkish state on Cyprus. When its allies refused to honor that request, the Turkish government unilaterally recognized the *de facto* existence of the Federated Republic of Northern Cyprus in February, 1975.

Nadji soon found there was not much need for the services of a reactivated 72-year-old general. A man with four stars on his shoulders could not be expected to command a brigade. For several months, he taught Turkish military history to classes at the War College. The following March, General Evren approached him with an exciting proposal. "Have you ever been to the United States, General Akdemir?"

"No, sir. I've made several American friends over the years. Aysheh and I've been meaning to go there, but we've never gotten around to it. Why do you ask?"

"May we speak in confidence?"

"Of course, Kenan."

"Our relations with America have deteriorated since the mid-sixties. Turkey's produced ninety percent of the world's legal opium for the past hundred years. In 1971, we agreed to an American plan to phase out cultivation. The U.S. agreed to compensate us for loss of foreign exchange and pay farmers who'd be deprived of the profits. Unfortunately, American money did not filter down. Most likely, it went into politicians' pockets. When the RPP came to power in 1973, Prime Minister Ecevit lifted the ban on poppy growing. Turkish farmers felt it wasn't their responsibility to police Americans' drug habits.

"As soon as Ecevit approved a return to poppy cultivation, the American Congress started debate on whether to cut off financial aid to Turkey. Then Kibris erupted. When Ecevit recognized Denktash's Turkish Federated State last month, the U.S. Congress imposed an arms embargo on Turkey.

"Our government is sending a delegation to Washington to try to negotiate a softening of America's position. We've not been able to upgrade our arms in fifteen years. We can't live with an embargo. I need a mature, balanced observer at these meetings."

"Would either side allow such a thing?"

"Yes. Turkish General Staff advised the government that the military must be represented."

"What was the response?"

"What could they say? Gürsel engineered the restoration of order in 1960. General Gürler warned the civilian officials in 1971 that unless the government could stop the violence and get this country stabilized economically, the armed forces would step in again. Frankly, I don't think either the Justice Party or the Republican Peoples' Party is in a position to question our authority now."

"You said I'd be an 'observer'?"

"Yes. Both sides understand that the negotiators will primarily be diplomats and politicians. There'll be a suitable contingent of generals and admirals on both sides. The Americans desperately want to maintain their combat base at Incirlik. They'd like to keep TUSLOG – the United States Logistic Command – and JUSMMAT – the Joint United States Military Mission for Aid to Turkey – in the capital. The Turkish General Staff has its own people in the U.S. I'd like my own man there in a less obvious status."

"Why Nadji Akdemir? Surely you've got enough influence to place someone on the negotiating team."

"I want to keep all my options open. You were a flag officer long enough to know that every colonel and brigadier who wants to get ahead attaches himself to a higher-ranking officer. Often, they tell their mentor what they think he wants to hear. You don't need to curry favor with me. You're retired, beyond ambition, and one of the few four-star generals who appears not to have made any substantial enemies."

"If you've read my personnel file, you know of Abbas Hükümdar."

"And I know of the safe house in Belgrade Forest and your discussions with the Russian, Mishkin. I said *substantial* enemies, Nadji."

"What am I expected to do?"

"Attend the meetings. Listen to what goes on. Report back to me at least once a month, more often if necessary, at your discretion."

"Will I be staying at the Embassy?"

"No. An acquaintance of yours, Richard Murchison, has a home in Bethesda, Maryland, with a guest cottage out back. He said he'd be delighted to have you and Aysheh stay with him while you're in America."

"I haven't seen Murchison in ten years. He was an American Air Force judge advocate when we first met. The last I heard, he'd gotten out of the military and gone to work for a Washington law firm."

"He's a partner in that firm now. He represents a large number of Turkish interests. I'm sure you'll have a lot to talk about during the time you're in the District."

"How soon would you want me to go?"

"Would two weeks be too soon?"

"I doubt it. Aysheh would kiss you. I'll try to live up to your expectations."

"Just be honest. You'll be doing me the favor."

"So I'm to be a diplomat's wife after all!" Aysheh said, pirouetting about their living room. "I'll need gowns to attend those Washington balls and an appropriate hairdresser for my dinners with Mister Ford."

"Hold on, Your Ladyship," Nadji said. "No doubt you'll be the most beautiful and elegant woman in the American capital, and I'll probably have to hire armed guards to keep the men away from you, but I'm not going as an ambassador. I very much doubt we can live the high life on a retired general's salary."

"I know, darling, but you're an *active* young four-star Pasha! Don't worry, my sweet, I've no intention of bankrupting us," she said, smiling.

Then, unable to keep her excitement in check any longer, she whooped like a young girl. "Oh, Nadji! I'm so excited! America at last! Will we have a car?"

"A car and a driver, Aysheh. General Evren doesn't want me to be conspicuous, so it'll be a Chevrolet. If it's got four wheels and gets us from 'Point A' to 'Point B' what more do we need?"

The Akdemirs arrived in Washington in time to see the cherry blossoms. They were used to the dry, brown hills of Ankara, and were elated, driving in from Andrews Air Force Base, to see the multiple hues of fifty different shades of green. Richard Murchison's home on Goodview Drive in Bethesda was a flowing mansion. The "guest house" had two bedrooms, a living room, kitchen, bathroom and a small library. The Turkish Embassy treated Aysheh as an ambassador in her own right. She was a striking, charming figure who spoke at meetings of the American Association of University Women, the Soroptimists, and numerous other service clubs. Everywhere she went, she disabused Americans' ideas about the "terrible Turks."

Nadji's ventures were not so successful. He watched in helpless frustration as Turkish efforts to improve relations with its huge ally faltered. Congress formalized the embargo on military arms "until there was substantial movement toward a Cyprus settlement."

"We made some progress," Nadji wrote in a confidential memo to General Evren. "The Americans seemed somewhat pacified when we told them the Turkish government would strictly control poppy harvesting by requiring the pods be removed and processed at a state-run plant. President Ford urged Congress to reconsider the embargo in light of our decision that the twenty U.S. installations in Turkey would be subject to a 'new situation' unless negotiations were reopened."

Evren responded, "Your reports confirm you were certainly the right man for the job. The government's announcement that it's placing

American installations under Turkish control because of Congress's embargo is not as harsh as it sounds. Incirlik won't be affected. All the installation commanders we're sending out are friendly to the United States. Do anything you can to get the arms we've already purchased."

In October, President Ford signed legislation partially lifting the embargo. A new defense cooperation agreement was initialed in March, 1976. Nadji was not optimistic about it passing through Congress, and wrote General Evren, "In the year I've been here, I've watched the two houses of the American Congress in action. Although it seems more orderly than our Grand National Assembly and there are only two parties to worry about, its members often cross party lines. Each legislator is primarily concerned not with the good of his party, but with being re-elected. Since members of Congress run for office every two years, they continually shuttle back and forth between Washington and their home constituencies. Americans are not afraid to write their Senators and Representatives. There are very vocal political action groups from every ethnic background. It's not like Turkey, where ninety-eight percent of the voters are Sunni Islamic Turks. There are very strong Greek and Armenian elements in the United States which I fear will interfere with the proposed new defense agreement for years. To make matters worse, this is a Presidential election year. Mr. Ford, who came to power by accident when Nixon resigned, is going to have to spend a lot of time, money and energy running for election. It's unlikely he'll want to alienate any substantial voting bloc. I regret to report there's no such thing as a 'Turkish vote.' Please let me know what you want me to do. Much as I'd like to remain here, I feel my usefulness is at an end."

In May, 1976, Nadji returned to Ankara and debriefed his superior. Evren was pleased. "You've been of more assistance to me than you realize. I suppose you'll want retirement again?"

"I think that's a good idea. A seventy-four-year-old warrior needs time to write his memoirs."

"Nadji?"

"Yes?"

"Thank you again. A good deed repays itself many times over. *Inshallah*, I can help you some day."

"Pasha, you've made Aysheh and me feel young again, and given us one of our finest and most useful years. Are you certain it's not I who should be thanking you?"

4

As the Mercedes pulled into the semicircular driveway and Abdullah Heper felt the crunch of well-tended small pebbles under the tires of his car, he marveled at how elegant Belgrade Palas still looked. The brick was rich ochre. Ivy climbed the walls of the two-story residence.

Turhan's appearance belied his years. He looked hale and hearty. His hair was grayer, but his eyes were clear and bespoke an alert interest in what was going on around him. "All right, Abdullah, what was so important it couldn't wait?"

"What do you do most of the day, Turhan?"

"Relax. Wait for calls. Work in the garden. Polish furniture. Watch television."

"Exciting?"

"At my age, I've had enough excitement. I simply want to enjoy living."

"I have an assignment that might interest you."

"Oh?"

"Turhan, have you read any of the books by your friends Ed Baumueller, Otto Grundig, Percy Phillips?"

"From time to time."

"What did you think of them?"

"Mostly self-glorification. 'I was in such-and-such a place, and I did so-and-so for Churchill,' or whatever other name the fellows choose to drop to show how important they were, even if only by association," Turhan chuckled.

"That's just it. I've read their books. *They're* the central characters around which the world revolved. But that's not real life. Do you ever read any of your old articles, Turhan?"

"Never. I fear I'd bore myself even more."

"That's where you're wrong. I've spent the last few weeks reading your writings, some of them going back nearly sixty years. What comes through in every one of them is a vivid, exuberant love of the Motherland. Turkey – not Turhan – is the main character. Your stories speak from the heart of the land. I'd like to publish a book of some of your best work from years past. I want you to pick out and edit the articles you think are particularly special."

"Who'd be interested in the ancient brayings of a cantankerous old donkey?"

"One never knows."

The Conscience of a Nation was published in February, 1977, to coincide with Turhan's eightieth birthday. Within a month, it became abundantly clear that a very great number of people were interested in "the ancient brayings of a cantankerous old donkey." The book became as treasured a possession as Lord Kinross' *Atatürk* had been a decade before. Within two months, "*Conscience*" was translated into seventeen languages. It was the subject of parlor conversation from New York to Vladivostok. Turhan was astonished at the book's incredible success.

On May 10, he received a call from Ed Baumueller. "What did I tell you, young man?" the New York World journalist said. "I told you that you had a future ahead of you."

"Yes, but you said that forty-four years ago! It was a long time coming, 'old man.' When's *your* next book coming out?"

"It's already been published here, but its reception's been nothing like *Conscience*. Listen, Turhan. You've been promising to come to the States for years. Now that we're both wealthy writers, why not do it? Pan Am leaves twice a week and flies Yeshilköy-Frankfurt-JFK. I'll even pay for the ticket."

"You're on. I've got to speak to the Foreign Press Club on May fifteenth. I'll fly out the week after that."

On May fourteenth, Turhan went to bed at his usual ten o'clock hour. There was a slight tremor in his right hand. He was not concerned. Probably just jitters, he thought. Although Turhan had always been able to express his thoughts on paper, he'd never quite gotten over his fear of speaking to a room full of people. When he awoke, it was still dark. Something didn't feel right. There was a curious, tingling sensation on his left side. He felt dizzy. He tried to shift position to find out what time it was. Odd, his body was not moving the way it should. With difficulty, he rolled to the right and looked at the lighted alarm clock. The clock seemed to be swimming in front of his eyes. White spots danced around it. Something was very, very wrong.

When Turhan tried to reach over with his left hand to pick up the telephone, nothing happened. He was still only half-awake, and thought he was dreaming. He thought to pinch himself awake. He willed his right hand over and squeezed the flesh. Two things became apparent. He was awake. And there was no feeling of any kind on his left side. Now he was frightened. He started to say, "What's happening to me?" It came out, "Whmm mmuh?" He tried again, with the same result. His heart pounded. It took him the better part of ten minutes to lift the telephone receiver from its cradle with his right hand. He slowly dialed Abdullah Heper's home. Praise Allah, he remembered the number. Abdullah answered by the third ring. "Hello? Hello?"

"Immm-dtt."

"I beg your pardon?"

Turhan took a deep breath and tried with the last burst of energy he had. "Immm-dahttt!"

"Who is this?"

"Tuhh... Tuhh."

"Turhan?" The voice sounded wide awake, alert.

"Immm-dahhhht!"

"You need my help?"

"Ehhh-ttt." Allah! He knew he was saying the words "Imdat!" for "Help!" and "Evet" for "Yes!", but even he couldn't understand himself.

"Stay where you are, my friend. I'm sending help right now."

"He had a stroke, Nadji, thank goodness a relatively mild one. His left side's paralyzed. His speech is slurred. With proper care and a lot of work, he'll regain his faculties. The doctors think he'll walk with a slight limp."

"It was fortunate you were there, Abdullah. Where is he now?"

"Intensive care unit of University Hospital. Baumueller sent a specialist from America."

"I'll take the mid-afternoon Turkish Airlines flight."

"I'll meet you at Yeshilköy."

The American physician, Harold Cowan, was a tall man, half Turhan's age, with thick, horn-rimmed glasses and a pleasant manner. "Well, young man," he said to Turhan. "No traveling for at least a year. I understand you're a best-selling author and everyone wants you to appear throughout Europe. Those plans'll have to be cancelled. I'm sure the book will continue to sell well without your presence. You must avoid all unnecessary excitement, take the medication regularly, and check your blood pressure three times a day. You'll have a lot of frustrating work ahead of you."

Turhan reached for a pencil and pad with his right hand. The doctor had fashioned a device which enabled Turhan to write. "Will I die?" he scrawled.

"Probably," the doctor said. Turhan's eyes widened. "But not from this stroke," Cowan continued easily. "Think of this as a very fortunate warning to you. We'll have to keep your blood pressure under control. You'll get back your speech and most of the movement on your left side."

Turhan wrote, "What happened?"

"You had a mild stroke. The blood pressure became too great and there was a small explosion in your brain. Some brain cells were destroyed. Now, other cells will have to learn to take their place. You'll be in charge of the training program."

"Will it be painful?" Turhan wrote.

"More uncomfortable and frightening than painful. But stick with it, don't give up. From what Ed Baumueller told me, there's little worry about you letting anything defeat you."

"Can I use a typewriter?" he wrote.

"Better than that. Baumueller insisted I bring you a new IBM Correcting Selectric."

With great effort, Turhan smiled and slowly mouthed the words, "Thank you."

5

While Turhan progressed toward recovery, the motherland he loved so dearly descended into chaos. The Turkish economy, battered by the dramatic increase in oil prices and the cost of the Cyprus intervention, was on the verge of collapse. Inflation exceeded fifty percent. One-third of the available work force was unemployed. Turkey's balance of payments deficit was five times what it had been two years before. There was no more "Turkish coffee" in restaurants, and precious little fuel for motor vehicles. Süleyman Demirel's Justice Party managed to hang on to leadership in the Assembly for almost three years, but by January, 1978, its support had eroded and Demirel's bitter adversary, Bülent Ecevit, became Prime Minister.

Totally unnoticed by anyone in Turkey who was not there, at the end of March of that year, a secret meeting took place in a private home on Ankara's outskirts. Turkey's president, the outgoing and incoming prime ministers, the chief of the Turkish General Staff, and the heads of the country's most prestigious universities were present. "So we've agreed that all differences are put aside for this project?" President Korutürk began, amiably.

"Fine by me," Demirel said.

"I concur, although none of my RPP must know," Ecevit said, clapping his "enemy" on the shoulder and smiling.

"Good. General?"

"The idea's superb."

"Let's go over the names again. Don't forget, our selection of the judges must be unanimous. There's been nothing like this in the history of Turkey. Professor Balaban, will you be so kind as to brief us on the details?"

The eyes in the room turned to the president of Istanbul University, a slightly paunchy man of sixty, who wore rimless glasses and had a thin, white moustache. "Thank you, Mister President." The speaker remained seated on the couch. "Those of us here today will select twenty-five men and women of absolute integrity and impeccable reputation from all segments of Turkish life. One rule is inviolate. Not one judge is to be a politician, a member of the Grand National Assembly, or anyone else who exercises authority in any legislative, executive, or military element of our government. Once these twenty-five judges have been selected, they will be asked to choose those people whose lives have made the most significant difference in twentieth century Turkey. They'll be given no criteria except that their agreement must be unanimous. Those men and women ultimately elected will be inducted into the Hall of Turkish Immortals.

"Once the panel of judges is selected, their work will be inviolate. At the end of their deliberations, they'll vote by secret written ballot. The ballots will be sealed under the supervision of the Clerk of the World Court. They'll be kept at The Hague until the results are tallied on July 1, 1983. The final list, which won't be known to anyone in Turkey before the honorees are announced, will be read aloud by the United Nations Secretary-General in 1983 at the presentation ceremonies, when our new museum will be completed."

President Korutürk then told the meeting, "As we speak, a special committee of architects is designing the project. The new Turkish National Museum in Ankara will be built directly opposite Atatürk's Mausoleum, the *Anıt Kabır*. It will contain our country's greatest treasures. There will be two wings adjacent to Atatürk's tomb. The left wing will house statues of 'Immortals' who attained historical significance prior to the Twentieth Century. Noah, Ibrahim – who our Western friends call "Abraham," – Homer, Alexander the Great, Cyrus of Persia, the Roman Emperors Constantine and Justinian, Bishop Nicholas of Myra, whom the western world calls 'Santa Claus,' the architect Sinan, and Süleyman the Lawgiver. Once the Twentieth Century immortals are announced, their statues will be commissioned and will grace the right wing. Whoever is President of the Republic will know the identities of the nominees, but no one, not even the judges, will know who was elected until the day the names are called.

"The museum and the two wings will be completed by spring of 1983, five years from today. Those nominees who are living at that time will be invited to the capital to participate in the opening ceremonies. We'll meet here one month from now with a proposed list of nominees for judges. Ideally, by October first, we'll impanel them. Their vote will be conducted no later than October 1, 1981."

"What if panel members get sick or die before they've cast their ballot?" Demirel asked.

"Then the vote will be left to the rest. If someone becomes disabled or dies after casting his or her vote, that vote counts."

"What if an elector personally knows a nominee or a candidate?" the Chief of Turkish General Staff asked.

"That's a matter of that judge's personal integrity," the president replied. "Any other questions? I see there are none. May Allah bless our historic venture."

6

Istanbul, January 10, 1980

Edwin Baumueller

Publisher Emeritus

New York World

New York. N.Y.

Dear Ed:

Doctor Cowan was right. It was a long, frustrating convalescence. Except for a slight limp, almost all the effects of my stroke are gone. I'm sending him a case of our best tea. It's hard to believe I'll be eighty-three next month. The number of my old friends seems to decrease almost monthly. Nadji's seventy-seven, still as strong as ever, and the Akdemir military line continues through his sons. Omer and Yavuz have each been promoted to major. If this country is still producing young men like those two, we'll survive, no matter how touchy it looks from both inside and outside our borders.

I was sorry to hear of Sascha's passing. He was a delightful man who lived life to its fullest. I have a collection of most of his recordings. It's amazing how fresh they sound, even by today's standards.

A hundred years ago, the Ottoman Empire was termed "the sick man of Europe." Now, we're the sick man of the western world. I wish I could tell you where it's all gone so wrong. It's too simplistic to say there's an undeclared civil war between "right" and "left," Sunni Muslims and Alevi Muslims, or between any factions. The whole situation is filled with random violence. It's nonsensical.

Heper was stabbed in the shoulder in the grand bazaar two weeks ago, for no reason except he was in the wrong place at the wrong time. Praise Allah, the wound was minor and he'll be all right, but what happened to Heper is symptomatic of the cancer eating at our country's innards. I don't know what figures the official Anatolian News Agency is giving the outside world, but Abdullah tells me – and I have no reason to disbelieve him – that five ***thousand*** *people have been killed during the last three years as a direct result of "civil disturbances."*

The declaration of martial law in thirteen provinces isn't having much effect. The country's bankrupt, the political parties are squabbling more than ever, and the Grand National Assembly is nothing more than a place where everyone blames everyone else for what's wrong. No one's trying to cure the underlying illness. Last week, I saw a cartoon in Cumhüriyet. *It pictured a bunch of cave men standing around a pile of dry bones. Their clubs were raised and they appeared to be shouting angrily at one another. The caption underneath read, "The assembly has determined there is no meat left. A motion has been made to quarrel over how to divide the bones."*

Just before the Balkan War broke out, sixty-seven years ago, I first heard the old Chinese curse, "May you live in interesting times." We both know where that war led. It seems that in Turkey the "interesting" times are back.

I hear that after the American elections are over you may have a movie actor running the United States. Our own entertainers are a strange lot.

Bülent Ersoy, one of our more popular singers, underwent a sex change operation and now he/she isn't allowed to perform in public. Adja Pekkan, that sweet young thing who cozied up to me at my party, is the most popular female vocalist in Turkey. The best we can say, my friend, is that we're still riding this great ball of mud as it whirls through the cosmos, and we're still alive to watch man's stupidity toward his fellow man. Be well.

Fondly, Turhan

The political merry-go-round whirled once again and Süleyman Demirel, who'd first come to power fourteen years before, assumed the dubious honor of Prime Minister for the third time when Bülent Ecevit was unable to keep his shaky coalition together. By the end of May, the situation degenerated to the degree that General Evren, now Chief of the Turkish General Staff, summoned both former presidents, Demirel and Ecevit, to a private meeting. The atmosphere was charged with tension as the general began. "Gentlemen, the Army's not going to stand for this foolishness much longer."

"Pasha, your military people forced the constitution on us when they intervened in 1960. They went too far in protecting everyone's 'civil rights' and insuring absolute democracy. When the political pie is cut in too many pieces, everyone goes hungry and unsatisfied," Demirel said.

"Bullshit!" General Evren swore. "This is a country, not a piece of pie. Fifty million people simply try to survive from day to day without the added worry they're going to be cut down in the streets simply because they happen to be alive. Süleyman, you were in power on March 25, 1971 when General Gürler's armed forces demanded a strong government."

"Of course, Pasha. I resigned that day because Gürler's action was entirely against established law. It was nothing more than a coup by memorandum and I wanted no part of it."

"Easy for you to say now," Ecevit rejoined. "You were back in power four years later."

"Only after the country was placed under martial law and no one else could hold a government together."

"Gentlemen!" General Evren broke in sharply. "Stop your petty bickering! I did not invite you here to replay your animosity toward one another and I will not tolerate it! Do you remember the statement, 'The Army is in its barracks?'" Each of the politicians was silent, recalling the traditional warning that prior Chiefs of Staff had given Adnan Menderes and Demirel himself just before the military assumed control of the country.

"Are we no better than the Greeks?" Ecevit asked, referring to the military junta that had seized control of Greece during the late 1960's and had fallen only after Turkish forces landed in Cyprus.

"You may take my statement any way you wish. The Greek colonels stepped in and seized power for their own ends. I'm simply warning you both. Whether or not you politicians can preserve the democracy we now enjoy is entirely up to your ability to bring order to this land."

"How long do we have, Pasha?" Demirel asked.

"That, gentlemen, is up to you. Despite your public outbursts, you're both intelligent, mature men of good will. We demonstrated our ability to work together when we appointed the panel to select 'immortals.' Whether you'll rule for a month or for the next fifty years is something we'll have to determine in the days to come."

General Evren's warnings were to no avail. The nation hovered between anarchy, chaos, and civil war during the summer of 1980. The explosive violence in the cities spilled into the countryside. When the Assembly openly criticized the military for not being able to keep order, Kenan met with Ecevit, Demirel, and key deputies of the Assembly at the end of August. His message was clear. "The Army is getting ready to leave its barracks."

By September, the Grand National Assembly, despite a hundred ballots, was unable to elect a new president. Parliament came to a standstill. Ecevit put together enough votes to force Demirel's foreign minister to resign. The next day, the ultraconservative religious National Salvation Party sponsored a massive rally in Konya, and demanded reinstatement of Islamic law in Turkey. The motherland was hemorrhaging. The ship of state not only had no rudder, but everyone was a mutineer and no one wanted to be captain.

Late in the evening of September 10, 1980, Turhan received a telephone call at his home. "Turhan? Nadji here. I can't speak for more than a few moments." Turhan heard some kind of commotion in the background.

"Where are you, Nadji?"

"Turkish General Staff headquarters. All flag officers, active and retired, have been recalled to active duty. The armed forces have seized control of Turkey."

"What??"

There was no answer. Turhan heard a click as the telephone disconnected.

7

"It's now exactly one year after the military takeover," Turhan said. "The measure of what's happened is why we're meeting in Geneva rather than Ankara."

"Aren't you over dramatizing a bit?" Nadji responded. "We left the country freely, using our own names and passports, with no interference from anyone. It wasn't any harder for us to fly here from Istanbul than it was for Ed Baumueller to catch the TWA plane at Kennedy. Could they have done that in Bulgaria, Iran, or Iraq?"

"Turkey is not an Eastern bloc country. We don't have the Ayatullah Khomeini or Saddam Hussein to direct our every footstep. But we're no better than Greece was under the colonels."

"Calm down, my friend," Baumueller cautioned. "I've been on this planet almost ninety years. Things always come around. You saw that in Germany. You've seen that in Turkey. Atatürk's republic has done political back flips a dozen times in the last thirty years."

"This time it's different."

"It's always 'different.' Someone once said, 'The more things change, the more they remain the same.'"

"I'm not a child, Ed. I asked you to meet me in Switzerland because I want your help, not because I want to be told how things remain the same. You're the three closest friends I've got left."

"Thanks for including me in that number," Abdullah Heper said.

Turhan looked at the publisher. Allah, he thought, Heper had been no more than a child when I met him, and I was already near retirement. Now he's pushing sixty! Where does the time go? Aloud, he said, "I give General Evren's National Security Council credit for restoring law and order, but at what price? I've got no choice but to do it."

"Don't," Akdemir said.

"Nadji, you're one of *them*. You've got to say that."

Akdemir rose to his feet, his face red with fury. "Don't you ever, *ever*, say that to me again! You and I have been 'family' since 1918 – sixty-three years next month. Just who the hell do you think put his career on the line to remain your friend when Abbas Hükümdar and his cronies threatened to expose your drug dealings? Who do you think was your supportive spokesman when you got your butt kicked out of Turkey the first time? Who was with you at Belgrade Palas when the Jews came through? Just who do you suppose held your hand when Rachela...?" He stopped in mid-sentence, abashed at the intensity of the anger that had caused him to push the one emotional button that remained sensitive forty years after the event. "I'm sorry, Turhan," he apologized. "That was very wrong of me to say."

"No, it wasn't," the journalist responded quietly. "I deserved that the moment I even spoke about doubting your loyalty to me. You've made me realize I have to make the ultimate decision myself."

"You've weathered many crises in your life, *arkadash*," the American said. "More than a man is usually asked to face. Starting back when you were a village boy."

"I know, Ed. I did it once before and went to jail for it. It was the thing to do back in the fifties. All of us risked arrest, Yalman, Heper, every editor and publisher who opened his mouth. It was a game. We all hung together. Despite what happened, we could count on one another. We had *news*papers back then, journals that helped shape *public* – not pubic – opinion. A few years ago, I became wealthy beyond my wildest dreams when *Conscience* became an international best seller. It didn't change my lifestyle one bit. Not because I didn't want all the good things," he chuckled. "Let's just say 'reasons of health' didn't allow me to have them."

"That's another consideration," Heper said. "You've had one stroke. You're not a young man."

"Anything's a risk, my friend," Turhan replied. "When you went into the Grand Bazaar, did you think you'd be knifed? Nadji, when you went on a reconnaissance mission during the War of Independence, did you expect you'd step on a land mine? This is a chance I've got to take. I don't hold any of you responsible."

"It's your money and your neck," Nadji said, shrugging.

"It may be my neck, but part of it's 'your' money as well, Nadji," he said, patting his oldest friend on the knee. "Just so you know, the money from the book is held in trust, right here in Geneva. If something happens to me, half of it goes to the Yujel Orhan Teachers' College. The other half goes to your heirs."

"I never asked..."

"Who else do I have to leave it to? I've really got no one. That may not be the right way, but, as circumstances turned out, it was my way. I've decided to draw down the trust for what I need to do. Ed, are you certain the *World* will run the ad?"

"We ran a full page for Khomeini just before he came to power. I own enough of the paper's stock to push the issue."

"How about the rest?"

"The L.A. Times and the Washington Post will run it. So will the London Times and the Economist. The Wall Street Journal won't say, but I got an affirmative response from *Der Spiegel* and the International Herald-Tribune."

"Abdullah?"

"I had the balls to run it for you when I was fifty pounds lighter and many years younger. You'll indemnify us when we're fined?" he asked, laughing.

"I didn't know that was part of the deal."

"Of course it isn't. I thought I'd inject a little heavy-handed humor. The answer is a gold-plated 'Yes,' my friend. *Cumhüriyet* and *Hürriyet* will run it, too, but they're understandably nervous. They want the right to edit it."

"If I say no?"

"Let them edit it if they must, Turhan. The message will get through. Give our countrymen credit for the ability to read between the lines. Can you survive what's sure to happen?"

"Jail again? Bread and water? Worms? The *Midnight Express* scenario?" Turhan said, referring to the motion picture that had infuriated both the Turks and the international community, but for different reasons. "They arrested forty *thousand* within a few weeks after the coup. A year later, twenty-five thousand are still being held without formal charges. So there'll be twenty-five thousand, plus one eighty-four-year-old curmudgeon. It won't make much difference to them and it won't make much difference to me."

"You're committed to this, Turhan?"

"Absolutely, Nadji."

"Allah's blessing on you, my friend."

"And Adonay's, Jesus Christ's, Buddha's and everyone else's," chimed in Baumueller. "'Cause God knows you'll need it."

8

On October 29, 1981, the fifty-eighth anniversary of the establishment of Atatürk's Republic, a full page article, surrounded by a thick black border, appeared on page six of the New York World. It was published simultaneously in the native language of each newspaper throughout the western world in which it had been accepted. Although *Cumhüriyet* and *Hürriyet* severely edited the statement, *Isharet* published it intact, and, to emphasize its support, printed five times its usual number of copies and distributed this edition throughout Turkey at no charge. Turhan's old friend at the B.B.C. prevailed upon that broadcast agency to let him read the article over the air in its entirety.

DEMOCRACY IN TURKEY: THE EXPERIMENT THAT FAILED

by Turhan Türkoğlu -- The Conscience of the Nation

I was born in 1897 in Diyarbakır province. I soon learned what it was like to live under an absolutist regime. My first exile came when I was eleven years of age because, in my juvenile way, I championed the right of ***all*** *the Ottoman Empire's citizens. In September, 1912, I had the good fortune to meet Ibrahim the Caravan Leader, who replaced my grandfather* *as my protector, and who taught me the single irreversible rule by which I have tried, with greater or lesser success, to live my life.* ***There is no such thing as 'relative' truth. Truth either is an absolute, or it does not exist****. I believe with all my heart that so long as there is one human being in the world who will tell the truth, no matter how brutal that truth may be, no matter what the consequences, society as we know it will survive. When I die, may the epitaph on my tombstone read simply, "He sought the truth and told it."*

I have been a reporter in Turkey since my first article appeared in ***Vatan*** *in 1915 – almost sixty-seven years ago. I was present in Samsun on a windy day in May, 1919, when Gazi Mustafa Kemal landed at a crumbling wooden wharf and declared he would convene a congress to set in motion the wheels of western-style democracy. When we nearly lost Ankara to the Greek enemy, I told our story to the world.*

When Adolf Hitler first came to power, I was the Gazi's eyes and ears. I was expelled from Nazi Germany within six months of the Reichstag fire, and I was banished from Turkey twice, once by the Gazi himself, and once at the behest of Adnan Menderes, who was later hanged. I lost a wife to the earthquake in Erzinjan. I lost a woman I loved more than life itself to a suicide caused by a government that acted within its self-proclaimed 'legal rights.' Except for my proud affiliation with the British Broadcasting Corporation, I have been employed by a single newspaper, ***Isharet****, for more than sixty-two years.*

Fifty-eight years ago today, Gazi Mustafa Kemal, whom the world has come to know as Kemal Atatürk, founded the Republic of Turkey on the ashes of the dead Ottoman empire. He pushed my countrymen forward five hundred years in the space of fifteen. He gave us a new nation, a new language, a new dignity. It was the Gazi's wish that every man and woman within our borders be entitled to the dignity of his or her own thoughts and the freedom fully to express those thoughts by means of a twenty-five hundred year-old concept called democracy.

Twenty-three years ago, I believed the Menderes government had shamed that democracy. I said so, and spent time in prison for those statements. But democracy survived, and in 1961 a new constitution gave birth to the Second Turkish Republic. Fifty million flowers bloomed, as each man and woman in the nation was afforded rights and protections as great as those in any modern western nation.

Perhaps we weren't ready for such freedom. Every hundredth man in Turkey wanted to start his own political party to protect his own private interests. I don't say this was the right thing. As the bloodshed and ruination of our motherland demonstrated in the late 1970's, it proved to be the wrong thing.

But right or wrong, such excesses do not excuse the authoritarian rule of the few, a situation which now exists in Turkey's Third Republic. Abuse of democracy does not warrant the arrest of forty thousand people – almost as many as were killed in the great Erzinjan earthquake of 1939. It does not merit that five out of every eight arrested remain in prison, without formal charges being filed against them, over a year later. A society does not benefit when the members of its parliament are barred from participating in politics for ten years, when political parties are abolished and their assets liquidated by the state, when trade unions are purged and strikes banned, and when the declaration of martial law in every province remains the only way to preserve order. The current regime is little better than that of the colonels in Greece we ridiculed a decade ago! Perhaps the constitution of 1961 was too loose of a shirt for Turkey to wear. But it need not have been exchanged for a strait jacket!

Is all this necessary in the name of law and order? We have become a pariah among nations, an embarrassment to our friends. The European community has begged the generals to restore parliamentary rule. We have been denied our seats in the Council of Europe. The one thing we cannot – we must not – become is a laughingstock among the nations, for then the stupid and tragic epithet, "terrible Turk" will come to have meaning.

General Evren, you are a good man. I believe you want only the best for your Motherland, which is my Motherland as well. Perhaps you know what is going on in the name of "national security," but more likely you cannot be in every jail cell any more than you can invade the heart and mind of every Turkish citizen. I call upon you to look at what is being done in your name. Pay heed to the voices of truth, not only those that tell you what you want to hear.

As I write these words, my heart breaks for my native land. What I say may be nothing more than the braying of an eighty-four year old ***eshek*** *– a donkey chewing the sparse thistles on a barren steppe. But in some quarters, I flatter myself that I have come to be called the conscience of my country. At this moment – this minuscule flyspeck on the windowpane of history – democracy, for what it is worth, has died in Turkey. Do not let it rest in peace. May Allah bless the works of your hands.*

-Turhan Türkoğlu, the Conscience of Turkey

9

Turhan was sitting quietly in the front room of Belgrade Palas when he saw the Cadillac limousine pull up in front of his door. Two smartly-dressed officers alighted from the black car and approached the entryway. He'd been expecting this ever since the article had appeared. He was not surprised. He waited a reasonable period after he heard the knock to answer. "Good morning, Colonels. How may I help you?"

"Turhan Effendim," the taller of the two said, in a surprisingly respectful voice, "our orders are to transport you to Ankara."

"Prison again?"

"No, Effendim. We don't know what will happen, Sir. We're to arrange for your movement to the capital."

"General Evren's orders?"

"I don't know, Sir. We're acting on orders from a special military court, convened under the authority of the National Security Council."

"Do you know anything?" Turhan asked. Then, more gently, he said, "I suppose not. You're only doing your jobs, correct?"

"Affirmative, sir," the second colonel replied. "May I say something off the record, while just the three of us are together?"

"Can I stop you?"

"What I wanted to say, that is, what *we* wanted to say..." The taller colonel nodded. "is that we have all the respect in the world for what you wrote. We read your article in *Isharet*. Allah bless you, Effendim." Turhan's "prison" was a room in the Kent Hotel in Ankara's "new city." While he was not free to leave the room, it was a far cry from his incarceration at Marmara or Aksaray. There was a comfortable bed, a television set, a console radio, and a modern chair and desk. He ate three excellent meals each day and caught glimpses of tree-lined Atatürk Bulvari from his window. The heating, hot shower, electric shaver, and the IBM typewriter provided him by the state, all worked. Unfortunately, he did not have access to a telephone. Thus, to all intents and purposes, he was in solitary confinement.

After three weeks, he was driven south in another Cadillac, to a large Army barracks. "Site twenty-three," the escort officer told him. "Twenty-three kilometers from Ankara. Originally designed as an American military base to get U.S. troops out of the center of the capital. While it was being built in the early sixties, the Turkish government threatened to cut off the Americans' Base exchange and private post office facilities on the grounds they facilitated smuggling. To quiet Turkish concerns, the U.S. gave us the installation."

"What's there now?"

"Special military court."

"Hear Ye, Hear Ye! The Provisional Military Court for the Sixth District is now in session, the Honorable Tümgeneral Yildizoğlu presiding. Be seated and come to order."

The courtroom was windowless. There were two electric ceiling fans in the room. A short, bald man, about sixty, wearing a black robe took his place at center bench. He was followed by a tall, angular looking man of forty-five, with a shock of graying hair and a long, lean face, who sat to the presiding judge's left. A middle-aged, nondescript man of medium height, sat to his right.

"Turhan Türkoğlu, please come forward, and sit at the table in front of you."

"What are the charges against me, Your Honor?" Turhan asked.

"We'll get to that momentarily," Yildizoğlu replied pleasantly. "First let's have a chat."

"I gather I'm not to be provided with legal counsel?"

"That is correct. In our proceedings, we've found lawyers interfere more with the pursuit of justice than help it along."

"Your Honor, I'm sure ninety percent of the free world would agree with what you said. However, there are times when one's rights should be guarded by those who know the protections conferred by law."

The general's face colored. "This is not a constitutional court. We're here to determine facts and, if they are true, to determine what would best serve the state's interests."

"Very civil words, General. Shall we drop the pretense of nicety here and be open with one another?" He heard someone in the room gasp. "I don't see a court reporter here. That means no record is being made of these proceedings."

"Be careful what you say, Türkoğlu. The powers given me are very broad."

"Given by whom, *Hakim* Effendim? Does General Evren know about this 'trial?'"

"Silence, Türkoğlu!" the tall man to the general's left snapped. "This provisional court is legally convened by authority of National Security Council emergency law 80-185."

"That's not my question," Turhan responded just as sharply. "Does General Evren know about *this* trial?"

"That's none of your concern," the presiding judge said. "This is a legally-constituted tribunal. I have the power to hold you in contempt."

"Then do so!" Turhan shouted. "What are you going to do? Imprison an eighty-five-year-old man? Beat me on the feet like the Menderes regime did? Withhold my medication so I have another stroke? Do you think I care about your ruling? You're damned right I'm in contempt of this body, which I will not dignify by calling it a court! Atatürk would be contemptuous of you for what you are doing in the name of Turkish justice!"

"Order! Order!" General Yildizoğlu banged his gavel. "Mister Türkoğlu will be shackled and gagged." Immediately a large bailiff came forward and politely asked Turhan to put his hands behind his back, then locked a pair of handcuffs over Turhan's wrists. The gag, a thick, rubber facial mask, allowed Turhan to breathe, but muffled whatever he said so that it was incomprehensible.

"Now, then," the chief judge continued. "I think we'll have no difficulty showing that you not only authored, but arranged for the publication of a treasonous document on October 29 of last year. Of course, this is only the latest in a line of crimes going back to the days of the Sultans. Need I remind you of them, Effendim? Drug-running for the Agha Khorosun and the Agha Nikrat? Insult to the Gazi's program of *Etatism*? Banishment for intemperate remarks? Imprisonment for failing to control your poison pen? Harboring enemy foreign elements in time of war? The list goes on and on. Rather a sad commentary." Turhan sat quietly. He'd heard the litany before. It meant nothing more to him than the grunting of an ox in the fields.

"In due time, you'll have a chance to explain your position on each of these charges. We have many cases to try, so we'll be absent when you make your argument. You'll be free to use a tape recorder that we'll provide for your convenience. Depending on our press of business we will, at our discretion, listen to portions of it before we pronounce appropriate disposition. We see you have no further objection to our procedure, since we've heard nothing from you. Please answer our questions 'yes' or 'no' by nodding or shaking your head. "First, did you author this article, which we will introduce as Exhibit One?"

Turhan made no response and maintained silence.

"There being no objection to the question, we consider your lack of response to constitute an admission. Second, did you intend to bring international disgrace upon the Third Republic by this article?" Turhan turned his back on the tribunal. "Deemed admitted. Finally, do you know of any reason why this court should not find you guilty of the charges against you?"

"There *are* no charges against me!" Turhan shouted into the mouth covering. "N *n* n n-n n-n n," came out the other end of the mask.

"Your statement appears to be you know of no such reason. We will take a three hour recess. During that time, you may use the tape recorder. Then you'll be returned to your hotel accommodations, which I trust are to your liking. You will hear from us again when we are ready to pronounce sentence. Good day, Türkoğlu Effendim." The three judges rose and left the room.

Turhan willed himself to remain calm, despite his last outburst. If he died of another stroke before justice was done 'they' would certainly have won. His gag was removed. For the next two hours, he concentrated on giving a quiet, well-reasoned defense of his position. When he got back to his hotel, he found that the bailiff had placed a scrap of paper in his pocket. The message contained two words, "Akdemir knows," and the initials, "K.H." written in pencil. When next he went to the bathroom, Turhan flushed the paper down the toilet.

"General Evren, General Akdemir is here to see you."

"Show him in!" The voice sounded hearty. "Nadji!" he said, giving his friend a great bear hug. "What can I do for you, *arkadash*?"

"Kenan, some years ago you said you owed me a favor."

"Of course, Nadji." Evren's face became more serious. "I don't have unlimited powers, of course, but if it's within my power..."

"I've learned confidential information. Don't ask me where. You don't even have to dignify it with a response. I understand that in 1978 a panel was set up to select certain twentieth century Turkish figures." He saw Evren grip the arms of his chair. The man's knuckles went white. So the information was correct. "I won't say anything further about it, *Pasha*. I must see a copy of that list as soon as possible."

"I have no idea what you're talking about, General?"

"Perhaps you don't, Mister President, but it's a matter of extreme urgency – of life and death, if you will – that I have access to that list by the end of this week. I don't want to embarrass either you or your government, Pasha Effendim, but *I need that list*."

"General Akdemir," Evren said, his voice edged with hardness, "would one old friend think to threaten another?"

"Not at all, General. I apologize if you took it as anything more than one old friend asking a favor of another."

When Aysheh returned home from shopping two days later, she was puzzled, when she opened the box of new shoes she'd purchased, to find a photocopied document that contained thirty names. She was even more surprised to see Turhan's and Halide's names on the single piece of paper. "Darling, I just found the strangest thing in a shoebox. Can you figure what it's all about?"

Nadji looked at the paper and smiled. "My love, it looks like I've got an incredible number of people to talk to in the next couple of days."

Within forty-eight hours, twenty-six people were assembled in Nadji's living room. The youngest was sixty-seven, the oldest ninety-two. One had come from as far away as Pittsburgh, Pennsylvania. Most lived within a day's journey of the capital. "Ladies, gentlemen," Nadji began. "I can't tell you how much it means to me, indeed to Turkey, that you've come here this morning. I'm sure all of you were pleasantly surprised to find out you're each being considered for 'immortality.' It's something you'd have learned in a few months anyway, but it's still flattering."

"I appreciate that Nadji Pasha," a soft-spoken, gracious woman, who reminded the general very much of Halide, said. "But why was it so urgent that we all be here today?"

"Because by tomorrow morning each of you will have your opportunity to prove how truly immortal you are, whether or not you're actually elected. Turhan Türkoğlu is a nominee for 'immortality.'" There was an approving murmur among the group.

"He's not here today for one simple reason. He's under house arrest. Tomorrow afternoon at two o'clock, he's to be sentenced by a provisional military court at a secret base outside Ankara." Now the murmur turned to anger. Nadji continued, "No doubt you all know about Turhan Türkoğlu's article condemning our present government. Just after the first of the year, Turhan was picked up and transferred to the Kent Hotel. I don't know what happened at this supposed 'trial,' but I've learned from an impeccable source that the so-called 'judges' intend to confiscate all his property in Turkey. That's not too much, since most of what he earned from the sale of the book is outside the country. However, I've also discovered the court intends to strike his name from the nominees. Thus, even if elected, he'd be ineligible to receive the honor."

There was an outbreak of hostile grumbling among the old people. "Has the vote been taken yet?" the gentle historian, who'd come from Pittsburgh, asked.

"Yes. Last September. The ballot box was turned over to the World Court on October first."

"Then how can they change the vote?"

"They can't. However, they can void his name from the list of nominees. That's exactly what they intend to do."

"I don't believe General Evren would let that happen," one woman said, angrily.

"I don't believe the President knows of the trial, nor of the proposed sentence," Nadji replied.

"Why didn't you just tell him directly, General Akdemir?" asked a small man, who wore very thick spectacles.

"Because if I did that for only one man, Turhan Türkoğlu, it would not protect the rest of you. If we stick together and make the presentation I have in mind, you are all guaranteed a level playing field, and we may yet be able to preserve the republic that Atatürk founded. There must be no dissent among us. Now here is my plan..."

The following Tuesday, Nadji telephoned Evren at six-thirty in the morning. "Mister President? Nadji Akdemir. It's absolutely essential you stop by my home on your way to work today."

"What are you talking about? You've exhausted any favors I owe you. Why can't you come to my office?"

"Kenan, I need to see you for less than an hour. For reasons I cannot disclose on the phone, it cannot take place at your offices or anywhere that's public. I can only tell you there will be more people here than you and me. It's critical that you come alone."

"Are you threatening me, General Akdemir?"

"No, Effendim. I'm transmitting information vital to your plans for the Turkish Republic."

An hour-and-a-half later, the Turkish president faced the same group who'd met at Nadji's home the day before. The gracious woman, who'd been first to speak at the private meeting, addressed General

Evren. "*Günaydin*, good morning President Evren. I've been elected spokesperson for our group. I'll be blunt, since General Akdemir told me you prefer the truth outright. The people in this room constitute every surviving nominee on the list of candidates for 'immortality.' We don't know which of us was elected any more than you do. We're aware that last October the World Court's representative sequestered the ballot box.

"We've recently learned that one of the nominees, Turhan Türkoğlu, was arrested in connection with an article critical of the government, which he published last Republic Day. He's been tried and found guilty of certain crimes – even he hasn't been told what they are – by the Sixth District Provisional Military Court at Site 23, outside Ankara."

The general paled. "I give you my word I know nothing about this, Hanım Effendim."

"We believe you, General. You can't be everywhere at once. Many things are being done in your name, ostensibly under the guise of 'national security.' Whether or not we believe the military court even had jurisdiction to try him is irrelevant. The point is that Turhan Türkoğlu is to be sentenced at two o'clock this afternoon. Our sources have informed us that part of the sentence is he will be stripped of his nomination."

"I'm shocked," Evren said. The group sensed his sincerity. "Unfortunately, even I cannot interfere with the military court. It was set up by the National Security Council. There's enough pressure on me already. I'm being called a dictator, a Führer, and many other names besides. I cannot interfere with the orderly administration of justice in Turkey."

"We were afraid you'd say that," the woman said, never raising her voice. "Mister President, if the sentence is carried out all of us in this room, every living nominee for the honor of 'immortality' is committed to do four things. First, we will call a news conference, both here and abroad. Three of our number have dual citizenship, so we cannot be stopped from leaving the country without protest from a number of embassies. At that news conference, we will tell the world about the secret 'trial' of Turhan Türkoğlu. Second, we will publicly demand that every one of our names be stricken from the list of nominees. We will refuse to accept the honor if it is conferred upon us. Third, we will publicly state exactly why we have refused the honor, and we will call upon the families of those who've been nominated but have died, to join us in refusing the honor. Finally, we will boycott the opening of the Turkish National Museum. That is our position, Mister President."

"You can't possibly mean that?" The general looked around the room at the other nominees. Each nodded his or her assent. "You wouldn't do that to Turkey."

"General," the spokeswoman spoke softly. "*We* wouldn't have done it to Turkey. Your government did. One other point, Mister President. We're united in this position because what happened to Turhan could happen to any of us. We know who's on the list. We trust there will be no deletions from that list, regardless of what happens."

The man who had become virtual dictator of Turkey looked down at the floor, then directly into the face of General Akdemir. "Very well, I'll see what can be done." Then, in a murmur only Nadji could hear, he said, "Now, truly, there will be no more favors."

"Hear ye, hear ye! The Provisional Military Court for the Sixth District is now in session, The Honorable Tümgeneral Yildizoğlu presiding. Be seated and come to order." The three judges filed in once again. The presiding judge and the tall associate justice on his left looked very agitated. The nondescript third man smiled benignly.

"Turhan Türkoğlu, come forward," Yildizoğlu said. "Are you ready for sentence to be pronounced?"

"This court has no jurisdiction over a free civilian citizen of the Republic of Turkey. I refuse to participate in these proceedings by any response."

The General said nothing. He looked toward the door from whence he'd come. When he spoke, it was quietly, with dignity. "Your objection is duly noted. This court has reviewed all the evidence presented, including the points raised in your recorded statement." The eyebrows of the third judge lifted upward. The presiding judge continued. "We have concluded that we do indeed have jurisdiction, as conferred upon us by the National Security Council, over every citizen of Turkey. We have determined that you are guilty of... of..." he looked down at a piece of paper he'd brought in with him, "disturbing the peace, and we hereby sentence you to be fined one lira. Court is adjourned." He banged the gavel, and the three judges rose as one. General Yildizoğlu and his tall associate quickly left the courtroom, so quickly they did not hear Turhan's exultant cry, "And I will appeal this 'judgment' to the highest court in the land!"

The third man, the only one who'd been a civilian judge before the coup, hesitated for a moment, as though he'd forgotten something at his bench. He looked directly at Turhan and winked. The slightest shadow of a smile played about the jurist's lips as he slowly left the courtroom.

Three months later, General Nadji Akdemir was killed in a mysterious and tragic hit-and-run automobile accident. The driver of the car was never found.

JULY 20-21, 1983

The small, high-winged turboprop, inbound from the East, dropped down over the hills that enveloped the Turkish capital. As the large city of Ankara gave way to the sere, dusty emptiness of the steppe, the plane began a series of left turns. It descended sharply, made the final tight turn and flared high for landing.

"Please remain seated with your seat belts fastened until the aircraft has come to a complete stop and the captain has turned off the no smoking sign." The flight attendant's perfunctory plea was drowned out, as a swarm of perspiring passengers jostled for position near the rear exit of the aircraft. The aged plane rolled to a stop. Two burly ground crewmen lethargically pushed a wheeled ramp to its side. As the door opened, the passengers shoved and elbowed their way onto the stairs. Turhan was last off the aircraft, a wizened old man, with wispy gray hair. He moved stiffly down the steps, holding onto the railing.

It was a fifty yard walk over cracked, buckling tarmac from the ramp to the terminal. A blue and white plastic sign proclaimed "Welcome to

Ankara," in Turkish, French, German and English. The sign sweated as profusely as the passengers. Droplets of moisture traced irregular lines through its covering of smoke-colored dust. The sun's broiling fierceness highlighted the chipped paint on the stucco walls of the boxlike air terminal.

A reedy female voice came over the loudspeakers in Turkish, then in English. "Your attention please. Turk Hava Yolları – Turkish Airlines announces the arrival of Flight 255 from Diyarbakır. We will be boarding momentarily for the continuation of this flight to Istanbul."

Inside, the terminal was hotter than outdoors and intolerably stuffy. Turhan hardly noticed. He'd endured eighty-five Turkish summers and did not miss air conditioning. Besides, there was something far more pressing on his mind. He walked slowly over to a concrete bench, sat down and closed his eyes.

Turhan Türkoğlu, indistinguishable from those shabby old people who populated the slum areas of cities around the world, wore a soiled, shapeless coat and carried a small, worn, cardboard suitcase. To his right, a fat, middle-aged, foreign woman, wearing a cloying, sweet perfume, rose, wrinkled her nose in distaste, and walked over to a facing row of seats. Her actions were meant to show the world that she was not associated with this derelict.

Turhan shared his countrymen's odors. Strong cigarettes smoked for a lifetime, clothes seldom cleaned, the sour sweat of one who has not bathed recently. A mustiness of old age hung about him, a sense of bones grown brittle, scars that no longer bothered to heal.

He heard a woman's voice, speaking American-accented English. "Darling, I'm so thirsty. There's a soft drink stand over there. Could they possibly know how to make real Coca Cola in this place? Where would they get the water?" He opened his eyes and saw a young couple to his left moving away from him. The man was in his late twenties, an

American military officer. He was overweight. His forehead glistened with beads of sweat. Another ten years and he'd have the belly of an agha, thought Turhan. The attractive, dark-haired woman with him appeared anxious. Turhan closed his eyes. For a moment he dozed.

A large, modern airliner braked to a stop a hundred yards away. The same disembodied female voice as before announced the arrival of Turkish Airlines Flight 136 from Paris and Istanbul. A sedate crowd descended politely from this plane. Suddenly, he saw a familiar face. Turhan rose as briskly as his age allowed and sauntered almost jauntily toward the arriving passengers, calling out to a small, elderly woman.

"Halide! Halide hanım! Hosh geldiniz! Welcome home, my wonderful friend!"

"Turhan Türkoğlu, you old scoundrel! You actually decided to come."

"No one's here yet," he said. "Come, let me treat you to a glass of tea."

"As always, trying to charm a girl off her feet! I accept the offer, you dear, dear rascal," she said, smiling. "Have you decided?"

He glanced around. "This is not the time or the place to talk." He signaled a young boy who was carrying a tray, asked for two glasses of tea, and extracted a coin from his pocket. The youngster handed him two tiny glasses of the hot liquid and two irregular lumps of sugar on small steel saucers. The woman took her glass and sipped daintily. Turhan placed one of the cubes between his crooked, stained front teeth and noisily sucked his tea through the sugar, Russian style.

"Praise Allah we still have tea, eh, my friend?" she said. "Where would we be without it these days, when the country can no longer afford to import our so-called 'Turkish' coffee?"

"True. Now that we're rusted hulks, and neither threatening nor useful, they want to put us on display like so many 'treasured' national monuments."

"Turhan, don't you think you could muster up some patriotic spirit for the event?"

"It's a bit hard after what happened. Besides, I think it's a damned waste to spend all that money on a grand spectacle. Why not reduce our national debt or care for our poor? If I were still writing for Isharet..."

"I thought you didn't want to talk about it now. Haven't you told our government once too often that their priorities were wrong? Why not look at the good that's happened? Our countrymen have come a long way in a very short time. Let them have their pride, Turhan. Every major world museum has plundered our land. Does it hurt to show our heritage to the world? If they want us for some sort of show, what harm does it do?"

"Bravo, hear, hear!" A single pair of hands clapped. "Is this a private party, or can a decrepit old military elephant join you high and mighties?" Turhan and Halide looked up to see the crinkled smile and gleaming eye of Nadji Akdemir in full dress uniform.

"Why, General Akdemir!" Halide smiled the coy smile of a young girl. "What lady would not feel special with such an honor guard - a four star General and Turkey's most respected elder statesman of the press, who, by the way, could use a lesson in courtliness and appreciation?"

"Teach Turhan Türkoğlu manners?" He grinned back. "Might as well try to teach a hippo how to fly. When we're all dead and gone, that old reprobate will be reaching for a pen from the bowels of hell to write one last scathing article about something of which he knows less than nothing."

"And you, great and noble Pasha! Your were a little snot-nosed military brat when I met you more than sixty years ago, and you still are!"

The three of them laughed uproariously. Turhan hugged his comrade of so many years around the waist and, in the Turkish tradition, kissed both cheeks. "Hosh geldiniz to you, my old friends. I'm so happy you're both here. I thought you were dead ... thought you were dead ... thought you were dead..."

"Turhan, wake up, you've been talking in your sleep."

He felt himself gently shaken. "Rachela?" he mumbled, in the dimness of half-sleep. He came to consciousness and found himself staring into the most beautiful pair of grey-violet eyes.

"No, Aysheh. Remember?"

"I'm sorry. I must have dozed off," Turhan said, embarrassed.

"That's all right, Uncle Turhan," said Omer. Turhan noticed that Nadji's eldest son was wearing the rank of Lieutenant Colonel.

"President Evren requested we come and get you," said Yavuz, also a *Yarbay*. "The others have already been here a day or so. Everyone's staying at the Büyük Ankara Hotel."

Turhan frowned. Under the circumstances, luxury treatment made him feel uncomfortable. As if she sensed his apprehension, Aysheh explained, "General Evren thought you might change your mind about coming. He told me to make sure you got to Ankara if I had to bring you in chains."

Outside the terminal, a full colonel clicked his heels and held open the door of a black limousine. Turhan thought back to the last time he'd been driven by a high-ranking military chauffeur. That day he, a civilian, had faced sentencing by the military court. "Cadillac," Türkoğlu said disparagingly. "Why couldn't we use one of our own for the big show?"

"What would you have us ride in, Your Elegance?" Aysheh asked. "That horse cart plodding up ahead? Or would you prefer to stuff yourself into a *dolmush*?"

"Neither," observed Omer dryly, looking toward a field to the right of the roadway. "Uncle Turhan would have us camp with the gypsies and ride into Ankara in their wagon tomorrow morning. He already smells like one of their dancing bears. No wonder Evren said to use chains."

"Watch how you talk to your elders, you miserable young whelp!" Turhan said, jovially pinching the young man's knee. *Allah, he's the image of Nadji. Talks like him, looks like him, has the same sense of humor. What a tragedy the father can't be here today.*

Five miles beyond the airport, the roadway narrowed to two lanes. No change in the last twenty years. Traffic slowed to a crawl. Trucks and buses inched their way the last ten miles into the most squalid section of the busy city. Ulus was still as ugly as when he'd first seen it so many years ago, but it was the soul of Ankara, Turhan thought. Why must it always be the first place the foreigners see? The limousine headed up Atatürk Boulevard toward the Grand Ankara Hotel. Turhan knew the Swiss managers of the hotel would make sure the bed sheets were free of lice. With a momentary stab of guilt, he told himself he'd still rather it were managed by Turks, even if it would not be so antiseptically clean.

"Where are they going to hold the festivities?"

"Out by the Atatürk Mausoleum," Yavuz replied. "No one's been allowed to see the place. It's been closed up and under guard for the past month. They've invited dignitaries from all over the world. The judges were told to select appropriate nominees without reference to politics and make the awards based solely on their morally honest judgment."

"And you expect that a panel formed before the takeover would risk offending our military overlords? Then you, young man, are more naïve than I thought. I can see Halide being chosen by anyone with a shred of sense. But me? The ancient curmudgeon of the press?"

"You're a bit hard on yourself, Turhan," Aysheh said. "The Turkish media refers to you as 'The conscience of the nation.'"

"Yes. Like any conscience, it's something you say *ought* to be there. You don't listen to it. When it starts buzzing around your head like a fly, you slap it away. If you think they really paid any attention to what I've said all these years, you'd believe they'd as soon drink horse piss as rakı." The limousine pulled up to the stark, slate gray tower of the Grand Ankara Hotel. The passengers disembarked. At dinner that night, the talk turned serious.

"Have you decided whether you'll accept?" Aysheh asked.

"It's very hard for me to say, even now. You know what happened as well as I."

"But that was over a year ago."

"It's easy for you to talk," the man answered, his voice edged with bitterness. "You weren't in my place."

"Uncle Turhan," Yavuz said. "That's all behind us, now."

"Is it really, Yavuz? You come from a long military line. Unquestionably, you owe your allegiance to the armed forces who run this country."

"And you," Aysheh snapped, raising her voice, "owe your allegiance to the motherland and to your two closest friends, both of whom are gone. Would you insult their memories by refusing the nation's recognition of what you made of your lives?"

"None of us has even been chosen, Aysheh. No one knows who's going to be an 'immortal.' The government that killed democracy in Turkey and would like to have killed me is still very much in power. That's what makes it so difficult for me to decide. If I'm elected to immortality and I accept the award, I dignify everything they stand for. And if I do that, they'll have won."

"Turhan," Aysheh said, Gazing at him evenly. "You said that if you accept the award, 'they' will have won. Turhan, dear, dear Turhan, you don't know how wrong you are. There's something you must know. And I think there's another person who should take part in our conversation." She looked across the room and nodded. A nondescript, middle-aged man approached their table. Turhan's eyes widened. It was the third jurist, the one who'd delayed his exit and winked at him after the trial.

Allah! Has Aysheh become one of them?

"Turhan, I believe you two have met?"

"Long ago, Madame Akdemir," the man said mildly.

"What do you mean? You were part of that unholy trio that sat in judgment at Site Twenty-three a year ago. How dare you say you knew me long ago!"

The man didn't change his expression. "Do you remember a piece of paper with the initials 'K.H.?'"

Turhan paled. "It was you?"

"Yes."

"Why? Why would you risk everything for someone who meant less than nothing to you?"

"Less than nothing?" The man pondered Turhan's words for several moments. "Turhan effendim," he said quietly, "Your name has had far greater meaning in my life than you'd ever imagine. Do the initials 'K.H.' mean anything to you?"

"Should they? Is this some kind of game?"

"You don't know my name then?"

"No. General Yildizoğlu was the presiding judge. I was not inclined to listen to much else."

"If you had known my name, it might have angered you more. Let me begin, if I may, by telling you that the old saying, 'The fruit doesn't fall very far from the tree' is not always true."

"More riddles?" Turhan said, becoming impatient.

"No, Effendim. Not a riddle. Many, many years ago you helped me to realize there are times when you must escape from under the shadow of your father. You knew mine. You wrote about him. More than once. You came back from the dead to help a friend, a lawyer named Zehavah Kohn. And when you did, a thirteen year-old boy discovered that there is justice. Like you, I've spent my whole life fighting for justice. Not the perversion of that word as practiced by my father. Nor what some – not all – of those in power today use to trample on the rights of those who don't agree with their point of view. Turkey's not a perfect place. There will always be those who believe they are better than those they are elected or appointed to serve. But it's a better place because you lived and fought for what you believed was right. I pray it will be a better place because I followed in your footsteps. And if I influence someone else because of what I learned from you, *Inshallah,* one day it may just be as perfect as we mortal men can make it. If we do not dare the absurd, how can we ever hope to achieve the impossible?"

Turhan stared fixedly at the man. The initials "K.H." danced before his eyes. Then the realization hit. He could only whisper the words, "*My God, you're...*"

"Kâzim. *Kâzim Hükümdar*. You helped save my life. Could I have done less for you?"

The following day dawned clear and warm. Limousines whisked the candidates to the Presidential Palace atop Chankaya Hill, where they shared breakfast with President Evren. Afterward, the General rose to speak. His speech was clipped, direct, no nonsense.

"Ladies and gentlemen, I'll not attempt to make a political speech, nor even a very long one. There has never been an assembly of more deserving people in the history of modern Turkey. Some of the candidates have passed on. You, the survivors, whether you're ultimately chosen or not, are the best our motherland has to offer the world. My respect is boundless. After breakfast, we'll proceed directly to *Anıt Kabır*, the Atatürk Mausoleum. This will be your first view of the Hall of Immortals and the National Museum. We arrive at eleven. You'll be the first to see the museum. We've tried to make it a place where history lives. The exhibition halls correspond to the most important periods in our nation's history. You'll be at liberty until four in the afternoon, when we'll reassemble next to the mausoleum. The United Nations Secretary-General will read the names of the chosen. Your accomplishments, whether or not you're elected, will be stated on plaques throughout the hall. Each of you will have a limousine at his or her disposal for the next several days.

"One thing more. For the remainder of your lives, whether you are chosen or not, each of you will receive a pension equivalent to fifty thousand American dollars each year." There was a delighted gasp. The general continued as though he'd heard nothing. "I thank you." He turned abruptly and strode from the room.

Turhan, scrubbed, shaved, wearing a well-tailored, natty suit, was barely recognizable. "Well, well, well, the conscience of the nation himself," the woman who'd been spokesperson for the group the year before, said. "Even you must be stunned by the General's last statement."

"Certainly," he remarked, looking sardonically around the room. "Fifty thousand American dollars a year. The average person in this room is more than eighty years old. At the very worst, they'll have to pay us for five years apiece. Most of us are too old, tired and feeble to do anything with the money except look at figures in a bankbook. The papers will sing the praises of our wonderful, humane government.

The money will sit in banks or be loaned out at the highest interest imaginable, to people who really need it. Jails will get dirtier, roads will have more holes, while we sit stiffly and starchilly encased in money we'll never spend."

"Bravo, my socialist friend. If you'll be so kind as to give me your share, I'll be pleased to distribute it for you," another old man, a retired general, gently mocked the journalist.

"Why? To watch you throw it away on tanks, old jet fighters and other toys? No, thank you, erstwhile warrior. I may as well keep the money in trust for the good of the nation."

The procession descended Atatürk Boulevard to Kızılay Square and turned onto the main entry road to Anit Kabır, the Mausoleum. Built long after Atatürk died, it stood in the midst of a formal park on a rise slightly above the floor of the City. The caravan stopped. General Evren emerged from the leading vehicle. An honor guard snapped to attention, crossed swords above the path, creating a gleaming metal latticework ceiling. Two young officers rolled a red carpet to the edge of the staircase, stood, brought their heels smartly together, turned sharply in opposite directions, and moved to the sides of the entryway.

On a signal from the chief of protocol, chauffeurs opened automobile doors in sequence. The nominees got their first glimpse of the shrine as they approached the stark, sandstone structure over the quarter-mile-long, lion-flanked walkway. The memorial was square, simple. The exterior of the new additions matched the spare style of *Anıt Kabır*. The museum, housed in a U-shaped series of buildings, resembled the caravanserais that had served Turkey for more than a thousand years. When they'd reached the entrance, General Evren cut a red ribbon in front of the museum's double brass doors. He said, simply, "By your leave, my friends, the next hours are yours. We assemble here at four o'clock."

As he entered the museum, Turhan was immediately struck by the feeling of vast openness. Large skylights and a high, domed ceiling descended to a three hundred sixty degree panorama of Turkey, from Edirne on the Bulgarian-Greek border, to Mount Ararat and the Valley of Mesopotamia in the East. The music of a single, unaccompanied flute played a haunting desert refrain. In the center of the rotunda was a simple, pale alabaster stele on which were written a series of words. As he read them, Turhan trembled, for these were the very words his mentor Ibrahim, the father of his heart, had written nearly eighty years ago.

> *"Since the dawn of mankind our land as been a bridge.*
> *East and West meet within our frontiers.*
> *Warrior and vanquished have spilled, shared and merged blood.*
> *The footsteps of forever have crossed our land.*
> *They have never diminished our spirit but have added to it.*
> *Come visitor. You are but the latest.*
> *Enter and look into the mirror of man's soul."*

Turhan Türkoğlu was quiet for an instant. Then he looked skyward and softly said, "We did it Halide, Nadji. You were right Grandfather, Shadran, Jalal, Ibrahim. The voice could not be stilled. Thank you Alkimi, Sezer and Zari for understanding me. Thank you Rachela, for teaching me I could love beyond our hopes, beyond our dreams. We won. For the little man. For all of us. *Praise Allah, we won!*"

Turhan turned and walked outside, into the sunlight, smiling. He'd made his decision. And whether he was chosen or not, he knew it was right.

High above Turhan, a mottled brown hawk circled slowly over new edifice. Finding nothing of interest, the bird flew south, circling the wrinkled dun-colored hills beyond the city, its eye ever alert for prey. Usually the outskirts of the great city provided ample fare – field mice, a rabbit, sometimes, if the hawk were lucky, a very young lamb. Today the fields were empty.

As it continued south, the hawk flew over a small village, with squat, mud buildings. At its center, a tall minaret attached to a white, stone building, rose proudly toward heavens. There was still nothing to spark the raptor's interest. The great bird dipped for an instant toward a large, noisy crowd of people, then rose sharply into the sky, wheeled about, and headed east, toward the high mountains.

EPILOGUE

Kenan Evren served as the seventh President of Turkey from 1980 to 1989. He assumed the post by leading the 1980 military coup. On June 18, 2014, a Turkish court sentenced him to life imprisonment and demotion of his military rank from army general to private, for leading the military coup in 1980, obstructing democracy by deposing the prime minister, Süleiman Demirel, abolishing the parliament, the senate, and the Constitution. His sentence was on appeal at the time of his death in a military hospital on May 9, 2015. He was 97 years old.

As this book is completed, Recep Tayyip Erdoğan, the twelfth and current President of Turkey, has served in office since 2014. He previously served as Prime Minister from 2003 to 2014 and as Mayor of Istanbul from 1994 to 1998. Under his administration, so many newspapers have been banned and so many reporters and intelligent people of goodwill arrested and held for interminable periods, for no "crime" other than speaking out, that freedom of speech and freedom of expression in Turkey have effectively ceased to exist, and the Turkish experience in democracy appears to have come to an end. For now.

Inshallah, may the time not be distant when those freedoms are restored and the next Turhan Türkoğlu arises to change the face of this astonishing, heroic, and tortured land.

THE END

Hugo N. Gerstl Collection

See below some of Pangæa Publishing Group's bestsellers by the same author:

Do not miss them on your shelf!

For Hugo N. Gerstl's complete novels list and descriptions, go to www.HugoGerstl.com

Pangæa Publishing Group
25579 Carmel Knolls Drive
Carmel, CA 93923
Email: info@pangaeapublishing.com

Printed in Great Britain
by Amazon